CRITICAL ACCLAIM FOR EDGAR AWARD–WINNING AUTHOR STEVE HAMILTON

ICE RUN

"Hamilton expertly delivers sharply etched characters, a vivid setting and a thoroughly enjoyable hero, leaving us breathless, perched at the edge of our seats for this chilly ride."

—*Publishers Weekly*

"Hamilton gives us mysteries within mysteries as well as a hero who simply won't be beaten down."

—*Miami Herald*

"An intense atmosphere continues to add to the riches of Steve Hamilton's well-plotted novels . . . Hamilton again excels at linking his traditional private detective novels with solid plots. A tender love story and a rude awakening of the past form the heart of *Ice Run* . . . *Ice Run* turns on edge-of-the-seat psychological suspense that Hamilton has honed to precision."

—*Florida Sun-Sentinel*

"Rougher, darker, sexier than previous installments, *Ice Run* raises the already noteworthy McKnight series to the next level and, in giving its hero a romantic companion, affords new insight into Alex's character."

—*This Week*

BLOOD IS THE SKY

"The best mysteries are about the past coming up out of the ground and grabbing the present by the throat. Steve Hamilton knows this. *Blood is the Sky* fills that bill and then some. This is his best yet."

—Michael Connelly, author of *Chasing the Dime*

more . . .

"*Blood is the Sky* takes us into the dark and brooding heart of Michigan's Upper Peninsula. It's got everything—tension, action, surprises. Alex McKnight is a believable hero who can also tell a good story."

—T. Jefferson Parker, author of *Silent Joe* and *Black Water*

NORTH OF NOWHERE

"Steve Hamilton writes the kind of stories that [one] can't resist . . . his tensile prose . . . reflects the dramatic, often violent contradictions of people who live on the edge of the world."

—*The New York Times Book Review*

"Superb! Hamilton keeps the action fast and furious and manages to keep the reader off balance."

—*Publishers Weekly*

"A brisk, well-plotted tale."

—*Kirkus Reviews*

"A bracing, sometimes sidesplitting . . . novel."

—*Booklist*

"A fast-paced book with wonderful characters . . . Hamilton writes great prose."

—*ReviewingTheEvidence.com*

"A robust entry . . . Alex is at his best and the support cast augments the isolated feeling of going north of nowhere that shows why Steve Hamilton is an award-winning author."

—*Internet Bookwatch*

THE HUNTING WIND

"Un-put-downable . . . exceptionally entertaining."

—*Publishers Weekly*

"Hamilton spins a smooth yarn."

—*The New York Times Book Review*

"The surprise ending delivers a satisfying jolt."

—*Booklist*

"Compelling."

—Los Angeles Times

WINTER OF THE WOLF MOON

"The isolated, wintry location jibes well with Hamilton's pristine prose, independent protagonist, and ingenious plot. An inviting sequel to his Edgar Award–winning first novel, *A Cold Day in Paradise*."

—Library Journal

"[Hamilton's] protagonist is likable as well as durable, his raffish cast is sharply observed and entertaining. Moreover, he knows how to pace a story, something of a lost art in recent crime fiction."

—Kirkus Reviews

"There's almost as much action in the book as there is snow—and there's heaps of white flakes. But Hamilton's first-person narrative has a lyric cadence and thoughtful tone that nicely counterpoints all the rough-and-tumble stuff."

—Orlando Sentinel

A COLD DAY IN PARADISE

"Ingenious . . . Hamilton unreels the mystery with a mounting tension many an old pro might envy."

—Kirkus Reviews

ICE
RUN

Steve Hamilton

St. Martin's Paperbacks

ICE RUN

Copyright © 2004 by Steve Hamilton.

Library of Congress Catalog Card Number: 2004041755

ISBN: 0-312-93296-0
EAN: 80312-93296-1

Printed in the United States of America

St. Martin's Press hardcover edition / June 2004
St. Martin's Paperbacks International Edition / March 2005
St. Martin's Paperbacks Regular Edition / June 2005

St. Martin's Paperbacks are published by St. Martin's Press, 175 Fifth Avenue, New York, NY 10010.

10 9 8 7 6 5 4 3 2 1

To Nonna and Donna

Acknowledgments

With a heavy heart I thank and remember Donna Pine of the Garden River First Nation, one of the most exceptional people I've ever had the pleasure of meeting. You will always be one of my heroes.

I owe much gratitude to Professor Phillip Mason of Wayne State University for invaluable assistance with the history of Michigan and Ontario, and to all the great people at the Ojibway Hotel.

Thanks as always to the "usual suspects"—Bill Keller and Frank Hayes, Liz and Taylor Brugman, Bob Kozak and everyone at IBM, Bob Randisi and the Private Eye Writers of America, Ruth Cavin and everyone at St. Martin's Press, Jane Chelius, Maggie Griffin, David White, Joel Clark, Cary Gottlieb, Jeff Allen, Rob Brenner, Larry Queipo, former chief of police, Town of Kingston, New York, and Dr. Glenn Hamilton, of the Department of Emergency Medicine, Wright State University.

And as always, I couldn't do anything at all without Julia, the love of my life, Nicholas the future gold medalist, and Her Royal Highness Antonia.

One

In a land of hard winters, the hardest of all is the winter that fills you with false hope. It's the kind of winter that starts out easy. You get the white Christmas, but it's a light snow, six inches tops, the stuff that makes everything look like a postcard. The sun comes out during the day. You can take your coat off if you're working hard enough. The nights are quiet. The stars shine between the silver clouds. You celebrate New Year's. You make resolutions. It snows again and you run the plow. You shovel. You chop wood. You sit inside at night by the fire. You say to yourself, this ain't so bad. A little cold weather is good for a man. It makes you feel alive.

That's what I was thinking. I admit it. Although maybe I had other reasons to believe this winter would be easy. Maybe this winter I could be forgiven for letting my guard down. One good look at the calendar would have put my head back on straight. Spring doesn't come until May, Alex. Which meant—what, winter had ten rounds left in a fifteen-round fight? That was plenty of time. That was all the time in the world.

When the storm finally hit, I was down the road at the Glasgow Inn. Jackie had the fire going and had just made a big pot of his famous beef stew. He had the cold Molsons, bought at the Beer Store across the bridge and stored just for me in his cooler, for the simple reason that American beer cannot compare to beer bottled and sold in Canada. That and a Red Wings game on the television over the bar were all I needed. On that night, anyway. I had plans for the next day. I had big plans. But for now I was happy just to be with Jackie, and to do everything I could to slowly drive him insane.

"Alex, you're gonna tell me what's going on," he said for the third time. He was an old Scot, God love him, with the slightest hint of a burr in his speech. Born in Glasgow sixty-odd years ago, the son of a tugboat captain, he came to Michigan when he was a teenager. He had been here ever since, eventually opening up the Glasgow Inn. It looked a lot more like a Scottish pub than an American bar, which meant you could spend the whole evening there without getting depressed or drunk or both.

"Don't know what you're talking about," I said.

"Like hell you don't. You've been bouncing in here, saying hello and how are you. Smiling and laughing."

"I'm happy to see you," I said. "Is that so bad?"

"Since when are you happy about anything?" He gave me that Popeye squint of his. "It's January, for God's sake."

"Almost February," I said. "How many inches have we had?"

"Don't even say that, Alex. You'll jinx it. You know a storm's coming."

"I had another cancellation today. There's not enough snow to ride on." This time of year, snowmobiling was the biggest business in Paradise, Michigan. Hell, it was the *only* business. Every rental cabin in town, and every motel room, was booked months in advance. On most January nights, Jackie's place would be crawling with men from downstate, most of them with their big puffy snowsuits zipped down to the waist.

And that sound. The whine of the engines, coming from every direction. It always drove me crazy. But this night was silent.

"Tonight," he said. "We'll get buried. You watch."

I shrugged and looked up at the hockey game. "Bring it on."

"And what's with the salad, anyway?"

"What salad?"

"Lettuce and vegetables, Alex. That salad."

"What are you talking about?"

"For dinner. You had a salad."

"I had the stew, Jackie. Since when can I pass that up?"

"You had a little bowl of stew and a big salad."

"Okay, so?"

"You don't eat salads for dinner. I've never seen you eat a salad in fifteen years."

"So I felt like a salad, Jackie. What are you getting at?"

"You're not drinking as much beer, either. Try to deny it."

I held up my hands. "Guilty. You busted me."

"You're working out, too. I can tell."

"You've been bugging me for years to take better care of myself," I said. "So now maybe I am. Is there something wrong with that?"

"You finally decided to listen to me? That's what you're telling me?"

"Is that so hard to believe?"

"Yes, Alex. It is. You've *never* listened to me. Not once."

The door opened at that moment, saving me from Jackie's third degree. It was my friend and neighbor, Vinnie LeBlanc, bringing in a blast of cold wet air.

"Holy Christ," Jackie said. "You can smell the snow coming. It makes my bones hurt."

"Who's winning?" Vinnie said as he took off his coat. It was a denim coat with a fur collar, the only coat I'd ever seen him wear, no matter how cold it got. He was an Ojibwa Indian, a member of the Bay Mills community. He had moved off the reservation a few years ago, and had bought the land down the road from mine and had built his own cabin. We were friends for a while, and then we weren't. Then I helped him look for his brother. What we found was a hell of a lot of trouble, but somehow we also found our friendship again. Just like that, without a word.

"Wings," I said. "Two to one. They just waved one off for Colorado."

He sat down next to me and asked Jackie for a 7-Up. The man never touched alcohol, going on nine years straight.

"Jackie's right," Vinnie said. "It's gonna snow. You better not be too far away from home when it does."

"That's a good one," Jackie said. "Since when does Alex go anywhere?"

Vinnie looked down at his glass. He rattled the ice. He had a smile on his face, a smile so subtle you wouldn't even see it if you didn't know the man as well as I did.

He knew. He was the only one who knew my secret.

I just couldn't tell Jackie about it. Not yet. I knew he had strong opinions about some things in life, and this was one thing he'd have a lot to say about. Maybe I wasn't ready to hear it yet. Or maybe I didn't want to ruin it. Maybe talking about it in the light of day would make it all vanish like a fever dream.

For whatever reason, I kept my mouth shut that night. I was happy to sit by the fire and watch the rest of the hockey game. The Wings gave up a late goal and after the five-minute overtime had to settle for a tie. Vinnie put his feet up and closed his eyes. There was still white tape on the side of his face, where the bullet had taken off part of his ear. I knew he was spending a lot more time over at the reservation now, looking after his mother. I didn't see him nearly as much.

We heard the wind picking up. There was a soft ticking at the windows. The snow had started. Outside this building, not a hundred yards away, lay the shoreline of Lake Superior. The ice stretched out a quarter mile, into the darkness of Whitefish Bay. Beyond that there was nothing but open water—water so cold and deep it was like a cruel joke to call it a lake at all. It was a sea, the Sea of Superior, and tonight it would feed the snow gods.

"You're gonna be plowing," Vinnie said. He kept his eyes closed.

"I'm ready."

He opened one eye. He started to say something and stopped.

"What is it?" I said.

He smiled again. Two smiles in one night.

"You're not going anywhere tomorrow," he said. "You're gonna be stuck here."

"We'll see about that," I said. But I knew he was probably right. God damn it.

We finally left around midnight. I said goodbye to Jackie and he dismissed me with a wave of his hand.

"You got him a little worked up," Vinnie said as we stepped out into the night. There were already three inches of new snow covering the parking lot. "He doesn't like not knowing what's going on."

"A little suspense is good for him," I said. "It keeps him young."

"I'm going to my mother's house," Vinnie said. "I'll see you tomorrow."

"I'll plow your driveway. Drive carefully."

We brushed our windshields off and then we were on our way, Vinnie to the reservation in Brimley, and me back up to the cabins. If you ever come to Paradise, Michigan, you just go through the one blinking red light in the middle of town, then north along the shore about a mile until you get to an old logging road. Hang that left and you'll pass Vinnie's place first, and then you'll find my place. My father bought the land back in the 1960s, and built six cabins. I live in the first cabin, the one I helped him build myself, back when I was an eighteen-year-old hotshot on my way to single-A ball in Sarasota. At the time, I never thought I'd be back up here for more than a visit. I certainly wouldn't have imagined living up here. Not this place, the loneliest place I'd ever seen. But all these years later, after all that had happened, here I was.

I put the plow down and pushed the new snow off as I went. It felt as light as talcum powder. I drove by Vinnie's place and then mine, and kept going. The second cabin was a quarter mile down the road. There was a minivan parked in front, with a trailer carrying two snowmobiles hitched behind it. A family, a man and his wife and two sons. I'd given them the chance to cancel, but they'd said they'd come up no matter what. Even with no snow, they looked forward to the trip every year. Now it looked like they might get some riding in after all.

Another quarter mile and I got to the third cabin. It was dark. Another quarter mile and then the fourth and fifth cabins together. They were dark, too.

One more quarter mile. The last cabin my father had built. His masterpiece. Until somebody burned it down. The walls were about half rebuilt now, a great blue tarp covering the whole thing, propped up in the middle to keep the snow off. Rising above it all was the chimney my father had built stone by stone.

I stopped and got out of the truck, made sure that the tarp was sealed tight. The wind died down and the pine trees stopped swaying. I took a long breath of the cold air and then got back in the truck. I plowed my way back to my cabin.

I went in and listened to the weather report on the radio. More snow was coming. A lot more. They didn't even try to guess the number of inches. That's always a bad sign.

God damn it all, I thought. I'm going to Canada tomorrow. I don't care if we get three feet. I'll plow again in the morning, and then I'm going.

I went into the bathroom and looked in the mirror. I ran a hand through my hair, then picked up the package and read the directions one more time.

"I can't believe I'm doing this," I said out loud.

I looked in the mirror again. Then I put on the plastic gloves and went to work.

The phone rang. I took the gloves off and wiped my

hands on the towel. I picked it up on the third ring, looking at the clock. It was almost one o'clock in the morning.

"Alex," she said. With that voice. It still hit me in the
gut, every time. She was Canadian, so she had that little
rise at the end of each sentence. That singsong quality, almost melodic, but at the same time it was a voice that
meant business. It had some darkness in it, a smoker's
voice without the smoke.

"Hey, it's late," I said. "Are you all right?"

"Yes, but I was just listening to the weather."

"A little snow. No problem."

"A little snow, eh? They're talking like twenty-four
inches. What are they saying down there?"

"They're not saying. You never know with the lake. It
could be less than that. Or more."

"I don't think you're coming out here tomorrow."

I thought about what to say. There was a distant hum-
ming on the line. "I think I can still make it."

"Don't be a dope," she said. "You'll kill yourself."

Out of a hundred different feelings I can have in one
minute when I'm talking to her, one feeling in particular
came into focus now. It was not the first time I'd felt it,
this little nagging doubt, that maybe I wanted something
out of all of this. Something real. And that maybe she had
woken up that morning not wanting anything at all.

And then the thing that always came right after that.
The certain realization that I was being a complete ass.

"Besides," she said. "Don't you have people staying in
your cabins? If it's snowing all day, don't you have to
stick around to plow them out?"

"I've got one family," I said. "The rest of the cabins are
empty."

"Okay, but even so. That one family will need you around, won't they?"

I closed my eyes and rubbed the bridge of my nose. "If there's a lot of snow falling, yeah. I can't be away for too long."

"So maybe it's time to try out your idea."

I opened my eyes. "What's that?"

"You know, about me coming to your place."

"Here?" I looked around the cabin. This was *my* idea? To have her come *here?*

"Yeah, why not? I've got four-wheel drive. And I've never even been there yet. You always come out here. I'm starting to feel guilty."

One single bed. The old couch, sagging in the middle. Two rough wooden tables. This sad wreck of a place, after fifteen years of living all by myself. This is what she'd see. My God.

"I don't know," I said. "This cabin—"

"You don't want me to see your bachelor pad?"

"I'm not sure I'd call it that."

"Yeah, I don't think anyone says that anymore. Bachelor pad, that was from the seventies, right?"

The seventies, I thought. Back when I was playing ball, and being a cop. And you were . . . God, were you in grade school then?

"Alex, are you still there?"

"Yeah, yeah, I'm just thinking. I don't want you driving all this way tomorrow if the weather's gonna be bad."

"It was just an idea. Okay?"

Think, Alex. Think.

"Hey, I know," I said. "Why don't we do something special?"

"Special like what?"

"Like I'll meet you somewhere."

"I thought you had to stay there."

"We could meet in the Soo," I said. "That'll keep me close enough to home."

"Soo Michigan?"

"There's a great hotel right on the river."

"A hotel?"

"It's called the Ojibway," I said. "You ever been there?"

"No," she said. "Never."

"They've got great food. And it's just . . . I mean, it's been there forever. It's the only fancy place in town."

"You want us to stay there?"

"I'm just saying . . ." You're blowing it, Alex. It's all gonna fall apart, right here.

"This is a nice place? In Soo Michigan?"

A little jab there, I thought. Sault Ste. Marie, Michigan, is so much smaller than its sister city across the river. Soo Canada has more of everything.

"It's a classy hotel," I said. "I'd really like to see you, okay? It's been a few days, and I wouldn't mind spending some time with you."

She didn't say anything for a long moment. There was the faint hum on the line and nothing else.

"Yeah, why not?" she said. "It sounds nice."

That's how it happened. That hesitation, that long silence while she thought about it, I figured that was just natural. Just part of the dance, the getting to know someone new.

Of course it wasn't that at all. It was something else entirely. But I didn't know her well enough yet. I didn't know the way she was, the way she has been for most of her life. The way she *had* to be. Above all, I didn't know the one most important thing about her—that she never, ever hesitated that long about *anything*. Not unless it was something big.

Really big.

Damn it all to hell. If I had only known.

Two

Natalie Reynaud. That was her name. Apparently, some of her friends called her Natty, but I never did. Not once. Natty didn't work for me. Natty didn't sound miraculous enough. To me she was always Natalie.

She was a constable with the Ontario Provincial Police, stationed in a little town called Hearst, way the hell up there on the last road in the world, the Trans-Canada Highway. The first time I saw her, she was jumping out of a floatplane, having flown back from a remote outpost to look for five missing men. She had dark brown hair pinned up under her OPP hat. She had green eyes.

She didn't find those missing men that day. Or the next. Vinnie and I found them, in a way I was still having nightmares about. Then a senior constable named Claude DeMers came looking for us. He was Natalie's partner, but he came without her. DeMers ended up dead and Natalie ended up looking like a bad partner. It was something I knew a little bit about myself.

There was something else I knew, too. Natalie's partner didn't leave her behind just to protect her from a little danger. He left her behind because he had a secret of his own out there, buried in the ground with the dead men. So he came out alone to try to keep that secret in the dirt, and he ended up with a bullet in the back.

Natalie took an administrative leave of absence from the OPP. I went back home to Paradise, but I kept thinking about her. I found out she was living in Blind River, just a couple of hours away from the International Bridge. So I went to see her. It was New Year's Eve, with only a trace of snow on the ground. I drove across the bridge and followed the King's Highway due east, along the shore of the North Channel. I arrived at her doorstep with a bottle of champagne and something else—what I thought would be a final answer to all the questions I knew she was living with. I had lived with the same questions, after all, with my own partner gunned down right in front of my eyes, on a hot summer night back in Detroit, in that one-room apartment just off Woodward Avenue with the tin-foil all over the walls.

I remembered the hell I had lived in for all those years afterward. I knew Natalie was in that same hell now. I thought I could give her a way out, the way out I never had.

Claude DeMers was buried a hero. He was the man who flew out to that lake to try to save the two Americans. When I told her the real story, I knew it would have to stay between us. When your partner's dead, you can't be the one to stand up and defame him. You can't point to his grave and say there lies a dirty cop. I knew that, but I figured what the hell. As long as *she* knew. Maybe she'd be able to sleep at night.

I had another reason to find her. I admit that. I sat in the dining room of that old farmhouse, watching what the antique light did to her green eyes, and how it picked up a faint hint of red in her hair. We talked and then we drank the champagne and made an awkward toast to the new year at midnight. She finally told me she wouldn't mind if I stayed the night, just so she wouldn't have to be alone.

"I don't trust many people," she said to me that night.

"But you trust me."

"How do you know that?"

"I can tell," I said. Although, of course, I couldn't. I had no idea what she was thinking. In another five minutes, I could have been back in my truck, heading home.

"That would be a miracle," she said. "I mean a real miracle."

"I think it already is," I said. "Look how we met. And now here we are."

"I guess I should thank you for coming out here, Alex. It was a completely insane thing to do. But I'm glad you did."

I didn't say anything then. I drank some more champagne and so did she. She had a way of looking up from her glass, eyeing me carefully, not like she was shy but maybe just the opposite. Like she was sizing me up. She asked me what sports I played, because it was obvious I was an old athlete. I shook off the "old" business and told her about my baseball career, such as it was. She told me she was a hockey player, back when a woman who played in college had nowhere to go with it. No women's hockey in the Olympics, just back to the frozen pond in the backyard. It surprised me a little. I would soon find out that the game of hockey fit her perfectly.

And then, for whatever reasons had brought me to this house, on this one cold night, after the grandfather clock at the top of her stairs chimed twelve times and the new year began, we stood up at the same time and met in the middle of the room. Because of the things that had happened to her, and to me. All these things we had in common. Hell, and maybe a little champagne on an empty stomach. It all came together in that minute after midnight. We kissed first, then she took me by the hand and led me upstairs.

We stopped in front of one room. Inside there was a canopy bed with white lace and stuffed animals all over it. "No," she said and pulled me past yet another room, with a double bed made up neatly, with more white lace. I saw two portraits, one on each end table, but I couldn't make out the faces in the dim light. "This one," she said as she pulled me into the third room. She was strong and the way she was pulling me, it felt like she was angry at me, and maybe she was. Maybe that was part of it.

The room she pushed me into was different from the others. The light was on, the bed was unmade, and there were two suitcases opened up on the floor with clothes spilling out of them. She turned the light off. As my eyes adjusted to the darkness, she struck a match and lit three candles. Then with her back to me she unpinned her hair and let it fall down onto her shoulders. She took her white shirt off and then reached behind and unhooked her bra. She kept her jeans on for the moment, turning around to face me in the candlelight. It's always been shoulders for me, more than any other part of a woman, and hers were perfect. She had small breasts and her nipples stood out erect in the chilled air of this bedroom in the corner of this old, silent house. I took my shirt off as she watched me, and then she came close and kissed me again. I felt her skin against mine. Her hair smelled faintly of smoke and something sweet like cinnamon.

She pulled away and left the room. I stood there, not quite sure what to do. When she came back, her white panties glowed in the candlelight. She put something in my hand, a foil wrapper, and in the half second it took to register, she knocked me backward onto the bed.

"That's two minutes for cross-checking," I said.

"Shut up and take your pants off." She climbed on top of me.

"I can't. That's another two minutes for interference."

"Just shut up," she said, and then she slapped me lightly across the mouth. It may have been a love tap, on her scale anyway, but it got my attention. "Okay, no more jokes," I said. I rolled her over and kissed her hard. She bit my lip and dug her fingernails into my back. Then it got serious.

Somehow, we ended up on the cold wooden floor with the sheets tangled all around us. She grabbed my hair with both hands when she came, holding on so tight it would make my head hurt for the rest of the night. Afterward, she sat back against the side of the bed. She didn't collapse on me, didn't put her head on my shoulder. She just rolled away from me and sat there with her eyes closed. In the candlelight I could see the beads of sweat on her neck.

We sat like that for a long time, until she finally opened her eyes. "So talk to me," she said.

"Okay," I said. But then I had no idea what to say.

"Tell me more about yourself."

I gave her the whole rundown. Growing up in the Detroit suburbs, my mother dying when I was eight years old. My old man getting up every morning to work for Ford Motors. Going to single-A ball right out of high school, four years in the minors without a call-up. Good hands behind the plate, but struck out too much. Went after too many bad pitches.

And then being a cop in Detroit for eight years. Getting married and living in that little brick house in Redford. I stopped when I got to the part about Franklin, my old partner.

"Can we move to the bed?" she said. "My ass is getting cold on this floor."

We got up onto the bed, under the thick down comforter. She was finally close to me again. I could feel her soft skin and the heat from her body.

I told her about that summer night in Detroit. Tracking down the man who was harassing people at the hospital. His apartment with the aluminum foil all over the walls. Then the gun he pulled out from under the table, the gun he had found in the Dumpster. It was an Uzi, the gun of choice in Detroit in the mid-1980s.

"I watched my partner die," I said. "He was on the floor next to me. I watched the lights go out in his eyes."

"It doesn't sound like you had any chance to stop it."

"I've replayed it in my mind a thousand times," I said. "Ten thousand times. I could have drawn on that guy. I could have at least tried."

She shook her head. "No way. He already had the gun pointed at you."

"He was spaced out, Natalie. I might have been able to beat him."

"Just keep going. What happened next?"

I told her about my own injuries. Three bullets, one in

the rotator cuff, the other nicking the top of the lung, the last one bouncing around like a pinball and ending up next to my heart. I showed her my scars. I told her that the last bullet, the one by my heart, was still there.

She touched my chest. "God," she said.

I told her about the bad years after that. Leaving the force, my marriage breaking up. Then those cabins up north, the ones my father had built, in this little town called Paradise, on the shores of Lake Superior. How I had gone up there, thinking I'd sell them off, but then deciding to stick around for a while. Something about the place. The absolute solitude. The desolate beauty.

I went fast through the rest of the story. Getting talked into trying out the private eye thing, and the wonderful experiences that brought me. Getting my ass kicked, almost freezing to death, watching my father's favorite cabin burn down. Right up to the recent business with Vinnie and his lost brother. She already knew that story. She was there.

"So how about you?" I finally said. "It's your turn."

"Tomorrow," she said. "I've got to sleep." She got up, wrapping herself in the sheet and leaving me the comforter.

"Where are you going?"

"The other room. I can't sleep with someone else in the bed." She left the room, then poked her head back in. "Good night, Alex."

"Good night," I said. I thought about maybe leaving, just getting in the truck and driving back home. Instead I just stared at the strange ceiling for a while. One of the candles burned down to nothing, making it even darker. I fell asleep.

That was the first night.

. . .

Having made our date at the hotel, all I could do was watch the snow fall and wonder how badly it would bury us. I tried to sleep, but the wind was whistling outside and making the windows rattle. I could hear a million tiny snowflakes being driven against the walls. At four in the morning, I got up and turned the outside light on. The snow was already up over the wheels of the truck.

"God damn," I said. My breath fogged the window. "We're gonna get buried."

I knew what I had to do. I threw on some clothes and my coat and gloves. The snow stung my face as soon as I opened the door. I made my way to the truck, stepping through drifts that came to my knees. It was the last thing I wanted to do at that hour, but I knew I had to get out on the road to stay ahead of the snow. Once it got past a certain depth, I wouldn't be able to plow it at all. This had happened exactly twice in the years I had lived up here. Both times, I had to wait for the county to send in excavators to dig me out. And a private access road with a few cabins was never at the top of their list.

I knocked most of the snow off the windshield, then climbed into the truck and started it up. The wheels spun a few times until they finally found some traction, thanks to a twelve-hundred-pound plow on the front and eight hundred pounds of cinder block in the bed. I pushed my way out of my driveway and started up the road, through the snow-covered trees.

My windshield wipers were fighting a losing battle. During the night the snow had turned into the heavy wet stuff that sticks to everything as soon as it lands. I cranked the defroster as high as it would go and tried to stay on the road, which was nothing but a rumor anyway. When I had finally worked my way to the last cabin, I tried to turn the truck around, got stuck a few times, used every bad word I knew and made up some, then finally got it pointed the opposite way. I pounded my way back, past the rentals, then my cabin, then Vinnie's, all the way to the main road.

The snow was mocking me. It was dancing in my headlights and covering up my tracks as soon as I could make them.

I turned around and went back in for more. At least I'd go down fighting.

We had breakfast that next day, the first day of the new year. We didn't talk about what had happened the night before. She went back to her work, wrapping up dinner plates and putting them in a cardboard box. This was her mission in life, she said. She wanted to use this time to pack up the old house, and to finally sell it. She had been putting it off for so long.

Her hair was pinned up again. She had gray sweats on. Working clothes. I offered to help her. She said she needed to be alone for a while.

She came over by the door and gave me a quick kiss on the mouth. Then I left.

By the time I got home, there was a message waiting on my machine.

"Sorry I was a little weird this morning," she said. There was a pause. "It's been a long time for me, if you know what I mean. Give me a call in a couple of days, eh?

If you feel like coming back out, I'll make you dinner."

That was it. I waited a couple of days. Three, to be exact. I tried not to think about her. It was one night. You were there and something happened and it was great and so what. You've got your own problems and she's got hers.

When I finally called her, she apologized again, and asked me if I wanted to come back out for her beef stew.

"I think you should know," I said. "My man Jackie does a beef stew that'll knock you out."

"So you're saying you've got some high standards."

"Yeah, but if you've got some Canadian beer in the house, you might win me over."

"Molson Canadian," she said. "A case in the fridge. Bottles, not cans."

"I'm on my way."

It was two and a half hours in the truck again, across the bridge and down the Queens Highway. Of course, up here that's nothing. You drive two and a half hours to buy your groceries.

It was still light out when I got there. She was wearing the same gray sweats. She had a white handkerchief wrapped around her head.

"You shouldn't have gotten all dressed up just for me," I said.

She pulled me inside and kissed me hard. A minute later we were upstairs, in the same bedroom. We went slowly this time. She took the handkerchief off her head and shook her hair. I ran my hands up her rib cage, caressing the soft flesh beneath her breasts. She closed her eyes.

She grabbed my hands as she moved against me. She worked at it harder and harder, all the while biting her lower lip. She looked at me once and then closed her eyes again. A great shudder ran through her body. Then she collapsed against me and whispered in my ear. "Oh God," she said. "What are you trying to do to me?"

We lay there without talking for a long time, as the sun went down and the light coming through the curtains changed the color in the room. It was the kind of light that usually makes you feel a little sad and tired, the light of a midwinter day that ends too quickly, with spring a long time away. But on this day it felt different.

"What's this from?" I said, running my finger along her eyebrow. I hadn't seen the scars on her face the first time, not in the dim light of New Year's Eve.

"Hockey, what else? I caught a stick there. Fourteen stitches."

"And here, too?" I touched the long line on her chin.

"I took a dive on the ice. Seventeen stitches."

"Don't they wear face guards up here?"

"In college you have to," she said. "But not out on the lakes. Face guards are for pussies. And Americans."

We rolled around a couple of times over that one. Then she got up and put her sweats back on. I couldn't help thinking, what kind of woman invites a man over and doesn't do anything to get fixed up? Maybe the kind who at the last moment was hoping nothing would happen between them? If that was it, her resolution lasted all of three seconds. Hell if I knew.

She served me her beef stew at the big dining room table, under the antique light with the five glowing lanterns. When she sat down across from me, I finally got her story. It's funny how you can distill your whole life down to a few minutes, telling it like it had a plot and a theme and a moral at the end. Or at least what will pass for a moral for the time being, until your whole life story is done.

"This house," she said, looking up at the ceiling. "It was my grandparents'. But it was my house, too. I grew up here. My father . . ."

She looked down for a moment.

"He was killed when I was six years old. He was shot in a bar. Apparently he was trying to protect somebody. Some woman was getting roughed up and he stepped in to help her. Anyway, I only have a couple of memories of him. Good memories, I guess. Him holding me up in the air and swinging me around. One Christmas when he bought me this big rocking horse. I think it's still in the attic."

She looked at the ceiling again.

"And your mother?"

She looked me in the eye. "What about her?"

"I'm just asking. I'm sorry, go ahead."

"My mother," she said, sitting back in her chair. "She didn't exactly get along with my grandparents. I guess it was kinda tough, living with your in-laws after your husband is dead, but she didn't try real hard to make it work. We moved out once when I was like twelve years old, but, well . . ."

She stopped.

"What is it?" I said.

"Alex, you've got to understand . . . Some things happened to me back then. I know it was a long time ago, but . . ."

I waited.

"Some things you don't get over," she said. "Maybe you get better at dealing with them. That's all."

"What happened?"

"My mother got remarried for a while. That's when we moved out of here. My stepfather . . . Well, for now I'll just say this, eh? He died a couple of years ago."

"Natalie, did he—"

"He made a lot of money, too—after he left my mother for somebody else. He became some kind of real estate big shot or something. I don't know exactly. All I know is that Albert DeMarco had a long and happy life. If there's any kind of justice in that, somebody is going to have to explain it to me."

My stomach started to burn. I wasn't sure what to say.

"I finally ran away," she said. "I came back here. My grandfather told Albert he'd have to kill him to take me away again."

"So your mother . . . Is she still around?"

"Yeah, she is. Although, hell, when's the last time I even talked to her? I think it was when she called me to tell me Albert had died. I think she actually thought I'd be happy enough to start forgiving her."

"I'm sorry."

"Don't be," she said. "My grandparents were great, okay? They were the best. My grandfather, you should have seen him . . ." She smiled at the memory. "He was so strong. So kind. He's been gone a long time now, but I still miss him."

She took a hit off her beer bottle and then put it back down.

"Anyway, as great as they were, I was still kind of lonely growing up. I was such an awkward kid. And shy, especially after everything that had happened to me."

I could see it in her. As beautiful as she was on that

night, I could see that kid in her face. A tomboy with a slight overbite and big eyebrows.

"But I loved playing hockey. I used to play with all the boys, and I was faster than most of them. When I started playing girls' hockey in high school and then in college, it was okay, but you could never really hit anybody. I led my women's hockey team in penalty minutes—I guess that sums me up pretty well, eh?"

I shook my head and smiled.

"After hockey, I wasn't sure what to do with myself. But you know, whenever I thought about my stepfather . . . I said to myself, why not become a police officer? Maybe help stop it from happening to somebody else. So I took the tests and joined the OPP. I don't know how it works down there, but up here a woman can do pretty well."

"You never got married?"

She looked at me. "No, Alex. I got close once. There was this other officer, Jimmy Natoli. That's right, my name would have been Natalie Natoli. But he really wanted me to quit the force after I married him. I didn't want to do that. Although maybe, looking back on it . . . I suppose I still had problems getting close to someone. After it fell apart, I was still on the force with him, so things got a little weird. That's when I got shipped up to the Hearst station. I was thinking, great, look where they stuck me, way the hell up here. They partnered me with Claude DeMers, too, this ancient guy. They must really want to bury me up here."

She took another drink.

"But then he turned out to be so great. It sounds kind

of dumb, but with my grandfather gone . . . It was like I really needed him, you know? He tried to make things good for me. Until that business at the lake."

"Yeah," I said. That part I knew.

"I swear, I'm cursed, Alex. Wherever I go, bad things happen."

"Come on, Natalie."

"But no matter what," she said, "I always had this place to come back to. When my grandmother died, she left it to me. I hired somebody to come in and keep things working. Run the furnace, make sure the pipes didn't freeze. But I was never sure what to do with it. I couldn't bring myself to sell it. It was like my refuge from the world. But now . . . I've been here for a few weeks, and I'm thinking maybe it's time."

"That's why you're doing all this packing."

She nodded her head. "Yeah. But after I sell it, then what? I don't know what the hell I'm going to do."

I didn't say anything. I sat there with her for a while until she got up to do the dishes. I grabbed a towel and dried while she washed. Later, we went to bed and this time we slept together, despite what she had said about always sleeping alone. I couldn't stop thinking about what she had told me that day, about her own scars and how they'd never heal completely. It helped me to understand her a little bit better, how she could be so close to me one moment and then suddenly a million miles away.

I worked with her on some more packing the next morning. Then I went home. I thought about her all the way home and all that day and that night. I sat at Jackie's in front of the fire and I thought about her.

I had been alone too long. To a starving man, this sudden feast.

"You've got to keep your head on straight," I said to the flames. "Or you're gonna be in big trouble."

I kept plowing. The sun came up, somewhere behind the snow clouds, giving the world a muted glow and no warmth. I rumbled down the main road to fill up the tank. There were a few poor souls out trying to shovel in the dim light, but aside from that it was quiet in Paradise.

I pumped the gas and paid Ruthie, the lady who owned the place. She told me I looked different and I agreed with her. "It's been a long night," I said.

"No, I mean there's something else."

I knew exactly what she was talking about, but I left before she could figure it out. I got back in the truck and pulled out right behind one of the county trucks. He had his big blade down and he was kicking that snow at least twenty feet in the air. I saw one car get completely buried, and I hoped the guy who had been dumb enough to park it by the road had a good memory.

I hit my road again and ran the plow through for the hundredth time. I had to keep at it, or I'd lose the road completely. With the new snow, the snowmobilers would finally be coming. As long as I had to put up with the noise, I might as well be making some money from it.

The snow started to let up. I finally got ahead of it, and made one more pass, down the road and back, before I stopped at my cabin. I had some coffee and splashed some water on my face. The phone rang. It was Natalie.

"Alex," she said. "Are you getting a lot of snow?"

"I don't know. I haven't noticed."

"Yeah, right. You still think we should try this today?"

"I'll be there," I said. "I promise."

Then a silence, another hesitation that should have told me something important, but didn't.

"Okay," she said. "I'll see you there. Drive carefully."

"You, too," I said. Then I hung up.

Now there's only one problem, I thought. Make that two. I look like shit and I feel like shit. I took most of my clothes off and collapsed on the bed. Plenty of time to grab a little sleep, I thought. A little sleep so I could feel human again, then a hot shower, get dressed, and go over there. Plenty of time.

When I woke up, the clock read 2:14 and it was snowing like crazy again. "Son of a bitch," I said. I got out of bed and looked outside. There was already another eight inches of snow on the ground. "Son of a bitch bitch bitch bitch bitch."

I called Natalie. There was no answer. I left her a message, told her I was still at home, and that I needed to plow again, and that I'd still try to make it. But hell, if it was this bad out her way, maybe she shouldn't even try. Assuming she hadn't left yet.

But if she wasn't answering her phone, she had to be on the road already. If she was on the road, then I was going to be on the road, too. Just plow a couple more times, I thought. Plow, then come in and call her again. Maybe call the hotel, see if she's there yet. If she is, get cleaned up, put some clothes on. Hell, go plow a couple more times if you have to, then head to the Soo. If the road gets buried, so be it. I'll deal with it tomorrow.

I headed out into the snow again. It was getting harder and harder to plow. There was no place to put the new snow, with the banks already four feet high. The road was getting narrower and narrower, but as long as one vehicle could get through, I figured I'd be okay. It's not like I'd ever have a lot of traffic.

I went back and forth three times, and then headed back inside. It was hard just to walk to my front door. The snow was up to my knees now, and the wind was blowing everything sideways. I fought my way inside and slammed the door. It was insanity to even think I'd be going anywhere. Absolute insanity. So of course I'd be going. I called Natalie's number again. I let it ring a dozen times.

"It's ringing," I said. "That means the phone lines are working, right? She's just not there."

I pictured her out on the road. I hoped she wasn't stuck somewhere.

I called the hotel. She hadn't arrived yet. It was after three o'clock now. God damn it, where was she?

Relax, Alex. She's on the way. She's taking her time.

I took a shower and shaved. I slapped some cologne on my face, felt it burning my skin. I put on an undershirt, took one look at it in the mirror and then tried to find a different undershirt. Twenty minutes later, I was finally dressed and ready to go.

I went outside and fought my way back to the truck again. The wind was screaming. The snow lashed at my face. "I'm going," I said to myself. "I'm going."

I had to brush the snow off the windshield again. I backed out and put my plow down for one more run. "I'm going. I'm going. I'm going."

I drove through town. There was nobody, no sign of life until I saw the lights on at Jackie's place. I kept driving. My wipers were clogged with snow already, and I could feel my tires losing traction every few feet. I fishtailed and swerved and swore at the snow.

There's a stretch of road a couple of miles south of town—it runs along a narrow strip of land, with the lake on one side and a pond on the other. It was totally exposed to the wind, so I figured it would be a little tricky. As soon as I got close to it, the truth finally caught up to me.

I wasn't going any farther.

I hadn't turned my radio on since the day before, so I hadn't heard it. I didn't *want* to hear it. But now as I looked at the great expanse of snow—I couldn't even guess where the snow-covered land lay, between the snow-covered ice of the lake and the snow-covered ice of the pond—I knew that there had to be a state of emergency all through the county. Even if I got through this stretch, and broke the law and tried to get to the Soo, I'd get stuck somewhere else. It was fifty miles if I stayed on the main roads, and even if most of M-123 was sheltered by the trees, as soon as M-28 broke out of the Hiawatha National Forest, it was all open ground. They wouldn't even try to plow it until the snow let up and the wind stopped blowing.

I hit the steering wheel with both palms, and then spent the next ten minutes trying to turn the truck around. When I was finally pointed north again, I drove back into town. There was no rush now. I went five miles per hour instead of my daredevil ten miles per hour. When I got to Jackie's place, I looked in again and saw the lights and pictured the fireplace and a cold Canadian. I pulled into the parking lot.

There were six people in the place, all locals who had walked down the road for a little company. They all looked up at me when I opened the door and cheered. It was that kind of night, when walking fifty yards was a cause for celebration.

"Alex!" Jackie said from behind the bar. "Did you walk all the way down here?"

"Can I use your phone?"

"Help yourself," he said, pushing the phone across the bar. As I got closer, he did a double take and stared at me.

"What did you do?"

"Huh?" I dialed Natalie's number.

"You did something."

I shook my head at him. Natalie wasn't answering.

"You did," he said. "Something's different."

I dialed the Ojibway Hotel again. I got the same desk clerk, and this time he told me, yes, Natalie Reynaud was there. I waited while he called her room.

"Alex," Jackie said. "You did something to your hair. That's what it is."

Yeah, I thought. My hair. The box said it would look totally natural, and that nobody would notice. Totally natural, my ass.

"It's just a little thing for my gray," I said.

"Just a little thing? You look like a lounge singer."

I gave him a look and wondered how the day could get any worse. Then I heard her voice on the phone.

"Alex, is that you?"

"Yeah, it's me." I tried to pull the phone off the bar, but the cord wasn't long enough. I waved Jackie away, but he didn't move an inch.

"Oh my God," Jackie said. "Now I know."

"They said the roads are all closed out your way," Natalie said on the phone. "I barely made it here myself. I think they closed the bridge right after I got across."

"This explains everything," Jackie said. "I should have known."

If I could have reached him, I would have grabbed him by the collar and choked him.

"I'm sorry," I said into the phone, trying to wave him away again. "It was a bad idea."

"Don't worry about it, Alex. It's kinda nice here, eh? A nice hotel. It's really good to be out of that house for a while. I was going stir crazy."

"I shouldn't have asked you to come out."

Jackie just stood there watching me, shaking his head.

"Alex, I'm fine," she said. "Really. I'll just go downstairs and get something to eat. Watch the snow for a while. If you think you might be able to get here tomorrow—"

"Yes," I said. "I'll be there tomorrow."

Jackie looked at the ceiling and sighed dramatically. I looked around for something to throw at him.

"Okay, then," she said. "I'll stay here tonight and I'll see you tomorrow. Call me in the morning, eh?"

"I'll do that," I said. Then there was a long silence while I tried to think of something else to say.

"I'll see you tomorrow," she said. We both said good-bye and hung up.

"A woman," Jackie said.

"I'm going to kill you."

"A woman. This is why you've been acting so weird lately."

"Yeah, and this is why I didn't mention it before, Jackie. I know how you are about women."

I didn't want to have the whole discussion again with Jackie, the man who lived through the worst divorce of the twentieth century. But it was coming whether I wanted it or not, so I just asked him for a beer and went over to the fireplace. As long as I'd be staying put in Paradise, I knew I should be back out there plowing my road. But a little break wouldn't hurt.

So that's where I was when the sun went down that evening. I was sitting by the fire in the Glasgow Inn, my usual spot, but on this day not at all where I wanted to be. The wind kept blowing and the snow was still coming hard, like it would never end.

This is why the Ojibwas prayed to the winter every year, asking for mercy, asking that the spring would come quickly, and that the old man and the young child would both live to see it.

The snow finally stopped around midnight. But the damage had already been done. I didn't even know it yet. As I slept alone in my bed, I didn't even know what I had done.

Everything that was about to happen would begin that night. And it would all be on my head.

Three

The time passed between the two of us, leading up to this night at the Ojibway Hotel. I had been going over there three or four times a week, for how long was it then? A month? Five weeks? You add up the actual waking hours we spent together, and it wasn't that much. But she was always there in my head. If I wasn't on my way over there or on my way back, I was thinking about what she was doing, and when I'd be seeing her again.

And me, I was virtually the only person she saw, the only person she ever talked to. She'd go down into Blind River, pick up some things, go right back home, work on the house. That's all she did. She said it helped her forget everything that had happened. She had to put it all behind her before she could think about what to do next. That's what she told me.

It made me wonder. Was I just a part of that? Another way to forget?

It got strange sometimes. She'd be doing something and she'd look up at me, like I had just shown up and she had no idea what I was doing there. I wouldn't hear from her for three or four days. Then she'd call me up and ask me how soon I could be there. She was hungry and she wanted to eat dinner with me right away.

Then we'd go upstairs. It was always the same room. The same bed or floor or a little of both. The last couple of times, we'd lain there and she'd be looking off at nothing, like she was a million miles away. She'd snap out of it and give me a quick smile, and then without a word she'd get up and go downstairs.

It wasn't real. That's what I finally started to realize. The whole thing was like a spell, or a daydream, or something you'd make up on a lonely night. Wouldn't it be nice if there were someone, right here, right now . . .

I've never left well enough alone, not once in my entire life, so I decided it was time to put this thing to the test, to get it out in the daylight and to see what happened. So I asked her if she'd like to come down to Michigan sometime. Just mentioned it. That she'd never seen the cabins, or Paradise, or the Glasgow Inn. She'd have to meet Jackie, and, of course, Vinnie she already knew. But it would be good to see him again, to see how well he was recovering.

She didn't say no. She said, yeah, that would be great. We'll have to do that sometime. Sometime soon. Maybe after she got some more work done on the house.

"Soon" never came, until the night the snowstorm hit and I was stuck here in Paradise. So it got postponed another day. Now, finally, maybe I'd find out if this whole thing was real after all. And maybe I didn't really want to find out.

That's the kind of soap opera nonsense that was going through my mind as I finally made my way out to the Soo.

I had called her that morning. She said it was a little strange sleeping there in the king-sized bed, listening to the snowstorm. Being a cop didn't help. If anything, it makes a woman realize all the more how vulnerable she can be. So she never did like staying in hotel rooms by herself. I told her I hoped we could change the arrangements that night. Just saying that out loud, seeing how it sounded, seeing how she responded to it. She told me to hurry up and get over there.

I had to plow again, of course, so I didn't get out until after lunchtime. Even then the main roads were still a mess. It took me a good two hours to get there, pounding my way through the new snowdrifts and then crawling along behind one of the county trucks.

In Sault Ste. Marie, Michigan, a six-story building is as big as it gets. That's how tall the Ojibway Hotel is, looming over everything else on Portage Avenue, right across from the Soo Locks. According to the sign in the lobby, it had been in business since 1927, and it was the only game in town if you wanted some real luxury. It had big red awnings over all the windows on the ground floor, and the dining room was like something out of another era. I always made a point of having lunch there when I was in the city, but I had never spent a night there. Until now.

As I finally found a place to park between the giant piles of snow, I knew she was up there in one of those rooms, waiting for me. I grabbed my overnight bag and crossed the street, trying very hard not to slip and fall on the hard-packed snow. That would be my luck, to break my leg twenty feet from the front door.

There was a young man out front, trying to shovel the

snow. He looked cold and miserable, and he was wearing a uniform that belonged on an organ-grinder's monkey. I watched him as I made my way to the door, wondering how long it would take him to split open the back of his red coat.

He stopped when he saw me coming, and opened the door for me. "Afternoon, sir," he said.

"Hell of a day to be shoveling snow in that suit."

"We do what we can."

I stomped the snow off my feet before I entered the lobby. It was the last place you'd want to track snow in, with all the fancy furniture and the Oriental rug and the display cases showing off the hotel's long history.

I didn't notice the man sitting there in the lobby. Not at first. I went to the desk and said hello to the woman behind it. She asked me if I had seen enough snow for one lifetime and I said that I had. When I asked for Natalie Reynaud's room, she picked up the phone and called her. I didn't take that personally, of course. You don't send a man up to a woman's room without calling her, no matter how friendly he looks.

I turned around while I waited. The doorman was still out on the sidewalk, struggling with the snow. The way he was lifting with his back instead of his legs, I knew he'd be sore as hell. It didn't matter how young he was.

Then I saw the old man sitting in the lobby. He was in one of the big chairs by the fireplace. He had a nice overcoat on, and it looked like he had a suit and tie on underneath that. He was wearing a hat, an old fedora. You don't see men wearing hats like that anymore. That's the first thing I thought. Then I noticed the boots he was wearing. They were like rubber fishing boots, going all the way up to his knees. They didn't go with the rest of his outfit, but with all the snow, what the hell.

He was looking at me. He smiled.

Before I could smile back, the woman gave me the phone.

"Alex, is that you?"

"Natalie. I'm in the lobby."

"I'm in room 601. Come on up."

"The top floor. I'm on my way."

I hung up the phone. I thanked the woman at the desk and headed for the elevator. My throat was dry.

I pressed the elevator button and waited. Then the door opened and I got in. The old man was right behind me.

I pressed six and asked him which floor he needed.

"Six is good," the man said.

I nodded and looked up at the row of numbers above the door. The door closed. I couldn't help noticing the man was looking right at me. It's the one thing you don't do in an elevator.

I looked back at him. He smiled again. Up close, I saw he was a little older than I had first thought. He had gray eyes with red rims, and a dark little mustache that had gone too thin. His lips were purple.

I returned his smile, then looked away. The elevator door closed. He kept looking at me.

I cleared my throat.

"Do you like my hat?" he said.

"Excuse me?" I said, looking at him again.

"Do you like my hat?"

I didn't know what to say. The elevator was moving now. "Yes," I finally said. "I do."

"It's rather old," he said. He kept looking me right in the eye. He kept smiling.

"I figured."

"Would you like to know how old my hat is?"

The elevator came to a stop.

"No, sir," I said. "I don't need to know that."

"Very well."

The door opened. I got out. Room 601 was just a few steps away, so I didn't have time to notice that the old man was still standing in the elevator. I was just about to knock, my hand in midair, when I looked back. He had stayed in the elevator, one arm extended to keep the door from closing. He was still smiling. Finally, he gave me a little nod of his head, pulled his arm away, and let the doors close in front of him.

I stood there for a moment, trying to figure it out. Then I thought, to hell with it. An old man slightly off his nut. Never mind.

His eyes, though. They were clear. They were focused. Never mind, Alex.

I knocked lightly on the door. Natalie opened it and let me in. She was wearing blue jeans and a red sweater. I had never seen her in red before. "You look great," I said.

"Your hair," she said.

"Oh God." I touched it, like I was verifying it was still on my head. "Okay, here's the thing. The box said it was supposed to look totally natural."

"You dyed your hair."

"No, no. It wasn't dye. Come on. It was, what do you call it, a rinse."

She came over to me and put her arms around my

neck. "You dyed your hair," she said. "Who'd you do that for, you jackass?"

I wrapped her up. "The box said—"

"Yeah, I know," she said. Then she kissed me. Everything seemed to run downstream at that point, right onto the bed. I lifted the red sweater over her arms and then she went to work on my shirt buttons.

"I wasn't going to do this," she said.

"Why not?"

"Because. God, Alex. I think we need to slow down a little bit."

"Too late."

"Why does this happen?" she said. "Every time I see you?"

She seemed genuinely angry this time. At me or at herself. I didn't know. I held her down and kissed her hard, and then everything happened again, just like the first time and every other time after that, like there was nothing either of us could do to stop it, even if we wanted to.

Afterward, as we were both lying there in the tangled-up sheets, I looked out the window and saw the snow falling. "Oh great," I said. "Just what we need."

She didn't say anything.

"Are you okay?" I said.

"I don't know."

"What is it?"

"We should talk about this."

"So go ahead."

"I need some air first," she said, sitting up. "Come on, it's not too late. I want you to show me around."

I laughed. "There's not much to see. Not this time of year."

But she was already putting her clothes back on. A few minutes later, we were both downstairs in the lobby, wrapped up tight in our coats, ready for our evening stroll. I looked around for my friend from the elevator, but he was nowhere to be seen.

"What is it?" she said.

"Oh, there was just a man down here before. He was acting kinda strange."

"An old guy, right? All dressed up?"

"Yeah, did he say something to you, too?"

"No, I just saw him in the dining room yesterday. When I was having dinner alone. He walked by and tipped his hat to me."

"I think he's got a screw loose."

"I'm sure he's harmless," she said. "He sort of fits in with the place, doesn't he? All these old artifacts in the display cases."

The young doorman opened the door for us. He still had the shovel, and it looked like he had almost finished the sidewalk. Until this new snow had started falling. Whatever they were paying him, today it wasn't enough.

We walked down Portage Avenue, toward the locks. They were closed for the winter, of course, so there were no ships to see. The entire river was frozen now, all the way across to Canada. I told her this street would be busy in the summer, when the shops were open and the tourists were walking around and watching the locks from the observation deck. It was hard to imagine now.

"What did you tell me?" I said. "That you've never been over here before? All those years you were living across the river?"

"I drove through a couple of times," she said, "but I

never came into town, no. I heard all the stories, though."

"What stories?"

"About Soo Michigan. What a wild town it is. At least, when I was growing up."

I looked down the empty street. The snow was falling and the wind was kicking up clouds all along the high snowbanks. Some wild town. At that moment, it was hard to imagine anyone even living here.

"My grandfather never wanted me to come over here," she said. "He told me there were gunfights and prostitutes and all sorts of bad stuff going on across the bridge."

"I think maybe he watched too many Westerns."

"Yeah, well, some Canadians think all of the States is that way."

We walked some more. The sun went down. From the end of the street we could see the International Bridge, the lights glowing in the darkness. It started to feel a lot colder.

We made our way back to the hotel, holding hands like schoolkids. What she had said back in the room, about wanting to talk—I kept waiting for it to happen. But it didn't. The lights were on outside the hotel and the doorman was there shoveling the snow.

We went inside with faces red from the cold air and snow all over our shoes. It felt good to sit down in the dining room and to feel the heat thawing us out. The room was elegant, with chandeliers and big windows overlooking the river. On a different night in a different season there would have been ships moving through the locks just outside, great seven-hundred-foot freighters on their way to Lake Huron. But on this night all we could see outside was the snow falling. Endless snow, that's what this winter had become.

When we had ordered our food, I noticed the old man again. He was sitting on the other side of the dining room, facing us, with a big cloth dinner napkin tucked into his collar. We were the only three customers in the place. He gave me a tip of his hat.

"There he is," I said.

"Who?" She turned to look and then gave the man a little wave when she saw him.

"Maybe he's a ghost," I said. "He died in this hotel and now he haunts all the guests."

She smiled for just a moment, then looked out the window. We were both quiet for a while. Just as she was about to say something, the waitress appeared with a bottle of champagne.

"Compliments of the gentleman," she said, setting up a stand with an ice bucket.

I looked back over at the old man. He was drinking something now. He raised his glass to us.

"Who is he?" I said.

"I don't know," the waitress said, pulling the cork. "I've never seen him before. But he sort of goes with the place, doesn't he? This hotel was built in 1927, you know."

When she had poured two glasses, Natalie picked hers up and raised it to the man across the room. He tipped his hat again.

"Veuve Clicquot," she said, taking a sip. "This is the good stuff."

"Yeah," I said, with a little edge. "We'll have to go thank him."

"What's the matter?"

"Ah, it's nothing. Like you say, he's probably harmless."

We drank the champagne until the waitress brought our dinners. The wind kicked up and rattled the big windows so hard we could feel it in our bones. But it was warm inside, and a full bottle of champagne was making everything look soft in the light from the chandeliers. Natalie was a little too beautiful to be true, her green eyes sparkling. The whole night seemed a little unreal.

When I looked over a few minutes later, the old man was gone.

"Guess our friend called it a night," I said.

"I hope he's not going outside."

"He's a ghost, remember? Ghosts don't get cold."

That's the line that would stay with me. That's the line I'd remember the next day, when we would find out what had happened. At that very moment, the two of us sitting there in the dining room, finishing the last of the champagne, the old man was out there. He had left the hotel. He had walked down Portage Avenue. He had taken a right onto Ashmun, and had made his way south, walking on the street lined with snowbanks and dark empty buildings on each side. It was snowing harder. He must have been walking slowly. He crossed the little bridge, over the frozen canal that cut off the downtown from the rest of Sault Ste. Marie. He made it as far as the bookstore on the right side of the road.

Was he already freezing at that moment, when I made my bad joke about ghosts not getting cold? I've been there myself. I know how it feels. You're disoriented, you start talking to yourself. Things from your past come back to you. You can't walk straight. Then finally, the ultimate irony. Or maybe the ultimate mercy. You don't feel cold anymore. You don't feel anything at all.

But, of course, we didn't know. We hadn't gone back to the elevator yet, feeling happy and full after the big meal, and still a little light-headed from the champagne. We hadn't kissed in the elevator and held tight to each other. We hadn't seen the present he had left for us, on the floor in front of room 601.

I hadn't gone back down to the lobby yet, looking for him, or asked the woman at the front desk if she had seen him. I hadn't looked for the doorman, or gone outside myself with no coat on, to look up and down the street for some sign of the old man.

We didn't know he was out there, the snow covering him at that very moment. Or that the snowplow would run over his frozen body early the next morning, nearly cutting him in half.

Ghosts don't get cold. I said it, and then we finished our dinner and went upstairs. The thing was sitting there on the hallway carpet, right in front of the door. The door he had seen me go to. Whatever it was, it was covered by the big dinner napkin he'd had tucked into his collar.

I pulled the napkin off. Underneath was a hat, upside down, filled with ice and snow.

The man had apparently gone out to the sidewalk, filled his hat to the brim, and then brought it back inside to leave it here by the door. The ice and snow were already starting to melt and leak through the material, a dark stain spreading onto the carpet.

"What the hell," I said. I bent down and picked it up.

"That's the hat he was wearing, right? The old man downstairs?"

"It is. But why?"

"Wait a minute," she said. "Is there something else inside there?"

She was right. I reached into the frozen mess and pulled out a piece of paper. It was the hotel stationery, and there were five words written in capital letters with an unsteady hand.

"What does it say?" she said.

I didn't say anything. I just turned the piece of paper around and showed it to her.

I KNOW WHO YOU ARE!

Four

I took the hat with me to Jackie's place the next day. I had come home that morning to plow the road again, having spent the night with Natalie on a strange hotel bed, after finding the hat with the ice and snow in it, along with the note, after going downstairs to look for the old man and then going out into the snowy night. I had come back to the room and we had talked about it.

"Are you sure you've never seen him before?" she had asked.

"I'm positive," I said. "I don't know the man."

"Well, he didn't leave it for me. I told you, I've never even been in this town before."

"He might be confused," I said. "Hell, maybe he has Alzheimer's. That's another reason to find him."

So I had gone downstairs again. Nobody had seen the man, or even knew who he was. There was no sign of the doorman, either. The woman at the desk seemed to think he had gone out to look for the man. But she wasn't sure.

I came back upstairs and found Natalie already in bed. When I lay down next to her, she told me she was feeling a little strange. "Just being here," she had said. "In this place. It feels like it's so far away from home."

I couldn't blame her. "Do you want to leave?"

"No," she said. "I don't want to leave." Then she proved it to me. The streetlamp below our window cast a dim light on the ceiling, just enough for me to see her face as we came together. It felt different this time, whether it was just the place and the circumstances I couldn't say.

The next morning, we left the hotel early, going our separate ways. I didn't even check out at the desk. I just took the bill that had been slid under the door and left.

I took the hat with me. I wasn't sure why. Maybe I thought it would help me figure out who the man was.

If we had stayed there a little longer, if we had gone downstairs and had breakfast, then we might have heard about the discovery down the street. But we didn't. We left before they found him.

Now I sat there at the bar and looked at the hat, rotating it in my hands. It had obviously cost some money, way back when. It was gray with a slightly darker band. The lining felt like satin. The crease ran perfectly across the top. It was in excellent condition except for the new stains on it. As the stains dried, they left the pale residue of salt.

"What's with the hat?" Jackie said. "Ashamed of that dye job you're walking around with?"

"I told you, Jackie. I was just trying to rinse out some gray hair."

"For this woman, I know. You did it for Natasha."

"Her name is Natalie."

"Let me see that hat," he said. He looked at the label.

"Borsalino, Milan and New York. This was a nice hat. What happened to it?"

I gave him the quick version of the story.

"You gotta be kidding me," he said, turning the hat around. "Some old bird ruins a great old hat just to let you know he recognized you?"

"What would you call that, a fedora?"

"This is a homburg," he said, trying it on. It fit him perfectly. "See how the brim is turned up all the way around? My father used to have one, back when men actually wore hats."

"I'm gonna call the hotel," I said. "See if they know anything more."

"Hell of a thing," he said, taking the hat off. "Doing this to a good homburg."

He kept fooling with it while I called the hotel. He wet a dish towel and tried to rub away the salt stains, but it wasn't working.

"Nope, this hat is a lost cause," he said, then he stopped short when he saw my face.

When I was done, I thanked the woman and hung up the phone.

"What is it?" he said.

"The old man's dead," I said. "They found him outside in a snowbank."

"Holy God."

"She said his name was Simon Grant. He was eighty-two years old."

"What happened? I mean, how did he—"

"He just walked outside. He went down Ashmun Street. They think he must have just got lost or got tired or something. They don't really know. A snowplow ran over his body this morning."

"Nobody should go that way," Jackie said. "Nobody should freeze to death like an animal."

I took the hat from him. "I have to call Natalie," I said. I dialed the number and waited while it rang.

"What are you going to do with this hat?"

"Hell if I know," I said. Her phone kept ringing.

"You should turn it in."

"What?"

"It belonged to the old man, didn't it?"

I held up my hand to him as Natalie finally answered the phone. When I told her what had happened, she didn't say anything.

"You still there?" I said.

"Yes, Alex. I'm here."

"Are you okay?"

"I can't believe it," she said. "Do you still have the hat he left on the floor?"

"Yeah, I've got it right here."

"You have to give it back. You know that."

"What? How can I—"

"His family," she said. "They should have the hat."

"I don't even know how to get in touch with them." I looked up at Jackie. He nodded his head at me like he knew exactly what she was saying.

"Take it to the police," she said. "They'll give it to the family."

"I guess I could do that," I said. Although driving back into town was the last thing I felt like doing.

"That poor man. What a terrible night."

"Natalie . . ."

"I'm sorry, Alex. I gotta go. I'll talk to you later, all right?"

"Okay," I said. And then she hung up.

"She agrees with me," Jackie said. "Am I right?"

"What'd you guys do, talk about this beforehand?"

"It's the only right thing to do."

That's how I ended up driving back to the Soo for the second time in two days, with the hat resting on the seat beside me. The sun was finally out, and it made the snow shine so bright it was hard to look at. Not that there was anything to see. The banks were piled five feet high all along the roads, and the plows were still out there trying to catch up.

When I got to the city, I saw a hundred people with snow shovels, trying to reclaim the sidewalks. I drove by the Ojibway Hotel, but I didn't see the doorman outside. I kept going, taking the right on Ashmun. This is where it happened, I thought. According to the woman at the hotel, this is where they found him.

I slowed down as I crossed the little bridge over the canal. A few yards beyond it I could see where they had dug out most of the snowbank, right in front of the bookstore. There were lots of tire tracks and sand and dirt and God knows what else. An empty paper coffee cup blew across the road.

You could tell that men had been there, working hard at something. But there was no crime scene tape, or anything to suggest that something bad had happened. But then, come to think of it, there had been no crime. It was just an old man who fell into the snow and froze to death.

Simon Grant. That was his name. I looked down at the

hat lying on the seat next to me. Simon Grant, whoever the hell he was, is no more.

The City County Building was back on the north side of the bridge, over on Court Street. I knew what I had to do next. But instead I kept going. I wasn't ready yet. On the spur of the moment, there was one thing I wanted to do first.

Simon Grant. I kept saying the name to myself. Simon Grant.

When I got to Three Mile Road, I hung a left and drove down to the Custom Motor Shop. They had just plowed the parking lot, and there was a mountain of snow to one side you could have used skis on. As I pulled in, I couldn't help feeling a little guilty. Sure, I had promised I'd stop in to see him the next time I was in town. But how convenient that I just so happened to have this little thing to ask him about.

I might have sat there thinking about it, but at that moment the man himself came out the door. Leon Prudell, my old partner. When a local lawyer talked me into trying out the private eye business, it was Leon who lost his job to me. It was Leon who showed up at the Glasgow Inn and called me out into the parking lot. That's how much he loved his job, and how much he hated me at that moment. When the whole private eye thing blew up in my face, he was there, and he actually helped me out, and proved that he knew what he was doing. Later, we had an off-and-on partner thing going for a while. When I walked away from it, he was still there to help me, whenever something would drag me back into the game. Now here he was, selling snowmobiles for a living, trying to forget all about those old dreams of being a private investigator.

"Alex!" he said when he saw me. I got out and shook his hand. He looked the same as always, with the wild orange hair and the extra pounds around the middle. In his down coat he looked as big as the Michelin Man.

"How's business?" I said.

"We had a busy morning," he said. "Now that the snow finally came."

I looked into the front window and saw a long line of gleaming snowmobiles. "I do love those machines. I just can't get enough of that noise."

"Snowmobilers pay your bills, Alex. What the hell did you do to your hair?"

"It's nothing," I said. "It'll wash out in a couple of days."

"I guess things are going well with Natalie?"

That stopped me. Then I remembered. Leon was the one who ran down her address for me, back when I had this crazy idea I should try to find her. That plus the hair, it was pretty basic detective work.

"Actually, I was with her last night," I said. "But something kinda strange happened."

That's all I had to say. He was already hooked. I could see it in his eyes. So I gave him the rundown, up to and including the old man being found in the snowbank.

"Do you have a name?" he said.

"Yes, the woman at the hotel told me. His name is Simon Grant."

"Hold on," he said, taking out a small pad of paper. You could count on Leon to always have a pad of paper.

"Simon Grant," he said slowly, writing it down. "Any other information on the deceased?" He was slipping right back into private eye mode.

"Leon, I'm just telling you what happened. I don't expect you to go to work on this." I hesitated. "I mean, I suppose if you still have the access to your database, whatever that thing was . . ."

"The P-Search," he said. "Yes, I still have it. I can do that, no problem."

"I'm sorry. I don't mean to do this. Every time I see you, it's like I want something from you."

"I'd be mad if you didn't ask me, Alex. Now what else can you tell me?"

"Nothing," I said. "I just have a name. And the hat he left in front of our door."

"You kept the hat?"

"Yeah, I did. I'm not sure why. I just . . ."

"What are you going to do with it?"

"I figure I'd better give it to the police. Maybe they can give it to the man's family or something."

"Do you have it with you right now? Can I see it?"

"Sure," I said. I opened the passenger's side door and brought it out for him.

"This looks old," he said. He examined it as closely as a jeweler appraising a diamond.

"You can see the stains," I said. "From the ice and snow."

"You said there was a note, too."

"Yes." I pulled it out of my coat pocket and unfolded it.

"I know who you are," Leon said, looking at the note just as carefully.

"I swear, I never saw this man before in my life."

"Here, hold these a second," he said. He handed me the hat and the note, and started writing on his pad again.

"What are you doing now?"

"The lining says Borsalino, Milan and New York," he said, writing it down. "There's no year on it. And no size. Although I'd estimate seven, seven and a half."

Good old Leon, I thought. Who else would stand in a parking lot and take notes on an old hat?

"Let me take some pictures," he said.

"What?"

"I've got my digital camera in the car."

"What do you have a digital camera for? I thought you were out of the private eye business."

"Everybody has a digital camera, Alex. It's no big deal."

It sounded like something he'd tell his wife Eleanor. No big deal, honey. It's just for taking pictures of our next vacation.

He went to his car, the little piece of crap Chevy Nova that somehow never got stuck in the snow, and found a black bag. "Here we go," he said, pulling out the camera. It looked a little too sophisticated for pictures of the kids, but I wasn't going to give him a hard time about it.

"Okay, let me take a picture of the note first," he said. "Put it on your hood."

I did as I was told. He bent down close and snapped two shots.

"Okay, now the hat."

I put the hat on the hood and watched him take nine or ten shots, turning the hat around and then tipping it over.

"Leon, is this really going to help us?"

"You never know," he said. "Now you can go give it to the police and we'll still have the pictures." He put the lens cap back on the camera.

"You're something else," I said. But I knew this is what

he would do. He'd grab on to this like a dog on a steak bone. It's what he lived for.

"I'll let you know what I find out," he said. "You wanna get some lunch now? I was just on my way."

I was about to decline, but then I thought, what the hell. Go buy the guy some lunch. He deserves that much from you, at the very least. Besides, look what's next on your to-do list. A visit to the police station means you might just run into your old friend, Chief Maven. The longer you can put that one off, the better.

"Okay," I said. "I'll take you to lunch on one condition."

"What's that?"

"We don't eat at the Ojibway Hotel."

We had lunch at the Chinese Buffet, then it was time for Leon to go back to selling snowmobiles, and for me to go back downtown. Chief Roy Maven of the Sault Ste. Marie Police Department can usually be found in the City County Building, which is basically a big gray cement block attached to the old courthouse. The building and the man go together, for me anyway, because they both have roughly the same amount of charm. Today, at least, I knew there was no need to see Chief Maven himself. All I was doing was dropping off a stupid hat. I figured I'd just give it to the receptionist and leave.

There was a truck working hard to clear the front parking lot, so I parked around back by the police entrance, right next to the jail's courtyard. It was a little twelve-by-twelve square, completely surrounded by a chain-link fence and razor wire. Ordinarily, there'd be somebody out sitting on the picnic table, having a smoke, but today the table was buried under two feet of snow.

The city police department shares the same building with the county, which puts Chief Maven somewhere near the bottom of the totem pole, below the sheriff, who owns the jail and the best part of the building, the state police, who have their own barracks down the road, and the feds, who run the Soo locks and control the border. That's half the reason why he's always so happy.

The other half is that he genuinely doesn't like me. We had this sort of chemical reaction to each other the first time we met, and we never found a way to get past it. Hell, for all I knew, he was a great guy, and under different circumstances, we would have even been friends.

But I wouldn't have bet on it.

I went inside, stomped the snow off my boots, and told the woman at the desk that I wanted to leave something for Chief Maven.

"Is he expecting you?" she asked.

"No, no," I said. "I just wanted to give him this hat. It belonged to the man who was found dead in the snow this morning."

"Oh my," she said. She looked at the hat like she wouldn't have touched it for a thousand dollars.

"I was thinking he could return it to the man's family. That's all."

"I'm going to call him."

"No, please, that's not necessary." I knew what would happen if she called him. He'd tell her to make me wait out here, and then sometime around spring he'd actually come out to see me. I'd played this game with him before.

"I'm sure he'll want to speak to you," she said, the phone already in her hand.

"I'll just drop it off at his office," I said. "I know where it is."

"Sir, you can't just go back there . . ."

But I was already gone. I went down the hallway and saw that his door was open. When I poked my head in, he was on the phone. No doubt the receptionist had called to warn him I was on my way.

"Hello, Chief," I said.

"McKnight," he said, slamming down the phone. "What the hell are you doing here?"

"I just wanted to give you something."

"The waiting area's out in the lobby. And what the hell did you do to your hair?"

I went in and sat down on the plastic guest chair. As always, his office was nothing more than a windowless box, with gray concrete walls and not much to hide them. One bulletin board. A calendar. It all went perfectly with Maven himself, with his drill sergeant haircut and his weather-beaten face that never changed.

"I've got snow up to my ass," he said. "Half the town I can't even get to. I got a poor old man found frozen stiff in a snowbank. Now you show up."

"It's good to see you, too."

"Just knock it off, McKnight. What do you want from me?"

"It's about Simon Grant."

He looked at me. "What about him?"

"I saw him last night," I said. "At the Ojibway Hotel."

"Yeah, so?"

"You see this hat?" I said, holding it up.

"What about it?"

"It belonged to Mr. Grant."

"What, is he a friend of yours?"

"As far as I know, I never met him before last night."

"So how come you have his hat?"

"He left it for me," I said. "Right before he went out and froze to death."

Maven thought about that one. "Okay, start at the beginning," he said. "What were you doing at the hotel? Having dinner?"

"Yes," I said. "Then staying the night."

"Staying the night? With who?"

"That's none of your business, Chief."

"Now I understand the dye job," he said. "McKnight, could you get any more ridiculous?"

"Do you want to hear the rest of the story or not?"

"Go ahead."

I ran through the rest of it for him. It was the third time I had told it that day, but it still didn't make any sense to me.

"So let me get this straight," he said when I was done. "You've never seen this man before, ever?"

"No."

"You're sure about that."

"Yes."

"And when you see this hat lying there on the floor outside the room, you go downstairs and chase this eighty-two-year-old man into the snow?"

"I didn't chase him into the snow. I was just looking for him."

"So you could . . . what?"

"So I could ask him what the hell he was talking about. Why he thought he knew who I was."

Maven closed his eyes. "You were involved in, let me think, the last three homicides in this city? No, four. Now we've got this poor old man who freezes to death in the snow. Even with that, you've got to show up holding the man's hat."

"Chief, I don't know why he did this. Okay? I've got no idea."

"Maybe my wife is right," he said. "Maybe it's time to retire. Move to Florida."

"I hear it's nice this time of year."

"Just give me the hat."

I looked down at it. For some strange reason, I didn't want to give it up. It felt like the hat itself was a message I still hadn't figured out yet. But hell, at least Leon had taken those pictures.

"You'll give this to his family?" I said.

"Of course."

"Can you have them give me a call? I'd like to talk to them."

"Why do you want to talk to them?"

"I just want to figure out why he thought he knew me."

"Oh no you don't," he said. "McKnight, if I find out you're bothering these people, I swear to God . . . Don't you think they're going through enough?"

"I'm not going to bother anybody."

"You're damned right you're not gonna. If I find out you're harassing this family while they're burying this poor man—"

"Chief, please. Give me some credit."

"I'll give you my boot up your ass," he said. "I've seen you do this before, remember? I know you. Please, Mc-

Knight, just go home and forget all about this, will you? Go dye your hair some more. I can still see some gray."

"It's been a pleasure," I said, getting to my feet. "As always."

"Promise me, McKnight." He stayed behind his desk. "Promise me for once in your life you'll leave something alone."

I raised my hands. "There's nothing to talk about, Chief. An old man is confused, he thinks he recognizes someone, he goes out in the cold, and he dies. It's just an unfortunate accident."

"So you're going right back to Paradise?"

"I'm on my way."

I caught one final glimpse of his face as I shut the door behind me. He didn't look like a man who believed me.

There were snowflakes in the air when I got back outside. For once it felt good to breathe in the cold air. I started up my truck and headed straight for home.

There was just one little stop to make on the way.

Five

I had already avoided eating lunch there. The last thing I wanted to do was sit in that dining room and remember the night before. But now as I headed back across town, I couldn't pass the Ojibway Hotel without stopping for one quick visit.

There was a different woman behind the desk. I asked her if I could see the manager. She told me I was looking at her. I introduced myself, and asked her if she had been around the previous night.

"I just got back into town today," she said. "I picked a great time to leave, eh?"

"Did you know Mr. Grant?"

"Not very well, no. But I know he's lived in this town forever. He used to come in here a few years ago and have dinner."

"A few years ago, you say?"

"Yes. To tell you the truth, I wasn't even sure if he was around anymore. I hadn't seen him in so long. When I found out he was here last night . . ."

"I was here, too," I said. "I'm wondering if I can talk

to somebody about what happened. The woman who was on the desk, is she going to be around today?"

"No, not until tomorrow."

"What about the doorman? The kid who was out there shoveling the snow?"

"No," she said. I could tell she was starting to wonder why I was asking all these questions. "He's not here."

"Do you know when he'll be working again?"

"I'm sorry. I don't understand. Were you here with Mr. Grant last night?"

"No," I said. "But I talked to him. Sort of. The doorman, he was here all day, and I know he saw Mr. Grant sitting in the lobby. I bet you he talked to him a lot more than I did. What was that kid's name again?"

She didn't bite. "Look, I really can't . . ."

"I understand," I said, taking out my wallet. What the hell, I thought. I still had some of these old business cards, the ones Leon had made up. God knows I wasn't actually in the game anymore, but she didn't have to know that. "But I'd really like to ask him a few questions."

She took the card from me and looked at it. Prudell-McKnight Investigations, with the two guns pointed at each other. "You're a private investigator?"

"I'm just trying to help out."

Help out what? I didn't know what I was talking about now. But somehow it seemed to be working.

"His name is Chris Woolsey," she said. "To tell you the truth, I'm a little worried about him. He's supposed to be here today."

"Chris Woolsey," I said. At that moment I wished I always carried a pad of paper like Leon. "He never showed up for work today?"

"No, he didn't."

"You know, when I came back down here last night, I didn't see him anywhere. I assumed he was out looking for Mr. Grant."

"The poor kid is probably traumatized."

"I'd like to check up on him," I said. "Would you happen to have an address and phone number?"

"Oh, now, I don't know . . ."

"I just want to ask him a few questions, ma'am. It's important."

She looked at my card again, then let out a long breath and did a quick run through a Rolodex. "He goes to Lake State," she said. "He's a senior, I think. This is the address and phone number I have for him. I think it's still current, but you know how it is when you're in college."

"Yes," I said. "Thank you. I appreciate it."

She wrote down the number and gave it to me. I thanked her again and left.

When I was back in the truck, I thought about calling on the cell phone, then decided I might have better luck just going over there. Lake Superior State University, or Lake State for short, was just south of downtown, right next to I-75. As I drove back down to Easterday, it occurred to me that I was seeing pretty much every inch of Sault Ste. Marie, Michigan, in one day. I thought about Roy Maven sitting in his office in the City County Building, and what he would have said at that moment if he knew I was still in town.

Easterday Avenue cuts right through the heart of the university grounds. Lake State's a fairly big school, bigger than anything else east of Marquette. If you grew up around here, and you wanted to stay close to home, it was the only game in town. Although when kids graduated from Lake State, more often than not they left the Upper Peninsula altogether. It's just the way things were. And the reason behind the old joke that the U.P.'s biggest export was its children.

I followed the street numbers past the student housing and the ice arena. Hockey was the only big-time sport at this school. I remembered the Lakers winning the national championship a couple of years back. The marquee out front announced that the University of Michigan would be visiting that night.

I finally found the apartment building I was looking for, another couple of blocks down the street. With all the snow piled up everywhere, I couldn't find a place to park, so finally I pulled into the alley next to the building. I heard the music playing inside as I knocked on the door marked 4, and then a young man opened the door with money in his hand.

"You're not the pizza guy," he said.

"Is Chris here?"

"No, I haven't seen him today. He's probably over at his parents' house."

"Can you tell me where that is?"

He stood there in the doorway for a long moment, looking all of fourteen years old in his sweatpants and his T-shirt. He had his long hair pulled up on top of his head and bunched together with a rubber band, and he was obviously trying to grow some kind of goatee on his chin. It wasn't working out so well.

"Who are you?" he finally said.

I dug out another card. "I'm a private investigator," I said. "It's no big deal. I just wanted to ask Chris a couple of questions."

"Is he in trouble?"

"No, not at all."

"That means yes."

"No. It means no. I just want to—"

"Look, I'll give him your card when I see him, okay? Then he can call you if he wants."

I was about to press him, but then I figured the hell with it. I wasn't going to stand there and argue with this kid. "All right," I said. "Just give him the card."

"I'll do that, man. I said I'll give it to him."

"Thank you," I said. "Have a nice—"

He slammed the door before I could finish. Okay, I thought. There's a nice young man. The future of America. Nice hair, too, sticking up like a damned flowerpot. When I got back to the truck, the pizza guy was there waiting behind me, and not looking too happy about it. I went to his driver's side window and apologized for being in the way. Then I gave him a twenty for the pizza and told him to keep the change. That seemed to make up for it. He drove away, I put the pizza on the seat next to me, and then I backed out of the alley.

It was getting late in the afternoon and the pizza smelled pretty good, so I had a slice while I drove back down Easterday. I stopped at a gas station by the highway and looked through the phone book next to the pay phone. There was one Woolsey listed, down on Twenty-fourth Avenue. Just for the hell of it, I looked up Grant and found a dozen listings, all over the city and out into the county. No telling who might have been a relative.

I'll wait and see what Leon comes up with, I thought. For now, I'll just go see if these Woolseys are Chris's parents.

I drove down to the southern edge of town, past Sanderson Field, one of the two old air command centers that had been turned into commercial airports. I followed the numbers on the mailboxes as they got smaller, until finally I found what I was looking for. It was a raised ranch sitting all alone in a wide open field, the snowdrifts climbing to the windows on one side. The driveway was covered by the drifts as well, with a serpentine set of tracks barely visible, where someone had fishtailed all over the place on their way to the garage. I put my plow down and pushed the snow off as I went. In this part of the world, it's the kind of thing you do for your neighbor, or even a stranger. You do it without even thinking about it.

I came up to the garage and pushed the snow to the side, then I got out of the truck and went to the front door. The walkway wasn't shoveled. When I rang the doorbell, nobody answered. I rang one more time. Just as I was about to turn around and leave, the inner door opened. I saw her face through the thick glass of the storm door, this woman with red eyes and a handkerchief pressed to her mouth. She was forty years old, maybe forty-five, and she was wearing a bathrobe.

"I'm sorry to bother you," I said.

She just looked at me.

"Are you Mrs. Woolsey?" I had to speak up to be heard through the glass. She was making no move to open the storm door.

She nodded her head.

"Is Chris here? His roommate said he might be."

"Who are you?"

"My name is Alex McKnight. I just want to ask him something."

She looked back in the house for a moment. "Ask him something about what?"

"He was working at the Ojibway Hotel last night," I said. "I just want to ask him a couple of questions about something that happened there."

She closed her eyes.

"He's not in any trouble, ma'am. Believe me. I just want to ask him if he—"

She slammed the door shut. That was two doors in one afternoon. And it made me wonder. I just wanted to ask this kid if he knew anything about the old man, but maybe I had stumbled onto something more significant. Either that or my chemically altered hair was scaring everybody.

I took out one more business card. "Chris," I wrote on the back, "please call me. I was at the hotel last night, and I just want to ask you if you know anything about Mr. Grant. That's all! Thank you. Alex."

I wedged the card into the doorjamb and left, slogging my way through the deep snow on the walkway and nearly killing myself on a hidden patch of ice. I got in the truck and plowed my way back down the driveway. What the hell, I thought. Maybe a little good deed will help.

I had a couple more slices of pizza on my way back home. There were thick clouds in the sky, and it was already getting dark. Somewhere in the world it was warm, and the sun stayed out for hours at a time. But I was here on the long straight road back to Paradise, thankful that the county trucks had thrown down some sand. Even more thankful that I'd be giving Natalie Reynaud a call when I got home.

I ran the plow down my road and back. When I got inside, I saw the light blinking on my answering machine. It was a quick message from Leon, asking me to call him when I got in. So I did.

"I found out a few things about your man Mr. Grant," he said.

"Leon, I hope you didn't spend too much time on this."

"Not at all," he said. "It occurred to me, this is going to hit the newspaper tomorrow, so I just called my friend over at the *Sault Evening News*."

"Yeah? What did he tell you?"

"Just some basic stuff for right now. Simon Grant was eighty-two years old, he was born in the Soo and lived in the area his whole life. Two sons, one daughter. He had a hundred different jobs, from shoeshine boy to union representative. He worked on the old railroad docks for a long time, right on the river."

"Yeah, the woman at the hotel told me she thought he'd lived around here for a long time. He used to come into the hotel fairly often, it sounds like, but then he stopped a few years ago."

"He might have been in some kind of senior care," Leon said. "Maybe he sneaked out and went back to one of his old familiar places."

"That makes sense," I said. "That would explain why they hadn't seen him for a while. There was one weird thing, though . . ."

"What's that?"

"I thought the doorman at the hotel might be able to help me out. So I tried to find him. He seems to have disappeared."

"What?"

I gave him the whole rundown. Chris Woolsey not showing up for work today, going to his apartment, and then his parents' place.

"That's a little strange," Leon said. "It might not be a coincidence."

"Well, I left a card at both places. Maybe he'll call me."

"You know, Alex, for a man who has no interest in being a private eye, it sure sounds like you're acting like one."

"I just want to know what happened," I said. "If I don't try to find out, it'll just keep bothering me, why this man would go to all that trouble, thinking that he knew me. Wouldn't you be doing the same thing?"

"I'd be all over it, yes."

I couldn't help smiling. "Yeah, I have no doubt about that."

"My friend at the paper said he's working on the obit this evening, so he may have some more information. If he calls me, I'll call you."

"You can stop, Leon. You don't have to do any more."

"It's no big deal, Alex. I'll let you know what he says."

"All right," I said. "Thank you."

"What are partners for?" It was an old line I had heard before, back when it meant something. It almost made me wish it still did.

When I was done with Leon, I called Natalie. Her answering machine picked up before she finally got on the line herself.

"Sorry," she said. "I was going through the stuff in the basement."

"You've got a lot down there."

"A whole lifetime's worth. It's gonna take me a long time to go through it all."

"Just let me know if you want help. My rates are cheap."

She didn't say anything.

"What's the matter, Natalie?"

"It's just too much sometimes. That's all."

"Okay," I said. "I can imagine."

"I'm sorry, so what did you do today?"

"I gave the hat to Chief Maven. Then I wandered over to the hotel." I gave her the same rundown I had given Leon—Chris Woolsey disappearing, and me trying to find him.

"Maybe he's just a little freaked out, Alex. This man was in the lobby all day, and then suddenly he's dead."

"I hear what you're saying. It's just kinda strange. And the way his mother looked today . . ."

"You went to his mother's house?"

"I just wanted to talk to him. I wanted to make sure he's all right, too."

"I don't know, Alex."

"Well, anyway, Leon will let me know if he finds out anything else."

"Who's Leon again?"

"My sort of ex-partner, remember? He's the one who found out your address."

There was a silence on the line.

"Okay, that sounds a little weird," I said. "What I mean

is, when I decided to contact you, Leon helped me do that. That's all."

Another silence. Then she said it. "Alex, I can't do this."

It was my turn to be quiet for a while. "Natalie," I finally said, "what are you talking about?"

"All of this, Alex. I'm sorry, I just can't right now."

"Wait a minute—"

"No, please, Alex. I've got to say this, okay?"

"Go ahead."

"I don't know why you came looking for me," she said. "I'm not saying I'm sorry you did. Because I'm not sorry. It was . . . The way things happened, it was like a miracle. I was in such a deep hole, Alex. You reached down and you pulled me out of it. I didn't even want you to do it, but you did. I'll always love you for that, Alex. I hope you know that. But right now . . ."

More silence. I didn't have any words to say. I just waited to hear the rest of it.

"Right now, it's just too much for me. I'm trying to get my life back together, and I can't do this. Yeah, coming out to that hotel to meet you, and having all that stuff happen, that didn't help any. That definitely made it feel . . . I don't know. Just not right. But it would have come eventually, you know what I mean? The whole idea of me coming down here, I was just going to clean up this house. I was going to sell it and go away and never look back. That's what I was going to do."

I looked out the window. I looked at the clouds and the snowflakes floating slowly in the air.

"I have to, Alex. Do you know what I'm talking about? Please, Alex. Please say something."

"I hear you, Natalie. I understand what you're saying."

"I'm sorry."

"Look, I know you're still dealing with what happened to you."

"It's not about that," she said. "That was a long time ago."

"I know, but it's still there. You told me so yourself."

"Just forget about that, okay? Forget I ever told you."

"I can't, Natalie."

"Okay, now I've got to get off the phone," she said. "Because I'm going to start crying here. Okay? I'm not going to do that."

"Okay," I said. "Okay."

"I'll talk to you later. Maybe I'll call you in a couple of days."

"That's fine."

"Please take care of yourself."

"You, too," I said.

Then she hung up.

You, too. That's all I could say to her. You, too.

I got up and went outside, because I'd be damned if I was going to sit there feeling sorry for myself. That wasn't going to happen, not for one single minute.

You met somebody. You did something good for her. She has her own life, but now it's going in a different direction. And all that other crap you tell yourself. All that worthless crap.

You were just fooling yourself, Alex. You should have known better.

I plowed the road and I chopped some wood. I didn't feel like going down to the Glasgow, so I just went back inside and had some more pizza. It was cold now. I sat at the table and ate cold pizza with a lukewarm beer.

The phone rang. For one instant I thought it might be Natalie calling me back, then in the next instant I hated myself for hoping that it was. It turned out to be Leon again.

"The funeral is day after tomorrow," he said.

"Yeah, so?"

"So you should go."

"Why?"

"Alex, are you all right? You sound a little down."

"No, I'm okay. I just don't understand why I should go to Mr. Grant's funeral."

"I'm just thinking," he said. "This is your best chance to find out more about him. Maybe you'll even recognize somebody there. At the very least, you can meet his family, tell them how sorry you are. If it goes well, you could even ask them to help you figure out why he thought he knew you."

"I don't think I want to do that."

"I'm not telling you to crash the funeral, Alex. I'm just saying, go pay your respects. There's nothing wrong with that."

"I'll think about it," I said. "Thanks again for your help."

"You sure you're okay?"

"I'm just fine, Leon. I'm just fine."

It started snowing harder. The wind picked up and whistled through the chinks in the walls. I put more wood in the stove.

The phone rang again. I went through the same routine again, as unavoidable as a reflex. Maybe it's her. But this time it was a man from downstate, asking me if there was enough snow up here to jump-start the snowmobile season. I told him there sure as hell was. He made a reservation.

I knew others would come. I'd be busy again. That was good.

The phone didn't ring again. I plowed one more time, then I went to bed. I lay there staring at the ceiling, listening to the wind.

Someday, I thought, that'll be me. The whole picture came into my head, all at once. I'll sit at the Glasgow Inn all day. Maybe Jackie will be gone by then. His son will own the place. But I'll still go down there and nobody will mind, because I won't be bothering anybody. I'll sit there and look out the window and think about things that happened a long time ago. Then one night I'll go outside into the cold, cold air and they won't find me until the next morning.

Just like Simon Grant. Frozen stiff in a pile of snow. All alone.

That'll be me.

Six

The men from downstate arrived the next day. They must
have gotten up at three in the morning to get here so early.
There were four of them in two SUVs, with four identical
Arctic Cat sleds on the two big trailers. I got them set up
in the third cabin and stacked a quarter cord of wood by
their front door. Then I went back to my cabin, split another full cord, then plowed the road again.

I cleaned my cabin within an inch of its life, throwing
out food from the refrigerator and picking up old magazines and books. I finally hung those extra shelves I
needed. I even cleaned the bathroom.

It kept snowing lightly all day long. I went out and
plowed again, then shoveled the walkways in front of all
the cabins. I knew they'd all be occupied before the week
was over.

Finally, I went down to the last cabin site and knocked
most of the snow off the blue tarp. I wished like hell I
could get back to work rebuilding it. That's the kind of
job I could lose myself in for days at a time. But that
would have to wait until springtime.

When the day was almost over, I went down to Jackie's place. He slid a cold Canadian my way. I asked for a little something else to go with it. He poured me a shot and watched me knock it back. He didn't say a word.

I had dinner by the fire. Vinnie LeBlanc came in and sat down next to me. His ear was still taped up and in the firelight I could see the scar on his cheek, the scar that he would carry for the rest of his life. It made me think about how he had gotten it, and how I had met this woman named Natalie up there, this policewoman from the OPP.

"You don't look so good," he said to me.

"What else is new?"

"Things okay with Natalie?"

"Things aren't okay. I'm not sure they're anything at all."

He nodded his head. "I'm sorry, Alex."

"It's all right."

Jackie brought me another beer and another shot. He stood above me like he was going to say something, but he never did. He put his hand on my shoulder for a moment, then walked away.

"I'm impressed," I said to Vinnie. "He didn't even say, 'I told you so.'"

Vinnie didn't comment on that, or on anything else. That was one of the best things about the man. He didn't try to make small talk. We sat by the fire and I picked up the *Sault Evening News* and read the lead story about Simon Grant's death. Then I turned to the obituary.

If I had read that obituary a little more carefully, I might have saved myself a hell of a lot of trouble. But I didn't.

"I'm going back," I said, folding up the paper. "I'll see you later." I tapped my fist on Vinnie's head.

"Calling it a night?" Jackie said as I put my coat on.

"I'm going to bed," I said, "right after I go dig out my suit. I'm going to a funeral tomorrow."

The next day was cold. There was a bitter wind from the north, the kind of wind that blew the snow into your eyes and knifed its way through your warmest coat. The snowmobilers were up early, tearing up the trails that run along the back of my property. I could hear the whine of the engines as I got up and got dressed. I put my suit on and my gray wool overcoat, which wouldn't be warm enough, I knew, but you can't wear a big mackinaw coat over a suit. Not even in the Upper Peninsula.

St. Mary's was on Portage Avenue, just a few blocks down from the Ojibway Hotel, and just a few blocks away from where Mr. Grant froze to death, for that matter. I got there around 12:30. The funeral mass would start at one o'clock. I sat in the parking lot with the engine running to stay warm, watching the people go into the church. Everyone kept their heads down against the wind and held their coats tight against their chests.

At ten after one, I got out of the truck and went into the church. It was an old building made of dark red brick, with a great black spire that was ringed on this day with a hard crust of snow all along the edges. When I got inside, everyone was standing up, reciting the Lord's Prayer. I slipped into the back pew just as they all sat down.

There was a closed coffin up front, covered in white lilies. The priest went through the ritual, and everyone seemed to know what was coming and when to respond. It finally occurred to me that everyone else in the place had a printed program. I followed along as best as I could, until the priest finally asked who would come up and speak of Simon Grant. There was a long silence, and then one man stood up and made his way slowly to the pulpit.

He was big, well over six feet tall and pushing 250 pounds. He looked like a former offensive lineman. His necktie was strangling him. He took a few moments to compose himself, then he began to speak. "I just wanna say a few words about Pops," he said. He went on to describe a long life filled with work and hardship. Growing up as an orphan during the Great Depression, having to act like the man of the house when he was only nine years old, going out every day to shine shoes and run errands or do whatever he could to make a little money for his family. Later joining the navy, and seeing action aboard a carrier in the Pacific. Coming back home and raising a family, working on the docks, back when the Soo Line ran all the way down to the river. Taking his kids out on the water every weekend.

"Pops loved this place so much," the man said, "even though the winters got harder and harder for him. He never wanted to move away. He said his heart was here and he wanted to be buried here."

The man stopped and looked down at the coffin. "You made us promise, Pops, that we'd never take you away from here. We kept that promise."

Another man came up next, a slightly smaller version of the first. He looked a few years younger. He tried to speak but he couldn't say a single word. His brother held on to the back of his neck and told him it was okay. He walked him back to the first pew and sat down with him.

Then a woman stood up. She walked up to the pulpit,

and as soon as she turned around, I knew who she was. God damn it all, I thought, it's the woman at the house. Chris Woolsey's mother.

She said a few words about her father, about how he was the strongest person she'd ever known. As I listened to her, I felt a little sick to my stomach. I had gone to this woman's house and asked to talk to her son about something that happened at the Ojibway Hotel.

The obituary in the newspaper, I thought. It probably listed her as one of the surviving children. Why hadn't I noticed it? God damn it, I'm such an idiot.

"It's a hard day," she said, looking out at all the people in the pews. "But I'm glad you're all here. Thank you." She looked back in my direction. For one instant, it seemed like she was looking right at me. Then she sat down.

The priest conducted the rest of the funeral mass. As it drew to a close he raised his hands and gave us the blessing. I got up and slipped out the door before anyone else.

I went back to my truck and got in, firing up the engine and the heater. "Okay, now what?" I said. I watched everybody gather by the church steps. After a couple of minutes, the coffin was brought out the front door, carried by four men. What a cold and bitter day to be doing this. Two were the sons who had stood up during the service, another I didn't recognize, and the fourth was Chris Woolsey. They carried the coffin down the steps and into the open doors of a hearse.

I should talk to them, I thought. Just go over to Chris and his mother, tell them I didn't realize it was Chris's grandfather.

The whole family was standing around in the parking

lot as they closed the doors to the hearse. People filed past them and hugged them and kissed their faces. I got out of the truck and crossed the parking lot. I'll tell them how bad I feel, maybe ask them about what had happened if they seem up to it. Maybe they'll have an answer for me. Yes, Mr. McKnight, he was doing that all the time. These past couple of years, he was always confused. He kept seeing people all over the place and believing that he knew them.

The biggest son was standing there with his wife, along with two teenage children. Then the other son with his wife, and a young boy hopping up and down in the cold. Mrs. Woolsey was there with the man I hadn't recognized, one of the pallbearers. It had to be her husband.

And Chris Woolsey, looking a lot younger without the hotel uniform. His face was bright red from the wind, or the grief of this day, or God knows what else.

"Pardon me," I said as I approached them. I wasn't sure who to talk to first, but Chris was closest, so I stuck out my hand. "Chris," I said. "I'm so sorry."

He shook my hand, but his mouth was hanging open like he had forgotten how to speak.

"And Mrs. Woolsey," I said, quickly moving down the line. "I have to apologize. I just didn't realize—"

"You're the man," she said, her face calm. "From yesterday."

"If I had known," I said, "of the . . . I mean, that this was your father, I never would have bothered you."

"Mr. McKnight is it?" Her husband stepped forward and shook my hand. "You're the one who plowed our driveway yesterday?"

"Yes. As long as I was there, I thought—"

"I appreciate the gesture," he said. "It made the day a little easier."

"I was at the hotel the other night," I said. "I saw Mr. Grant. That would be your father-in-law, right?"

"Yes," he said. "Let me introduce you to Michael and Marty, Simon Grant's sons. His daughter, I see you've already met. And his grandson."

Chris hunched his shoulders against the cold wind and looked down at the ground.

"I don't want to keep you," I said. "I just wanted to offer my condolences. And, well . . ."

"Yes?"

"There's something else I wanted to ask you about, but it can wait, believe me."

"No, no," Mr. Woolsey said. "Here, come with me." He turned to the rest of the family and told them to get the cars warmed up. Then he put a hand on my back and steered me toward the side of the parking lot. "It's so damned cold out here," he said. "Let's get out of the wind."

"Actually, it's about Mr. Grant," I said, walking with him. "Something he said that night. Or rather, something he wrote in a note to me."

"Yeah? So maybe you're thinking one of his sons might be able to answer your questions?" He pulled a pack of cigarettes out of his coat pocket. "Do you smoke?"

"No, thanks," I said. "And yes, I mean obviously his sons might have a better idea—"

"You saw how they were in there," he said. "They're kind of in a bad way today. Maybe if you tell me what you want to know, I can pass it on." He took one of his gloves off and tried to shake one cigarette out. "God, could it get a little colder, do you think?"

"I can't imagine."

He looked behind him as he fumbled with the lighter. "I'm feeling a little self-conscious lighting up here, eh? Come on back here a bit." He took a few more steps toward the back of the building. I hesitated, and as he came back to me, I had just enough time to hear the little alarm bell ringing in my head. He threw the lighter and the cigarettes at my face, and as I reached up to block them he grabbed my arm and swung me around hard. He stuck his leg out in one smooth, practiced move that sent me falling backward onto the hard pavement.

I tried to roll right through it and back onto my feet, but the other two men were all over me before I even knew what was happening. They came from behind the building—they had obviously sneaked around the other way to meet us. They each grabbed me by one arm and dragged me all the way to the back so that nobody in the world would see what they were about to do to me.

They didn't say anything at first. They just went to work on me, methodically pumping their fists into my ribs. I tried to fight back but I didn't have a chance against three of them at once. They knocked the wind out of me and I started to go down, but they pinned me up against the red brick wall of the church and kept hitting me again and again, in the face now and then back to the body and then to the face until I couldn't do anything but try to roll myself into a ball, anything to cover myself. That's when they finally started talking to me.

"How's this, tough guy?" one of them said. "Little different than roughing up an old man, eh?"

"Stop," I said, trying to catch my breath. "What are you talking about?"

I took another blow, then heard a voice that might have been the same or different—it was all just noise now, mixed in with the ringing in my ears. "We were gonna come find you, McKnight. Right after we buried him. Who'da thought you'd actually show up at the fucking funeral?"

"No," I said.

"You've got some balls. I'll say that much."

"Stop," I said. "You're making a mistake."

The voice came closer. "You think *we're* making a mistake? That's a good one."

It wasn't making any sense. I tried to say something else. I tried to breathe.

"We should kill you," the voice said. "We should kill you right here."

"Take it easy," another voice said. "Come on, guys. Don't do something stupid."

"We should do it, man. We should kill him and dump him in the river."

"Think about what you're doing, guys. Come on."

I felt someone grab me by the shoulders. His voice was hot in my face. "You bother my sister again, or my little brother, or my nephew, or anybody, man. My fucking next-door neighbor, and we will find you and we will fuck you up. You got that, man?"

The other man stepped in close to me. I ducked and heard him hit the brick wall just above my head. He let out a quick scream of pain and then another man was battering me with uppercuts one after the other, some hitting me in the elbows and others finding their mark until the last one cut me right in half.

I took one more shot. No protection now. No defense. One more shot and my head was snapping backward until it hit the cold bricks. Then everything turned upside-down.

"Come on, guys. Look at you. We gotta go bury your father, for God's sake. You're messing up your suits now."

I heard those last words from somewhere far away. Then there was the sound of snow crunching under heavy footsteps. Then it was just me all by myself, leaning against the red bricks, going down inch by inch, until I finally touched the dead frozen ground.

Then there was nothing.

Seven

I woke up shivering. I don't know how long I had been lying there. At that moment, I barely even knew what had happened. All I knew was that I was cold and I was in pain. Cold and pain, that's all there was in the world.

The first thing I saw when I opened my eyes was red brick. I was lying curled up against a wall and there was a light layer of snow melting on the side of my face. I tried to get up. That wasn't going to work. Very bad idea. I tried rolling over. Another very bad idea. I lifted my head. Worst idea yet.

This is it, I thought. I'm gonna freeze to death right here. Just like . . . somebody. I couldn't think straight. Just like who?

Like Simon Grant. It all started to come back to me. The funeral, meeting the family, walking back here with Chris Woolsey's father, then everything that happened after that.

Behind a church yet. I had gotten beaten within an inch of my life behind a church.

Okay, now what? I tried to think. My cell phone . . .

Where was it? In the truck. I tried to roll over again. I just had to see . . .

Damn it, that hurt. God damn it. I saw another building, just beyond the plowed parking lot. It looked like a garage. Some trees. An empty swing set half buried in the snow. Beyond that, the backs of more buildings, over on Maple Street. Too far away.

I've gotta move, I thought. Move now or die here.

I rolled again. God, that hurt. I was on my hands and knees now. I was bleeding. The blood was getting in my eyes. Son of a bitch.

As I shook my head to clear my eyes, everything went out of focus and my ears rang like I was underwater. Okay, I thought, no more shaking my head.

I wiped my eyes, felt the cut above my left eyebrow. Not good. Not good at all. I tried to push myself up with my hands. My head started pounding again.

"Help," I said. "I need some help here . . ."

But there was no sound except the wind.

I know somebody will come by eventually, I thought. If I can get around to the front of the church, somebody will see me. The street is busy enough, even in the dead of winter. I just have to . . . have to . . .

I wobbled and rolled back down to the ground.

"No," I said. "Get up. Get up, Alex." I pushed myself back up to my hands and knees. "Now move."

I worked my way toward the corner of the building. I left a path in the snow as I moved, a jagged line of red running down the center. My jaw started to ache. My nose. My ribs. Then the bells went off in my head again. I stopped in my tracks and waited for it to pass. Then I started moving again. I fought inch by inch until finally

I could see around the corner. The rest of the parking lot was empty now, everyone else gone. They had all left for the cemetery. No vehicles in sight, except for my truck. My truck, with the heater. And the cell phone. A hundred feet away.

I didn't see any cars moving on Portage Avenue. But somebody would come eventually. I started moving. I had to get closer to the road. Or to my truck. That was closer. No, the road.

I kept crawling. A car came by, moving slowly.

"Help," I said, too weakly for anyone to actually hear me. "Please stop."

The car passed and was gone.

Get to your feet, I thought. Get up and walk. Go to the truck and call somebody. It's the only way you're gonna get out of here. Just get up and walk.

Okay, okay. Just have to catch my breath. Breathe, damn it. Breathe.

On the count of three, I'm gonna get up.

One.

Two.

Three. I pushed myself up, tried to move my weight back onto my legs. I fell forward, caught myself with my hands, leaned all the way forward this time, letting my legs catch up.

Just like that, Alex. Just like that. Now stand up.

I pushed up with one arm, then the other. I was crouching now, bleeding into the snow, the red drops free-falling now, making little red specks.

Stand. Up.

I tried to straighten out my body. Everything went into a whirl, all the colors spinning around me, all the sounds like instruments playing at once, the trombones and the tubas and the bass drums.

Get to the truck, Alex. Get to the truck. Where is it?

I saw it in one direction, then another. It was moving all around, taunting me. I took one step, another step, and then I was falling down a hill sideways, putting my hand down to keep from falling again.

The truck is there. It's right there.

But I couldn't walk straight. I pointed myself in one direction and moved in another, east instead of north. I tried to double back. God, my head. My aching head.

I didn't know where I was going now. I was moving and everything kept turning around me and then there was nothing but sky above me and then snow all over the ground, wherever I looked. Nothing but white, white snow.

Then I heard something. One of the instruments in the band playing a long note, louder and louder. Something was coming for me. Something big. It got closer and closer until it was right on top of me and it was all I could see.

I reached out one hand to it.

"No more," I said. "No more."

I went down. All the way. I tasted the salt on the road.

"No more."

There was a light shining into my eyes. It hurt like hell. I blinked and then I tried to sit up. I felt a hand on each shoulder, holding me down.

"Don't get up, Mr. McKnight," a voice said. "Please, just stay right there."

I blinked a few more times. Then I saw a face. It looked familiar.

"Do you know who you are?" the voice said.

"What?"

"Your name. Tell me your name."

"McKnight. You just said it. My name is Alex Mc-Knight."

"Okay, good. What day is it?"

"I don't know." I tried to sit up again. The hands kept me down.

"Please, Mr. McKnight. You have to lie still."

Everything else started to come into focus. The white ceiling, the fluorescent lights. I was in a hospital room. The doctor was looking at a medical file. He had a white coat on, and a stethoscope hanging around his neck. He had a beard. I knew this man.

"What happened?" I said. "How did I get here?"

"You tell me," he said. "Someone brought you into the emergency room. The man said he almost ran over you."

"Where have I seen you before?"

"My name is Doctor Glenn. I treated you once before. That time it was cracked ribs and a collapsed lung. Do you remember?"

"Yeah, I remember." That meant I was in War Memorial, on Osborn. I was just a few blocks away from the church.

"This time it's your head. Are you going to tell me what happened?"

"It's all kinda fuzzy, Doc."

"I bet." He held his pen in front of my face and moved it from side to side. I followed it with my eyes. He seemed satisfied and went back to his notes.

"Do I have a concussion?"

He looked up at me. "You're kidding, right?"

"I'll take that as a yes."

"Grade three, Mr. McKnight. Do you know what that means?"

"I'll be sitting out a few games."

"You have a hairline fracture in your right eye orbital. Another hairline fracture in your cheekbone. The cut above your eyebrow took twenty-seven stitches, ten internal and seventeen external. And you have fifteen stitches in the back of your head."

I reached up and felt the bandages on my head. "What about the rest of me?"

"You have bruises all over your torso, but no broken ribs this time. I guess that's the good news."

"Some of my bottom teeth feel a little loose."

"They may tighten up on their own," he said. "If they don't, you'll have to see your dentist."

"So aside from all that, I'm just fine."

He shook his head and flipped a page. "I see we found a little something in your chest last time," he said.

"The bullet. That was from a long time ago."

"The eighties, you told me."

"Yes."

"I believe I asked you then if you'd been having your annual chest X-ray, to make sure the bullet hasn't migrated."

"Doctor, can we talk about this later? No offense, but your voice is like a drill in my head right now."

"Everything's going to hurt for a few days," he said. "Sounds, lights, you name it. Now that you're awake, we can start some medication."

"How long am I gonna be here?"

"At least two days," he said. "Maybe three. Is there somebody you'd like me to contact?"

I thought about it. "Yeah," I said. I gave him two names—Vinnie LeBlanc and Leon Prudell, along with the phone numbers. I thought about adding Natalie to the list for about a second and a half, but then I thought, no way. No way in hell.

"I'll send the nurse in with the meds," he said. "In the meantime, try not to move. The police should be here in a few minutes."

"Doctor—"

"This one's automatic," he said. He closed the file and tucked it under his arm. "Last time, what did you tell me? You hurt yourself skiing?"

"I think I might have said sledding."

"Yeah, well, I let it go then. I probably shouldn't have. This time, somebody really did a number on you, Mr. McKnight. I'm not just going to send you back out there. Even if I wanted to, the law wouldn't let me."

"Whatever you say, Doc." I put my head back on the pillow and immediately regretted it. Damn, it hurt to do *anything*. Anything at all. I looked over at the other bed in the room. It was empty. A dark television screen looked down at me from just below the ceiling. I thought about turning it on, but no, I was sure watching television would hurt, too.

My clothes. Where were they? I was wearing a paper hospital gown beneath the covers. God, I hated hospitals. Every bad thing in my life had something to do with a hospital. Watching my mother die when I was a kid, and then my father many years later. Being older didn't make it any easier. Then when I got shot. Lying there with all those tubes stuck in me, my soon-to-be-ex-wife looking down at me and then around the room, like she was thinking of escaping out the window.

And somewhere in that same hospital, on that hot summer day way back when in Detroit, in the basement, my partner Franklin was lying on a bed of cold steel, a white sheet over his head.

Yeah, I hated hospitals. The last time around, I had promised myself I would never spend one minute in a hospital again. Yet here I was.

A nurse came in and gave me some drugs. I asked her to help me up so I could use the bathroom. She told me I'd be better off with the little urinal bottle, but I disagreed with her right up until I actually tried to sit up straight. "Bring on the bottle," I said. Even using that hurt.

A little later, Chief Maven appeared at the door, just to make the day complete. "You realize," he said as he came in, "this is the third time I've seen you in a hospital bed."

"And it never loses its magic."

"Cut the crap, McKnight. What happened?"

"You didn't have to come over here yourself," I said. "You could have sent an officer."

"No, this one I had to see for myself. What did you do this time?"

"I don't think I *did* anything, Chief. I think it was all done *to* me, you know what I mean?"

"Who are we talking about?"

I hesitated.

"Come on," he said. "They found you on Portage Avenue, right in front of St. Mary's. Just a couple of hours after Simon Grant's funeral."

"You know how Catholic funerals are. They can get a little rough."

He didn't smile. "McKnight, God damn you," he said, moving closer. "Were you listening when I told you to leave that family alone?"

"I actually was, yes."

"Then what the hell were you doing there?"

I started to feel dizzy again. I closed my eyes and waited for it to pass. "Chief, I went to the hotel and I asked about Chris Woolsey. He was the doorman that night, the night Mr. Grant died. I had no idea that he was the man's grandson. Then later, I stopped by his parents' house—"

"Why did you do that?"

"I told you, I just wanted to talk to him."

He closed his eyes and rubbed his forehead. "Okay, and then?"

"I figured I'd just go to the funeral, to pay my respects. That's when I found out Mrs. Woolsey was Simon Grant's daughter."

"Then the Grant brothers beat the living shit out of you."

I didn't say anything.

"I know those boys," he said. "Believe me."

"Yeah, well, now I know them, too."

"Listen," he said, "did it ever occur to you that maybe I was looking out for you when I told you to stay away?"

"No. Not really."

"I'm serious, McKnight. I know you think I'm just a hard-ass, but for once in your life did it occur to you that I was trying to do you a favor?"

"No, Chief."

"Look at you," he said. "God damn it. Nobody deserves to get beaten up like you did, McKnight. Nobody."

I didn't know what to say to that. He was starting to sound almost human.

"Did they say anything to you? Did they give you any reason?"

"I'm trying to remember. They were saying something like . . . Like, how's this, not the same as roughing up an old man, eh?"

"They said that?"

"Something like that. It's a little fuzzy."

He shook his head. "So the two Grant brothers and who else? Their sister's husband, was he there, too?"

"How did you know?"

"I'm just assuming. If he was at the funeral, I'm sure he got into it."

"So now what?"

"What do you think, McKnight? I'm going to arrest all three of them."

"Chief—"

"We arrest people for aggravated assault, McKnight. Even if it's you who gets assaulted."

"I'm touched."

"Just stop," he said. "Okay? I'm not in the mood. I'll bring a complaint by later so you can sign it. You might as well, because I'm charging them no matter what."

I hesitated. Here's where the young version of me would have protested. Hell, even the me of ten years ago. Don't cooperate, tell him I'm not really sure who was there. Wait until I get better and then go find them myself. Get back my own way.

I didn't know if I had gotten a little wiser, or if I was just too tired and sore. If Maven was really gonna go out and arrest them, I didn't feel like stopping him.

"I'll sign it."

"Good," he said. "Then you just get better and you go home, all right? Stay the hell away from them. In fact, you know what? Doesn't your friend own that bar in Paradise? What's it called?"

"The Glasgow Inn."

"That's the one. He's got beer there? And good food?"

"Yeah."

"So you're all set," he said, putting his face close to mine. "There's no reason to ever leave Paradise again."

I tried to smile. But that hurt, too.

"I'm going," he said. "Goodbye."

"Nice talking to you."

He paused at the doorway. "Have you seen yourself yet?"

"What?"

"You know, in a mirror. Has somebody shown you what you look like?"

"No."

For the first time since he had come in, he smiled. "Just wait a couple of days," he said. "You'll be able to sell tickets."

The next forty-eight hours passed like slow death. Leon stopped in to see me. Then Vinnie. Leon was happy to hear that Chief Maven was on his way to arrest the three men. Vinnie wanted to cut out the middleman and just go find them himself. I told him to back off for now. When the time came, I'd let him know.

I tried to watch television, but that made my eyes hurt. I couldn't read anything at all. I sure as hell couldn't sleep. They brought me drugs every four hours and I'd sit there for a moment looking at the pills. I had my own reasons for thinking twice about taking them. But those reasons weren't enough to stop me.

I got out of bed on the second day and made it to the bathroom before throwing up in the sink. By the end of that day I could sit up in the bed and turn my head without making the room spin. I slept a few hours that night.

On the third day, Dr. Glenn came through on the morning rounds and gave me three random words to remember. Then he went through all his tests. When he was done, he asked me to repeat the words back to him.

"What words?" I said.

He looked at me.

"Table, bicycle, chair," I said.

"Congratulations. You get to go home and rest for the next seven days. Then you need to come back for another checkup, and to have your stitches taken out. If you start to feel worse, you need to call me right away." He gave me his card.

"Thanks, Doc."

"You lead an interesting life," he said. "I'll give you that."

Vinnie showed up not long after that to take me home. I put my clothes on. Then they stuck me in a wheelchair and rolled me out of the place.

"To the ice arena," I said. "I feel like playing hockey."

The sun was out, glittering all over the white snow and making my head hurt enough to die right there in the parking lot.

"Come on," he said. "Let's get you home."

"Take me to my truck."

"No way."

"Vinnie, just take me to my truck, all right? I can drive it home."

"It's not gonna happen," he said. Then I saw his cousin Buck pull up in his beat-up old Plymouth Fury.

"You gotta be kidding me," I said. "I'm getting a ride home in this?"

"No, just to your truck," Vinnie said. "Then I'll drive you home."

Vinnie climbed into the backseat and gave me the front. Buck looked me over a couple of times and gave a low whistle. "Man, you got run over," he said. He pulled out and drove down the street toward the church.

"You ever get your license back?" I asked him.

He shrugged that one off. He was a big, round man, with dark hair falling halfway down his back.

"It's one thing to drive around the rez," I said. "They catch you in the Soo, it's gonna be a different story."

"Alex, give him a break," Vinnie said from the backseat. "He's doing you a favor."

"I know that, Vinnie. I just don't want the man to go to jail over it."

"All that working over you got," Buck said, "and they didn't bust up your mouth? You're still talking too much."

"Right here at the church," Vinnie said. "His truck's on the side there."

Buck pulled into the parking lot and stopped next to my truck. It was covered by six inches of new snow, and circled by more snow on the ground where the snowplow had worked around it. I let Vinnie and Buck clean it off for me while I walked just far enough to see around to the back of the building. There was no trace of what had happened here in this one patch of ground next to the red brick wall. The snow had covered up everything.

"Alex, what are you doing?" Vinnie had started up my truck and was scraping the last of the ice from the side window. "Let's get you home."

I thanked Buck for bringing Vinnie over, suspended license and all. He surprised me by grabbing me by the shoulders and hugging me. "Take care of yourself," he said. "You've got too much trouble in your life. Vinnie can't watch over you all the time, you know."

I wasn't about to argue with that one. I thanked him again and watched him rumble off in his old Plymouth. Then I got in the passenger's seat of my own truck. It felt strange not to be driving. But I figured what the hell. I closed my eyes and waited for Vinnie to pull out of the parking lot.

It didn't happen. I opened my eyes and saw him looking at me.

"What?" I said.

"You gotta promise me something."

"What is it?"

"You don't go after them alone."

"Who?"

"You know who I'm talking about."

"How stupid do you think I am?"

"Alex . . ."

"Vinnie, look at me. Your mother could kick my ass right now."

He shook his head and smiled. "On another day, when you're better . . . promise me you won't do anything stupid."

"I don't know what to tell you, Vinnie. Right now, I can't even think about it. But later . . ."

Later what? Maven was going to arrest them. At this point, that had probably already been done. Was that enough?

Or would I still want to settle things myself? When I was strong again, would I want to go find them, one by one? I knew their names. I knew their faces. I could find out where they lived.

"I'll promise you this," I finally said. "If that day comes, I won't go alone."

He put the truck in gear. "You're damned right you won't."

As he drove, I kept my eyes closed and listened to the wind whistling past my window. I dozed off for a while. When I woke up, we were just hitting Paradise. He drove through the blinking light, past the Glasgow Inn, then down the access road.

"Looks like somebody plowed while I was in the hospital."

"My other cousin, Henry. He's got a plow on his truck now."

"I guess I owe all of you," I said.

"It's nothing." He pulled into my driveway and stopped the truck.

"Especially you," I said. "Thanks."

"Do you have your pills?"

I rattled the bottle in my coat pocket. "Right here."

"You're gonna take them?"

"Why wouldn't I?"

"Alex, it's okay to take painkillers when you're in pain."

"I know that," I said. "How come you're so inside my head today?"

"Because I'm your blood brother, remember? I feel what you feel."

"Get out of here, Vinnie. I don't need you to—"

"Alex, damn it. Do I have to take those pills from you? I'll take them and come over and make you swallow one every four hours, I swear."

Once again, he knew me too well. He knew that there had been a time, back in Detroit, after my partner had been shot, and I had taken those three bullets myself . . . The pain in my shoulder, where they had tried to put my rotator cuff back together, not to mention the thought of another bullet left inside me, right next to my heart.

Worst of all, the sight of Franklin lying on the floor next to me, the life fading from his eyes as I looked into them. Those long nights when I couldn't sleep. Those dark hours all by myself. That's how it started.

"You know as long as you're in pain," Vinnie said, "you can't get addicted to painkillers."

"Yeah, that's what they say."

"Alex—"

"I'll take them," I said. "Okay? I'll take them as long as I need to, and not one day longer." I opened the door and got out of the truck. He did the same.

"I'll come by later to see how you're doing," he said.

"You don't have to do that."

"Says you."

I thanked him again. He walked away, down the access road toward his cabin. It was a good day for a walk if you had the strength for it.

When I went inside, there were five messages on my machine. Three were from downstaters wanting to make reservations, one was from Leon, a few days back, wanting to know where the hell I was. And one was from Natalie. Just calling to say hello. Wondering how I was doing.

"If you only knew," I said. I didn't call her back yet. I couldn't deal with it. Not yet.

My bruises had reached their full-color peak, and as I stood in the bathroom looking in the mirror, I thought to myself, Maven was right. I should sell tickets. The skin around both of my eyes was black now, and my eyes were both streaked blood-red. There was tape above my left eyebrow, and tape on the back of my head, where they had shaved the hair. The same hair I had dyed, standing right here just a matter of days ago, thinking that I could knock off a few years by hiding some of the gray. God, what a fool I was.

"You really did it this time," I said out loud.

I took the bottle of pills from my coat pocket. Vicodin. My old friend Vike. I shook the bottle. Thirty of them.

On the spur of the moment, I almost flushed them down the toilet, every last one of them. I stopped myself. "You're gonna regret that," I said to myself. "It's okay to take one now. It's okay."

One more look in the mirror, at the ugliest face I'd seen in a long time.

I took a pill, chased it with a gulp of water, and went to bed.

I stayed in my cabin for the next couple of days. I sure as hell wasn't going to go down to the Glasgow and let Jackie see me looking like this. I took the Vike when I needed it. I ran hot showers and stood there for a half hour at a time, letting the water work on me. A lonely man's massage. I watched my bruises turn yellow, purple, and green. Vinnie came by a couple of times, bringing in bags of groceries for me. I told him he was a good man.

On the third day, I got out of bed and almost fell right on my face. I had to hold on to one of the kitchen chairs until the room stopped spinning. The pain, which had been losing ground on me, was making a big comeback. I couldn't eat much that day. The dizzy spells hit me every time I stood up.

The phone rang. I couldn't stand the sound of it, so I turned off the ringer. I turned the volume down on the answering machine, too. It would take the messages, and I'd play them back later, when I felt like a human being again.

God damn it all, I thought. I took another Vike.

That afternoon there was a knock on the door. I didn't answer it. Just the thought of getting up made me sick to my stomach. A few minutes later, there was another knock on the door. I stayed in bed. This time, an envelope came sliding under the door. When I finally felt a little better, I got up and opened it. It was a check from the family in the second cabin, God bless them.

Later, as the sun was going down, there was another

knock on the door. I stayed in bed. If it was renters, they could leave me a note, or put money in an envelope like the family in the second cabin had, or just skip out on me without paying. I didn't care.

One more knock, and then whoever it was gave up and went away. Or so I thought.

The door opened a few seconds later, so quietly I didn't even hear it. My eyes were closed. My ears were ringing. I had no idea that someone else was in the cabin.

Until I opened my eyes and scared the hell out of both of us.

Eight

"Oh my God," she said.

"Natalie."

"Oh my God."

"How did you get in here?" I sat up too fast and paid for it.

"The door was open," she said. She reached her hand toward me, stopping just before she touched my cheek. "Alex, what happened to you? Oh my God."

I didn't say anything. Her face was inches from mine now. She was looking at me with those eyes. She finally touched me, just the tips of her fingers on my face.

"I'm sorry," she said, her voice low. "Alex, I'm sorry."

"For what?"

"Look at you."

"You didn't do this."

"This wouldn't have happened to you if we hadn't been there at that hotel."

"Who told you that? How did you—"

"This is what you get," she said. "Just for being around me. First I hurt you and then you get beat up."

"Stop, Natalie."

"You really look terrible."

"Thanks a lot."

"I mean really, really terrible."

"How did you find me, anyway? You've never been here before."

"Vinnie gave me directions," she said. "I called him and asked him what had happened to you. I left a couple of messages on your machine."

"I couldn't talk to you yet," I said. "I mean, I just couldn't—"

"It's all right. I don't blame you."

"But why did you come all the way over here?"

"I had to, Alex. Okay? I don't even know why. I just had to see you."

"Well, I guess I'm glad," I said. "A little surprised, but glad."

"Vinnie told me something happened at the funeral. He said you ran into some trouble."

"Yeah, I suppose you could say that."

"Who did this, Alex?"

I sat up. "I can't even think straight right now. I haven't eaten anything today, and all of a sudden . . ."

"Here, just stay there," she said. "I'll get you something."

I didn't fight her. I watched her as she banged around in my kitchen for the next few minutes, trying to find something edible.

"The place is kind of a mess right now," I said.

"Don't worry about it. Where are your pans?"

"I don't think any are clean. It's been sort of a tough week."

She picked up a pan from the pile in the sink, then put it down again. "Alex, put your coat on," she said. "You're coming with me."

"I don't feel like eating out, Natalie."

"We're not eating out, Alex. I'm taking you to my house."

"I can't."

"Come on, get up."

"No."

"Alex . . ."

"I can't leave, Natalie. I've got the cabins, and I've got to plow the stupid snow."

"I already talked to Vinnie about it. He's going to take care of your cabins. You're supposed to leave your keys in your truck so he can plow."

"Figures Vinnie would be involved in this. You had this all planned out?"

She came over to me. "No, Alex. Not all of it."

"Well, let me tell you something. Nobody else could get me out of bed today."

She smiled for the first time that evening. It was good to see. "Whatever you say. Now come on."

She put a hand under my arm and helped me out of bed. When I was on my feet, I went into the bathroom and splashed some cold water on my face. She was standing by my desk when I came back in the room. She had a framed picture in her hands, the only framed picture in my whole place. "Is this your father?"

"Yeah, that's him."

"Good-looking man."

"Yeah, he was." I picked up my coat and put it on slowly.

"You should pack some clothes, too."

I stopped. "How long am I staying?"

"Until you're better."

"I don't have that big a suitcase."

I settled on a few days of gear and we went outside into the cold and the dying light. Her Jeep Cherokee was parked next to my truck. It felt strange to be leaving the truck behind, but I got into the passenger's side and we were off.

We breezed right through Canadian customs. Even though she was on leave, she could still identify herself as an officer of the Ontario Provincial Police. The man asked about me and they exchanged a quick joke about me being her prisoner, and then we were sailing through Soo Canada.

It was getting darker by the minute, another winter day ending, this one in a way I would have never guessed. Neither of us said a word as the quiet streets passed by.

"So are you going to tell me?" she finally said.

"What's the question?"

"Who did this to you?"

"Let's just say I shouldn't have gone to Mr. Grant's funeral. His family didn't make me feel very welcome."

I could see her gloved hands working hard at the steering wheel now, like she wanted to pull it right off. "Did you call the police?"

"The doctor did. My old friend Roy Maven paid me a visit."

"The Soo Michigan chief?"

"Yeah. The same guy who told me the day before to stay away from the family."

She shook her head. "So why didn't you?"

"I didn't know the Woolseys were part of the family. It was a mistake."

"So for that they get to assault you? Because you made a mistake?" She turned to look at me, trying to keep one eye on the road. "Just because you showed up at the funeral? Imagine if you were still a police officer and you found somebody beaten all to hell and they said something like that."

"I'm not saying that, Natalie. I'm not saying I deserved it."

"I'm sorry, Alex. I've just heard it too many times. I'm sure you did, too, when you were a cop."

"Yeah," I said. "But it was always a woman. Black eyes, teeth missing. Whatever. It was her fault, not his."

"Yes," she said. "You're right. It's always a woman."

She kept driving, following the King's Highway due east, past the Garden River First Nation, past the old railroad bridge with the message written in white paint. We went through the small town of Echo Bay, and passed McKnight Road. It made me remember the first time I had come this way, and how that road had seemed like a good omen to me.

We drove through Bruce Mines, then Thessalon, past the abandoned motel on the side of the road, then the great expanse of the North Channel opening up to the south of us, through Iron Bridge and past the Mississauga Reserve, then finally into Blind River. A small spotlight lit up the monument next to the town hall—two men riding the logs, a testament to the great logging years on the channel. A couple more miles east of town we turned up her long driveway. With the four-wheel-drive Jeep, she crunched her way through the five inches of new snow without a second thought.

When we were inside, she made me a quick dinner. Then she took me upstairs and ordered me into bed. It was the same damned bed we had rolled around in every other time I'd been there. But now she just watched me lie down, never moving from the doorway.

"That was bad," she said.

"What?"

"In the car. I was taking it out on you. I'm sorry, I'm just . . ."

"It's all right."

She closed her eyes. "I don't know anything anymore," she said. "Look at me. I've got no idea what I'm doing, Alex."

"Come here."

I held up my hand. She came to me and took my hand and then I pulled her down on top of me. Her hair fell in my face.

"I'm sorry," she said, in a voice so low I could barely hear her. "I'm sorry."

"Stop saying that."

"But I am."

"It's okay."

"No," she said. "No."

"It's going to be all right. I promise."

"Tell me the truth, Alex. How bad did they hurt you?"

"I'm fine."

"Tell me the truth, God damn it."

"Okay," I said. "Everything hurts. Inside and out. Absolutely everything."

"Everything?"

"Yes."

"Then I'll try not to make it any worse."

She took her clothes off, shivering and suddenly covered with a million goose bumps. She started to take mine off, but didn't get far. We made do and we went slow. It felt good and bad at the same time.

Afterward, as she lay next to me, she touched the bandages over my eyebrow, and on the back of my head.

"You should sleep," she said.

"I will. Are you gonna stay?"

"Yes," she said, getting up. "I'll be right back."

I was out before she could keep her promise.

I woke up alone. It took me a second to remember where I was and how I had gotten there. It took me yet one more second to remember how much my head hurt. It was the first night I had slept all the way through since leaving the hospital.

I picked my watch off the bedside table. It was almost noon. I said her name once, then again a little louder. She didn't answer. But I knew she had spent the night here in the bed with me. There was another pillow next to mine, and I could smell her scent, her hair, the soap she used. I figured at this hour she was already downstairs.

It was quiet. Something about that fact bothered me, until I realized what was missing. There were no snowmobiles outside, no constant buzzing all over the place, the sound I was accustomed to waking up to every winter morning.

I got out of bed slowly, like my head was a bomb that

could go off at any second. I went into the bathroom. When I was done washing my face, I took a good hard look in the mirror. Maybe I looked a little better, I thought. Maybe one notch below Quasimodo now. But I still had the full array of bruises and the red streaks in my eyes that made me look possessed.

She came back, I thought. She came back to this face. I can officially believe in miracles now.

I went down the hallway, passing the other upstairs bedrooms—the master bedroom with the portraits of Natalie's grandparents, the bedroom with the canopy bed and the frilly white bedspread. Everything had a slightly sad and dusty smell to it. I didn't know how she could spend so much time here in this big empty house.

The grandfather clock was ticking at the top of the stairs. Aside from that there was no other sound.

"Natalie!"

No answer.

I went down the stairs, the old floorboards creaking with each step. The dining room table was completely taken over by moving boxes. All the china had been carefully packed away. All the curios and souvenirs of a family's long life in this house. The living room was just as empty. Or maybe it had been called the "parlor," once upon a time. There was a sofa, two matching chairs, a coffee table, and more boxes.

I parted the curtains and looked out the front window. Her Jeep was parked in front of the house. There was no garage to park it in.

"Natalie!"

Still no answer.

Then I noticed the old barn outside, across the snow-covered field, with an open side door fluttering in the wind. I found my boots. I swore as I bent over to pull them on to my feet. When I stood up straight, the blood was pounding in my ears. I was so dizzy I had to lean against the wall. I needed some more drugs, or hell, maybe an early beer or two, but first I had to find out where Natalie was.

I grabbed my coat and went out the front door. The sun was shining, but it was cold and the wind was kicking up so much sparkling glitter, it was like it was snowing all over again. I didn't see any tracks, but I tromped all the way through the deep snow to the side of the barn. The door was still swinging in the wind, but I saw that it was just barely open, stopped by the packed snow on the ground. I pulled it hard until I could squeeze through.

"Natalie!"

My voice reverberated through the high rafters. It took my eyes a while to adjust to the dim light, after the brilliant snow outside, but when they did, I saw the vast emptiness of that old barn, with the light shining through in thin slits here and there. A swirl of powder hung in the air as the snow worked its way through the cracks. It collected in a light layer on the floor, covering the ancient wood and the hay dust. There were a few farm tools hanging on the walls—a hoe and a pickax and some other metal contraptions I couldn't have named to save my life. Everything was rusted to the point of disintegration, and an old leather horse collar was eaten away to almost nothing. If someone had told me this barn had been used in the last fifty years, it would have been a surprise to me.

I pushed the door open again and made my way back across the field to the house. I was starting to get genuinely worried. When I was inside, I knocked the snow off my boots and called her name again.

Nothing.

Then I saw the door. It was in the corner, behind the old wood stove. I tried it, and it opened to a set of stairs.

"Natalie, are you down there?"

I didn't hear anything, but it looked like there was a light on, so I went down, holding on to the wooden rails. There was a strong smell in the air, a cellar smell, of moisture and rot and mildew.

It was dark, the way cellars used to be before they started building them with high windows. The stairs led to a small room filled with stacks of wooden crates and an old metal bicycle with long wooden fenders. The room led to another room, and then to another, the light growing stronger and stronger.

"Natalie, where are you?"

I went through one more room, this one with piles of old magazines on one wall, and on the other wall a set of shelves filled with mason jars. There was a door. It was half closed, the light streaming out onto the floor.

"Natalie?"

I pushed the door open.

She was sitting on the floor, surrounded by more boxes.

"Natalie, didn't you hear me calling you?"

She didn't answer me. She held an old photograph in her hands, its edges curled with age.

"What's the matter?" I said. I winced as I bent down beside her.

She didn't say anything. A single tear ran down her right cheek.

"What is it?" I said. "What are you looking at?"

She didn't show it to me, but I could see just enough of it to make out three men. The photo was in color, but it had that washed-out look to it, the way color photos looked in the sixties. I was guessing the older man was her grandfather, and one of the other two men was maybe her father. She had come down to pack up all these boxes of old photographs, and had stopped to look at this picture of the grandfather she loved and the father she had hardly known. And that this had gotten to her, in the same way it would have gotten to me or to anyone else.

I was wrong.

"I talked to the doorman," she finally said.

"What?"

"At the hotel."

"What are you talking about?"

"The first night I got there. I talked to him. What did you say his name was? Chris?"

"Yes, but what does—"

"He helped me with my bag," she said. "He rode up in the elevator with me, and he asked me how bad the roads were. I told him I had a Jeep, and that I knew how to drive in the snow. He asked me how far I had come."

"Yeah?"

"So I told him I came from Canada. I'm pretty sure I said from Blind River. That old man, the man who left the hat, the man who died in the snow . . . You told me he was the doorman's grandfather, right?"

"Natalie, I'm sorry. I have no idea what you're talking about."

She looked down at the picture and swallowed hard. "I need to tell you something, Alex."

"What is it?"

"When you asked me to come over to Michigan, the first thing I thought of was this promise I had made to my own grandfather."

"What did you promise him?"

She looked up at me. "I promised him I would never set foot in Sault Ste. Marie, Michigan."

"What? I don't get it."

"He hated that city so much, Alex. Once, when I was a teenager, a bunch of us went over the bridge to go to this bar. God, I thought he was going to have a heart attack when he found out. I never saw him so mad."

She looked back down at the picture.

"Why did he feel that way?" I said. "I mean, I remember you telling me he thought it was a wild place."

"There's one thing we never talked about in this house," she said. "My father's death was the one forbidden topic. But now, I think it makes sense."

"What? Tell me."

"My father was killed in Michigan, Alex. In Sault Ste. Marie."

"Why didn't you tell me?"

She shrugged. "I thought it was time to grow up, you know? My father's been gone for thirty years now, and my grandfather's been gone for fifteen."

"Okay, so go back. What does all this have to do with the doorman at the hotel? Or his grandfather?"

She handed me the picture. I flattened it out. There were three men. The man on the left was the oldest of the three, maybe in his fifties. He was robust and he had a stern smile, and he was dressed in an old suit with a string tie. He stood with his hands on his hips, like he wasn't quite sure whether he approved of the scene before him. The man in the middle of the picture was young, in his twenties. He had a big wide smile and he was wearing a light linen suit. He was moving toward the camera, his arms spread as if he were about to embrace the photographer. The man on the right was just as well dressed, his suit coat unbuttoned to show off his suspenders. His hands were in his pockets, and he stood watching the man in the middle with a thin smile.

"It was meant for me," she said. "I'm the one he left it for."

"What are you talking about?"

"Look," she said. She pointed at the man in the middle of the picture. "Look at what's on my father's head."

It was the same shade of gray, the same band. The same shape. Forty years later, it would end up filled with ice and snow on the floor of a hotel hallway, but in this picture, it belonged to a young man from Canada. Sure, there were thousands more just like it. That much we knew. But somehow, we knew something else—the way you know in your gut that the most improbable thing in the world has to be true.

This was it.

This was the hat.

Nine

"It was my father's hat," she said. "But why? Why would that old man go to all that trouble just to tell me he knew who I was?"

She finally looked up at me. It was like she was seeing the damage on my face for the first time.

"Alex." She reached out to me. "This all happened because of me."

"No," I said. "Come on. It's not your fault."

"It is," she said, looking back down at the photograph. "Of course it is. It was my father . . ."

I looked more closely at the three men—starting with the old man on the left, who had obviously worked hard his entire life, who had seen so many long Canadian winters. Then the younger man in the middle, Natalie's father, with the big easy smile, all charm and optimism. He was stepping toward the camera, drawing the attention to himself. Then the third man.

"This man on the right," I said.

"Albert DeMarco. My stepfather."

I felt a sick flutter in my stomach. "The one you told me about?"

"Yes, he was my father's best friend back then. His family lived just down the road."

I bent down closer to look at him. "You say he's dead now?"

"They all are," she said. "All three of them are gone. Two of them left too soon, and Albert not soon enough."

"Do you recognize where this picture was taken?"

"It's right here at the house, standing out by the driveway."

"When was it taken?"

"I don't know exactly. I think I remember that car, though. It was still here . . . Years later, I mean. It was a beat-up old thing by then, just sitting in back of the barn."

Behind the men I could just barely make out the tail end of a car. "So this must have been what, late sixties maybe?"

"Yes. Somewhere around then."

I touched the photo where the corner was peeling away from the backing. "This is a Polaroid," I said. "One of the early ones. The picture would come out and you had to stick it on the cardboard and smooth it out."

She shrugged. I might as well have been talking about a box camera with the big black hood and the gunpowder flash.

"What else is here?" I said. "Any other pictures?"

She pushed open the lid on the box. "There's all sorts of old stuff here. Pictures. Souvenirs."

"What about these other boxes?" There were six or seven in all, lined up against the wall in this small room.

Above them there were shelves with dusty old radios, lampshades, one of those old milkshake mixers with the steel canisters like you see in diners.

"More history," she said. "Most of all this was from before I was born. God, Alex."

"Why don't we bring some of this stuff upstairs?"

She wiped her face on the back of her sleeve and stood up. "I'm almost afraid to. What else are we going to find?"

"Come on," I said. "Let's go up. It's freezing down here."

She picked up the box in front of her. I grabbed two more. I was afraid the cardboard would give way in my hands.

"This is all falling apart," I said. "It's a bad place to keep stuff like this."

"I didn't put it down here, Alex."

"I know that. I'm just saying."

She turned and headed for the stairs. I followed her. When we were back upstairs, I took a big breath of the warm dry air. We made room on the empty dining room table to put the boxes down. I left her there and went back down to grab another box. It felt strange to be down there by myself.

When I picked up the box, the flimsy cardboard started to come apart. Another photograph fell out at my feet. Another faded color picture, this time of a woman's face. I bent down, picked it up, and looked into the eyes of a woman who had to be Natalie's mother. She was fairer than Natalie, with red hair and green eyes. This was where Natalie's Irish side came from, to go with the dark features inherited from her father.

The woman was turned slightly sideways. She looked

into the camera with a shy smile, perhaps a little too knowing at the same time. She seemed aware, most of all, that she was taking a damned good picture.

When I got back upstairs, Natalie was sitting at the dining room table, a dozen photographs spread out before her.

"Here's some more," I said. I took out the picture and showed it to her. "I'm guessing this is your mother."

She put her hand to her mouth. "My God."

"I shouldn't even be looking at this stuff," I said. "I mean, you should go through it yourself."

"Look at her," she said, ignoring me. "She was so beautiful." She took it from me and held it in front of her.

"This was back in the sixties, too?"

"Yes."

"What's her first name, anyway?"

"Grace," she said. "Her name is Grace."

"That's a good name."

"God damn it, what did she do to herself?"

"Natalie, has something bad happened to her since then?"

"Just herself, mostly. Not to mention marrying Albert after my father was gone. Plus a lot of alcohol." She put the photograph face-down on the table. "I'm sorry, I can't even look at this now."

"There are a couple more boxes," I said. "I'll go get them."

I made two more trips to the basement. Whatever had caused such a strong reaction to seeing her mother's picture, she seemed to put it behind her quickly. By the time I brought up the last box, she was busy sorting through all of the contents.

"I guess I was saving the basement for last," she said. "You can see why I was dreading it."

"Natalie, are you all right?"

"I'm fine, Alex. Here, look, I found another photo from that same day."

She showed it to me. Her father was standing in the middle of the shot again, the gray hat on his head. He had one arm around Natalie's mother now, the other arm on his father's back. The old man was smiling now, like he had finally given in to the occasion.

"Where's DeMarco?" I said. "Is he taking the picture?"

"I think so. That first one must have been taken by my mother."

"That hat . . ."

She shook her head. "It's hard to believe, but I know it's the same hat. I know it. And if Simon Grant had that hat . . ." She stopped.

"What?"

"Maybe he killed him, Alex. Maybe Simon Grant killed my father."

"You can't know that."

"It all fits," she said. "We never found out who did it. Now maybe I finally know."

"Tell me again," I said. "What do you know about how your father was killed?"

"I told you, my grandfather never talked about it. Not ever. It was my mother who told me what little I knew. He was in a bar in Michigan and somebody killed him. I think that was her way of telling me to stay away from bars. Which was kind of ironic, coming from her."

"Nobody was ever arrested?"

"Nobody."

I picked up the photo again.

"Natalie, didn't you ever ask her to tell you the whole story?"

She looked up at me. "What, ask my mother?"

"Didn't you want to know?"

"He was protecting somebody, some woman in the bar. He was just an innocent bystander. That's what my mother said, anyway."

"That's all? If you wanted to find out more, couldn't you just call her right now?"

"Alex, it's not that easy."

"Why not?"

"You gotta understand," she said. "I can't just call my mother and ask her something like that. Not if I really want to know the answer."

"What do you mean?"

"She lies, Alex. Every other thing she says is an outright, complete lie. It's her gift. It's the reason she was put on this earth."

"She lies even to you?"

"*Especially* to me. She saves her best work for me. Her masterpieces. You want an example?"

"Okay."

"Let's see. There were so many of them . . . Okay, how about this one? When I was twelve years old, when she and Albert got married, she moved out of this house and took me with her. We were living down by Toronto, in this really big house. The guy was already pretty rich by then. I'm in this huge house with a gigantic bedroom of my own and it was the absolute worst time of my life. I don't even like to think of it now. But the one thing I had going for me was I had a dog. That was the only friend I had in the world, the whole time I was there. This little beagle mutt named Keon."

"You named your dog Keon?"

"After Dave Keon, from the Maple Leafs. I was a big hockey fan, even back then. Anyway, one day I come home and Keon's not there. I asked my mother where he was and she said he ran away. She gave me this whole description of him getting off the leash and her running down the street chasing after Keon, going through everybody's backyard."

"Let me guess. The dog didn't really run away."

"No, he didn't. But it wasn't enough for her to just tell me that lie. She had to go crazy with it. We were out there putting up posters, Alex. We put an ad in the newspaper. We were driving in the car, all over the neighborhood, me with my head out the window calling Keon's name. We did that for five days. Until finally, the guy across the street comes over with one of the posters in his hand, and he says to my mother, 'Hey, didn't I see you run over a dog in your driveway?'"

"Oh, no."

"She kept lying, Alex. She said no, that wasn't Keon, that was another dog. And this guy was saying, 'Well, he looked just like this dog on the poster.' So my mother yells at him and tells him to mind his own business. But, of course, then I knew what had happened. I wasn't an idiot. After all that time, I finally got her to admit that she had killed the dog. She says to me, 'I didn't want to tell you because I knew it would make you sad.' Like going through this charade for five days was somehow better than just telling me what had happened."

"That's pretty bad."

"How about one more?" she said. "When I told her about what Albert was doing to me, she promised me she'd make him stop. She promised me he'd never touch me again."

She didn't look up at me. She picked up a photograph and ran her fingers along the edge.

"My mother promised me, Alex. Never again, she said. Never again, my sweet little daughter. If she had to, she'd take me with her and run away forever."

I sat there and watched her, not sure what to say. She picked up a few more photographs and sorted through them.

"I grew up with lies," she finally said. "To this day, I cannot stand for someone to lie to me."

"For what it's worth," I said, "I'm not too crazy about lies, either."

"If you ever lie to me, Alex—"

"Not going to happen. That's one thing I can promise you."

"Okay, good."

"So what do we do now?"

"We call my mother. We take our chances."

"Are you sure?"

"It's time to find out," she said, picking up the original photo. Three men, almost thirty years ago. "I want to know what happened to my father."

She got up and went to the kitchen phone. As she dialed the number, she closed her eyes like someone waiting for a bomb to go off. There was a long wait. Apparently, nobody was answering.

"Hello, Mother," she said, opening her eyes. I could tell she was talking to the answering machine now. "This is Natalie. Um, hope you're doing okay. Give me a call. I want to ask you about something."

She paused. She closed her eyes again.

"I saw a nice picture of you today," she said. "I'll talk to you later. Goodbye."

She hung the phone up and let out a long breath.

"She'll call you back, right?"

"Oh yes. She'll call me back."

I felt like holding her just then, but she went back into the kitchen. She returned with a bottle and two glasses.

"I could use a drink," she said. "How about you?"

She poured a couple of fingers' worth of Wild Turkey in each glass and handed one to me.

"Have you eaten anything today?"

"Don't worry, Alex. Just one, okay? It's been a bitch of a day already."

She kissed me on the mouth and clinked my glass with hers.

"Cheers?"

"Cheers," I said.

I watched her take a long swallow. She made a face and put the glass on the table.

"I actually called my mother," she said. "Without a gun to my head. Can you believe it?"

I didn't say anything.

"This is the other thing my mother does. She drinks. After my father was gone, she and Albert would hang around all day, seeing who could get drunk first."

"Natalie, maybe you shouldn't—"

"My mother always had the advantage, you know? Less body weight, the liquor works faster."

"Come on," I said. I tried to take her glass from her. She gave me a little elbow check and took another drink.

"Here's to mothers, eh?" Half a glass of bourbon and her Canadian accent was already getting stronger. "Which reminds me . . . If we want to find out more about the past, I've got one idea who we can talk to."

"Who's that?"

"You'll see," she said, putting her glass down. "Follow me."

The house was next door, she said. Next door meaning the next house down the road, a half mile away. There was a path that led across the field behind the barn, then into the trees. I didn't like the sound of a half-mile hike in knee-deep snow, in the beat-up shape I was still in that day, so we took her Jeep instead.

"I'm sorry about all that," she said as we pulled down her driveway. "Just talking about my mother, I turn into a twelve-year-old again."

"I didn't have a mother when I was twelve."

"At the time, I wished I didn't either, believe me."

"Who's this woman we're gonna see?"

"Mrs. DeMarco, Albert's mother. She's been here forever, Alex. Practically her whole life."

"How old is she?"

"If I'm counting right, she's ninety-six years old now."

"Good Lord," I said. "I thought Simon Grant was old."

"She blew by eighty-two a long time ago."

"Did she know your family well?"

"Yes, the two families were pretty close. Albert and

my father, they spent so much time together—they'd use that trail between the houses to meet up so they could go get in trouble."

"What kind of trouble?"

"Just kid stuff. Setting fires, shooting off guns. At least that's what my mother told me. So God knows if any of it's true."

It was a short trip down the road, heading due east. The wind was still blowing, but the bright sun from that morning was long gone. More snow was on the way.

"Later on, when I was growing up," she said, "I'd come over here a lot myself. I remember that one time, when my mother was trying to move out, I ran over here and hid, so she couldn't take me with her."

She pulled into the driveway. It needed a good plowing.

"I always loved Mrs. DeMarco. She was always so glad to see me. I think maybe because she didn't have any grandchildren of her own."

"So Albert and your mother . . ."

"Never had any kids of their own, no. Thank God. I can't imagine having Albert DeMarco as your natural father."

"But his mother still lives here in Blind River? All by herself?"

"Yes," she said. "I was stationed up at Hearst for so long . . . When I came back, I was surprised to see that she was still here."

Natalie pulled up to the house. It was another farmhouse, but about half the size of Natalie's, and in much more need of attention. I could see from fifty feet away that all the wood on the porch was rotten. The shutters didn't look any better. The one hanging cockeyed from the hinges was the crowning touch.

"I've only been here once since I've been back," Natalie said. "I know I should come more often, but God, it's so hard seeing her like this. Apparently she has this nurse who comes to check on her every afternoon, but I haven't met her."

"Shouldn't she be living somewhere else now?"

"She should be, yes. Most of the time she's sort of living in the past. I don't think she even knows what year it is."

"If that's true, then is she really going to be able to answer your questions?"

"Who knows?" Natalie said. She pulled the key out of the ignition. "If her mind is really stuck in the past, maybe she's the best person of all to tell us about it."

I couldn't argue with that. I got out of the Jeep with her and walked up to the front steps. It looked like someone had made a half-hearted attempt to shovel the walkway.

"The nurse must have been here," Natalie said. She knocked on the front door and peeked inside the little window. She pushed it open and stuck her head inside.

"Hello! Mrs. DeMarco?"

I didn't hear any response, but she pushed the door all the way in anyway and went inside. I was right behind her.

"Mrs. DeMarco?"

I was expecting a shambles, based on the way the place looked from the outside, but it was surprisingly neat and well ordered. We passed a set of stairs with a great polished railing, an antique phone table next to the stairs, a faded Oriental rug over hardwood floors, then another larger rug as the hallway opened into the living room. There was more old furniture in fairly good shape, a sofa that probably would have been called a divan, and a long chair that I'd guess you'd call a settee. Stuff so old even the names had been retired. There were white lace curtains on the windows and a pair of portraits on the walls in oval frames. A man and a woman, taken a hell of a long time ago. The air was warm, and smelled of mothballs and something medicinal like liniment.

"Is that you again, Flo?" A woman came into the room from the kitchen, moving slowly. She was wearing a quilted robe and slippers. She looked all of ninety-six years, and maybe seventy pounds, if that. But what the hell. If you're still on your feet at ninety-six, you're doing pretty damned well.

"It's me, Mrs. DeMarco. I hope I'm not bothering you."

She came closer to us, holding on tight to the back of the chair. "Where did she go now, eh?" She certainly sounded like a lifelong Canadian.

"Mrs. DeMarco, this is my friend Alex," Natalie said. "We've both come to visit you."

She came closer. When I bent down to shake her hand, she stared into my face. Her thick glasses magnified her pale blue eyes, and her white hair was pinned up on her head. Around her neck was a long silver necklace with what looked to be one of those medical alert tags. One push on the button and the ambulance would be on its way, although way the hell up here, I couldn't imagine how long it would take to show up.

"Alex?" she said. "Is that your name?"

"Yes, ma'am." I took her right hand carefully in mine.

"That's a good name," she said. "What happened to your face?"

"It's a long story, ma'am."

"My son is named Albert. That's close to Alex."

"Alex and I would like to ask you a couple of questions," Natalie said. "Would that be all right?"

"Of course, dear." She put her hand on Natalie's shoulder. "I'm sorry, dear."

"Yes?"

"Tell me your name."

"I'm Natalie."

"Natalie! There's a little girl next door named Natalie. Her grandparents are dear friends of mine."

Natalie closed her eyes for a moment. She cleared her throat. "Mrs. DeMarco, I wonder if I can ask you something."

"Please sit down, eh? Can I get you anything?"

"No, please," Natalie said. "Let me. Have you eaten lunch yet?"

"Oh yes. Flo was here before. She comes every day."

"Your nurse, you mean? I thought her name was Celia. When I was here before, remember? You told me her name was—"

"She's the woman who comes over every day. Her name is Flo."

Natalie took her by the hand and led her to the couch. "Are you sure I can't get you something else? Maybe some tea?"

"No, I'm fine, dear. But thank you."

She took her time sitting herself down on the couch. I offered my hand to her, but she waved me away.

"Sit down," she said. "Please."

I sat down next to her. Natalie knelt down on the floor.

"Mrs. DeMarco, you do remember me, right? I came over to visit you a couple of weeks ago."

"You didn't have your friend with you then," she said, looking at me. "Him I'd remember."

"No," Natalie said. "Alex wasn't with me."

"You've got to learn how to duck, young man."

I couldn't help smiling at that. It had been a long time since someone referred to me as a young man.

"We have a question to ask you," Natalie said. "It might seem kind of silly. Are you ready?"

"Yes, dear. Go ahead, eh?"

Natalie took the photograph out of her coat pocket. "Can you see this picture all right?"

Mrs. DeMarco took it from her and held it a few inches from her face. "Can you turn on that lamp, dear?"

Natalie reached over and pulled the cord on the tassel-shaded lamp on the end table. "Is that better?"

Mrs. DeMarco squinted and moved the picture back and forth a little bit. "Is that snow on the ground?"

"No, I think this was taken during the summer."

"I remember that hat," she said.

Natalie looked at me. "The hat? You remember it?"

"That was an expensive hat, eh? You have to take good care of a hat like that."

"Were you here in the yard the day this was taken?"

"How much snow is there?" she said, looking closer. "This is right before New Year's Eve."

"No, Mrs. DeMarco—"

"I told them, New Year's Eve you should spend with

your family, eh? You shouldn't be going out all night like that."

"Mrs. DeMarco, I don't understand. What New Year's Eve are you talking about?"

"There wasn't much snow, eh? It was a strange winter. And them going down there like that. There was no reason for it. You shouldn't be away from home on New Year's Eve. It gave me a bad feeling, you know. A woman knows these things."

"Down there? Where's down there?"

"It's bad business. Any fool knows that, eh?"

"What's the bad business about, Mrs. DeMarco? Can you tell me?"

"New Year's Eve," she said. "Of all the nights in the year, eh?"

"What happened on New Year's Eve?"

Mrs. DeMarco looked at the picture again. "Luc Reynaud certainly knows how to wear a suit," she said. "Who are these other men?"

"That's my father," Natalie said.

Mrs. DeMarco looked at her, shaking her head in confusion.

"Your father, dear?"

"I mean to say, this is Jean Reynaud."

"No, dear. Jean's just a little thing."

"The other man was . . ." Natalie stopped. What could she say? Your dead son?

"Where did he go now?" Mrs. DeMarco said, looking around the room.

"Who, Mrs. DeMarco?"

"Albert. He's always getting into things."

"I don't know," Natalie said, blinking. "I don't think he's here."

Mrs. DeMarco turned to me. "What was your name? Alvin?"

"Alex, ma'am."

"Have you seen my son?"

"No, ma'am. I haven't."

"If you do, will you bring him home?"

I looked at Natalie. "Yes, ma'am. I will."

"Good," she said. She patted me on the hand. "You're a good boy. You shouldn't get into fights, though. It's not a smart thing to do, eh?"

"You're right about that," I said.

We sat with her for a few more minutes. It was obvious she wasn't going to talk any more about the hat or anything else from the past. She was getting tired, too, so we made our goodbyes and promised her that we'd come back again soon. She made Natalie promise to say hello to the Reynauds next door if she saw them, and she made me promise to keep an eye out for her son. And to not get into any more fights.

Natalie wrote out a note to the day nurse, asking her to call her. Then we left. The air felt painful after the warmth of the house.

"That was bad," Natalie said as she got into the Jeep.

"I know."

"I've got to do something to help her. I can't just leave her in that house like that."

"Isn't there somebody you can talk to?"

She shook her head. "She doesn't have any family left, Alex. And she doesn't even know it."

I didn't say anything. There was nothing to say. She

started up the Jeep and backed it down the driveway. When she was on the road, she gunned it and drove west, past her own driveway.

"Let me guess," I said. "We're going to Michigan now?"

"You up for it?"

"Yep."

She nodded her head and kept driving. She didn't say anything else for a while. The snow started to fall.

"Mrs. DeMarco couldn't help us," she finally said. "But I *am* going to find out. I want to know what happened."

"If this man really did kill your father," I said, "this Simon Grant, the man with the hat . . ."

"I know, Alex. They just buried him."

"I'm just saying—"

"He's gone now. I can't touch him, I know. But I still have to find out."

I heard the determination in her voice. It was something I recognized, the same thing that would be driving me if I were in her place. She'd have no peace until she got her answer.

I wanted to help her. I wanted to watch her back, wherever this thing would take her. And of course I wouldn't mind finding out some answers myself. Why the hell I got triple-teamed behind the church, for starters.

I wasn't quite sure where we'd begin, but I did know one thing. Sooner or later, we'd end up spending some more time with the Grant family.

Ten

The snow kept coming. We hit a bad patch on the road and for one instant I could feel everything moving sideways. Natalie slowed down just a little bit, but otherwise barreled right on through it. Then the snow stopped, just like that. Neither of us said anything about it. We didn't want to jinx it. Or maybe we just didn't feel like talking yet. A few minutes later, I picked up my cell phone and dialed Leon's number.

"How old is that thing?" she said. "It looks like something from World War II."

"It works," I said.

"Do you have to crank it by hand first?"

"At least I have a cell phone."

"Yeah, so anybody can call you, no matter where you are."

"If I left it on, yeah."

She smiled and shook her head. Before I could say anything else, Leon came on the line.

"Leon," I said. "Are you at the store? I hope I'm not bothering you."

"Of course not, Alex. What's going on?"

"I'm just wondering if you could give me the name of your friend at the newspaper. We've got something we want to look up."

There was a pause. "Why don't you just tell me what you need? I can talk to him."

"All right," I said. Like there was any other way. "This is what we're looking for. A man named Reynaud was murdered a long time ago, in Soo Michigan. Most likely in a bar."

"What's the full name?"

I pictured him getting out his little notepad, standing there among the snowmobiles with the phone to his ear.

"I'm sorry," I said to Natalie. "Did you ever tell me his full name?"

"Jean Sylvain Reynaud." She kept staring straight ahead. We had just driven through Iron Bridge, and now we were back out on the open road.

"Jean Sylvain Reynaud," I said into the phone.

"When was the murder?"

"Natalie, do you remember—"

"Nineteen seventy-three," she said, her eyes still straight ahead. Her voice was flat. "I don't know what date. Sometime early in the year."

"Leon, it was early 1973."

"Do you have anything on the cause of death? Shooting? Stabbing?"

I looked over at her.

"Leon," I said. "That should be enough to go on, shouldn't it?"

"Yeah, yeah. No problem. I'll give my guy a call, see

what he can find out. If it was here in the Soo, I know the *Evening News* will have a record of it."

"Thanks, Leon. You're the best."

He told me he'd keep in touch. Then he was off to sell more snowmobiles. I put the phone down and looked out the side window.

"This Leon," she said. "He's good at this stuff, eh?"

"He is."

"How long will it take him to find out?"

I looked at my watch. It was 3:15. "We'll be down there by what, 4:30?"

"Before that."

I looked over at her speedometer. With the snow stopped, the needle was back up to 120 on her Canadian dial, which meant she was going somewhere around 75 miles per hour. She was driving just like a cop.

"If his newspaper friend is in the office," I said, "Leon will call me back before we get there."

"That fast?"

"He's like a pit bull when he wants to find out something. That's why he's such a good private eye."

"And you're not?"

"He loves this stuff," I said. "He lives for it."

"He sounds like the perfect partner. You ever think about trying it again?"

"Not really, no."

"Why not?"

"You're serious?"

"What else are you going to do? Sit around in your cabin all day?"

"With a blanket on my lap, yeah. In my rocking chair."

"That's not what I meant."

"Actually, right now that sounds pretty good."

She reached over and touched my arm. "Sorry."

"It's all right."

She kept driving. We hit Thessalon, and she had to slow down for a while. When the town was behind us, she blew by a big truck and got back to cruising speed again.

"So what do you want to bet?" she said.

"About what?"

"About whether Leon calls you back before we hit the bridge."

"I don't want to take your money," I said.

"Who said anything about money?"

"Hmm, you might have something there."

"Unless you're too sore."

I looked over at her. After everything that had happened that day, finding the picture of her father, having to think about his death, having to work up the nerve to call her mother of all people in the world, the visit to Mrs. De-Marco—after all that, here she was trying to pull herself out of a blue mood. She was *willing* herself to be happy again. It was something I needed to learn.

"We're almost there," she said. We were coming up to Bruce Mines.

"He's got plenty of time," I said. "All the time in the world."

There was more traffic on the King's Highway now. She passed three cars in a row and kept going.

"No fair," I said. "You're cheating."

"Nobody said I had to drive like a civilian."

"He'll still make it. I know he will."

We passed the Garden River First Nation. I looked at

my watch. It was 3:45. Leon hadn't been on the case for more than thirty minutes.

"I'll take dinner first," she said.

Then the phone rang.

"Hello, Leon," I said as I picked it up. "What took you so long?"

"I've got something," he said.

"What is it?"

"You said early 1973, right?"

"Right."

"How about a few minutes into the year?"

"How do you mean?"

"It was New Year's Eve. He died just as 1972 was turning into 1973."

That stopped me cold. New Year's Eve. I thought back over all the jumbled references Mrs. DeMarco had made to New Year's Eve.

"It happened here in the Soo," Leon went on. "Just like you said. You want to know exactly where?"

"Yes, tell me."

"Right outside the Ojibway."

"My God." I looked at Natalie. She was back to her straight-ahead stare.

"I've got the old news article here," he said. "Reynaud was found around the corner, right next to the building, on Water Street."

"On the side overlooking the locks?"

"Yeah. He was shot in the back of the head. They never found out who did it."

"No leads even?"

"No, at least there aren't any mentioned in the paper.

You'd have to talk to the police about it. Maybe some-body remembers the case."

"Okay. Can I get a copy of that article?"

"Of course. You never bought a fax machine, did you?"

"Why would I buy a fax machine?"

"Just stop by the motor shop," he said. "I'm here for another hour."

"Thanks, Leon. I really appreciate it."

I hung up the phone. I told her everything he had given me.

"So I lose," she said. Then nothing else. She just kept driving.

We rolled through Soo Canada, then crossed the International Bridge. High above the St. Marys River, I looked down at the locks and the thin stretch of rapids between the Canadian and American sides. The whole scene was cast in a gray, muted light, the clouds hanging low and dark over our heads. The snow would start falling again. It was just a matter of time.

When we cleared customs, I gave her directions to the motor shop on Three Mile Road. As soon as we got out of Natalie's Jeep, I saw Leon coming out to meet us. I made the introductions.

"Pleased to meet you," Leon said to Natalie. He bowed a little bit and did everything else but kiss her hand. "No wonder Alex is so loopy these days."

"Leon, the only thing making me loopy is my concussion. Now who's this guy over at the newspaper who can—"

I stopped and looked into the showroom.

"There's like a dozen people in there," I said. "Don't you have to go back in?"

He took a quick glance behind him. "They're fine in there. Everybody's just looking."

It made me feel a little guilty again, taking up his time like this. But he was already off and running.

"I've got a copy of the article right here," he said. He took a piece of paper out of a manila folder.

I took it from him and started to read it.

"Leon," I said. "This isn't a fax. It's a photocopy. How did you—"

"I ran over to the newspaper office and got it. Only took me a minute."

I shook my head and kept reading. It was a front page article dated January 1, 1973, with the same lighthouse that had been on the masthead of the *Evening News* since forever. The headline read "Canadian Man Slain," and the text went on to describe the discovery of a frozen body on Water Street, behind the Ojibway Hotel. The man was identified as Jean Sylvain Reynaud of Blind River, Ontario. His wallet was still on his person, robbery ruled out, no suspects at the time. It was all pretty straightforward reporting, and I wasn't sure if it gave us anything we could use. Except for one detail.

"Leon, it says here he was seen drinking in the hotel bar that evening. I don't remember there being a bar in the hotel."

"There was, way back when. I remember my dad going in there when I was a kid."

"Where the dining room is now?"

"Yeah, I think it was on that side of the building. They redid the place a couple of times since then."

I passed the paper to Natalie. She read through it quickly and gave it back to me. "Shot in the back of the head," she said, "behind the bar. That doesn't sound like he was protecting somebody."

"No," Leon said. "Did you have reason to believe he was?"

"Just part of my mother's story," she said. "Another lie."

"I'm sorry," Leon said to her. "This can't be easy."

She pulled her coat closer to her body. "I'm okay."

"Leon, how can we find out more about this?" I said. "You think the police record is still lying around somewhere?"

"I'm sure it is," he said, "in some storage room. Probably take forever to find it. You know any old Soo cops who might have been around back then?"

"You don't suppose . . ."

"One way to find out."

"Sure," I said. "This'll be fun."

"You know, if you're talking about the seventies, you're going back to a pretty strange time around here. Like I said, I was only a kid then, but I heard about it later."

"What do you mean?"

"You gotta remember, the air force base was still open then. There were a lot of men stationed up here. You add up everybody, I think it was like ten thousand. That's a lot of people, Alex. With a long hard winter. You can imagine . . ."

"So you're saying, what, there were a lot of prostitutes around, and what else?"

"You name it," he said. "You remember what happened to the chief of police up here."

"No, what?"

"He was arrested by the state police for taking bribes from the Detroit Mafia. I forget what year that was."

"I didn't know that," I said. "I was downstate back then."

"What my grandfather said about this town," Natalie said. "I guess he knew what he was talking about."

I looked at the article again. "It's hard to even imagine."

A man stepped out of the shop and stared daggers at Leon's back.

"I think you're wanted inside," I said. "Thank you again, Leon. You're the best."

"Yes," Natalie said. "Thank you. Alex told me you were a good partner."

That seemed to make Leon's day, even though he was headed back inside to deal with an unhappy boss.

We got back in Natalie's Jeep. "So now what?" she said.

"Take a right here," I said. "It's time for you to meet somebody."

"Another friend of yours?"

"No, I wouldn't say that."

We went up Ashmun to the north end of town. When we hit Portage, we could see the Ojibway Hotel, three blocks down. The red awnings seemed to glow in the fading light.

"This way," I said.

We turned right, away from the hotel. It was going on five o'clock when we got to the City County Building. We pulled around back, just in time to see Chief Maven leaving.

"Chief," I said as I opened my door. "Can we have a minute of your time?"

"What is it, McKnight? I'm on my way home."

"It won't take long," I said. "This is Natalie Reynaud of the Ontario Provincial Police." I figured the official title wouldn't hurt, but it probably didn't matter. His face brightened as soon as he looked at her. Turns out he was human after all.

"Officer Reynaud," he said, taking her hand. "A pleasure to meet you."

"Likewise, Chief. If it's not too much trouble, can we go back inside for a moment?"

"Certainly. Right this way."

He opened the door and showed her into the building. I followed, watching this unnaturally charming clone of Chief Roy Maven asking Natalie which detachment she was based out of, and how long she had been in the OPP. We went straight to his office and he went a couple of doors down to get a comfortable guest chair for her. I sat in my usual rock-hard plastic chair.

"So," he finally said when we were settled in, "what can I do for you? Alex, your face is looking a little better, at least. Relatively speaking."

"About that," Natalie said. "What's happening to the men who assaulted Alex?"

She wasn't wasting any time. Maven threw his hands up in surrender. "Let's not get off on the wrong foot here," he said. "I arrested all three of them, right after I saw Alex in the hospital."

"How did you charge them?"

"Felonious assault, naturally."

"What class is that in Michigan?"

"Well," Maven said, "that's actually a class three felony."

"That's one step away from a misdemeanor," Natalie said. "Am I right? Is that how it works here?"

"It's a mighty big step," he said. "Believe me."

"Three men beat him and left him for dead. You're telling me that's not a class two at least?"

"For a class two assault, you need intent to rob or else some sort of criminal sexual contact. For class one you need intent to kill or maim."

"Chief Maven, if you're telling me they had no intent to maim him . . ."

"I know what you mean, but you've gotta understand how it works around here. Intent to maim is strictly interpreted. With no weapon, and no admitted intent, it just doesn't get prosecuted as class one."

"Can we stop talking about me like I'm not even here?" I said. "Just tell me what they said when you arrested them."

Maven looked at me, then opened a file on his desk. "We arrested Mr. Woolsey at his residence, and the two Grant brothers at their place of business."

"Where's that?"

He hesitated for a moment. "It's no secret," he said. "It's an auto glass shop over on Spruce."

"Grant's Auto Glass," I said. "I've seen it."

"That's the place," he said. "We arrested all three men without incident, questioned them here at the station, charged each of them with felonious assault. They were arraigned later that day and released on bail. The trial date is pending."

"Go back to that questioning part."

He cleared his throat. "If you'd like me to summarize—"

"Just tell me," I said. "I want to know why they jumped me."

"Mr. Woolsey and the older of the two Grant brothers exercised their Fifth Amendment rights," he said, looking back down at the file. "Marty Grant, on the other hand, had a few things to say."

"Marty Grant," I said. "He was the big one, right?"

"He's a big boy, yes. His hand was in a cast."

"I seem to recall ducking and somebody hitting the brick wall."

"Yes, well, according to him, the events of that day were caused by an account given to him by his nephew, Christopher Woolsey. Apparently, there had been an altercation at the Ojibway Hotel three days before."

"That's the day Simon Grant died. What kind of altercation was he talking about?"

"It involves you, McKnight. He says you contacted Mr. Grant and asked him to meet you at the hotel."

"What?"

"Despite the fact that Mr. Grant is not supposed to be out alone, especially in bad weather, you told him to meet you at the hotel. Then you made him wait around there all day, and young Mr. Woolsey was unable to convince him to go back home."

"You are kidding me, right?"

"Finally, you had words with him in the dining room. After which time you must have told him to leave the hotel immediately."

"I must have told him? What does that mean?"

"Apparently, Mr. Woolsey was not present at that exact

moment. When he came looking for his grandfather, he was gone."

"Because I made him go out in the snow? An eighty-two-year-old man?"

"I'm just telling you the story as it was told to me, McKnight."

"You got all of this secondhand from Marty Grant. Did you talk to Chris Woolsey directly?"

"I tried to, yes. So far, he hasn't agreed to talk to us. He wasn't charged, after all. Only his father and his two uncles. But I'm sure he'll be subpoenaed for the trials."

I didn't have anything to say. I was completely dumbfounded.

"This kid is lying," Natalie said. "Did you talk to anyone else at the hotel about this supposed altercation?"

"As yet, nobody else at the hotel can corroborate the story."

"Yes," she said. "Big surprise."

"Chris is covering his ass," I said. "His grandfather comes to the hotel and instead of keeping an eye on him he's hitting on one of the maids or something. Then when the poor old guy wanders out and gets lost in the snow, Chris makes up this story so the rest of the family has someone else to blame for it."

"I'm not saying I believe the story, McKnight. Okay? I'm not saying that. But if this is what he told his family, then it helps explain the state of mind those men were in the day of the funeral. They honestly believed that you were to blame for their father's death. Not in a way that they could do anything about legally, but responsible just the same. Then later, when you were driving all over town trying to talk to them—"

"What does that have to do with it?" Natalie said.

"Ms. Reynaud," Maven said. "Did Alex tell you that he went looking for Chris Woolsey the day before the funeral? That he went to his apartment on campus and then to his mother's house?"

"He didn't know," Natalie said. "At the time, Alex had no idea Chris was related to Mr. Grant."

"Okay, fine," Maven said. "But to the Grants and the Woolseys, here's this man who they think drove old Simon Grant out into the snow. Now here he comes around bothering them, trying to . . . They don't know what. He's leaving private investigator cards around. Whatever he was harassing Simon Grant about, now he's after them."

"For God's sake," I said. "Can we please—"

"Then when this same man shows up at the funeral," he said to her, "to harass them even further . . ."

"You keep using that word," Natalie said. "Alex wasn't harassing anyone."

"It's *their* word," Maven said. "I keep trying to tell you that. This is what the Grants are saying right now."

"Listen," I said. All of a sudden I was getting another big headache. "This is not even why we're here, okay? We want to ask you something about Natalie's father."

That stopped him cold. "I don't understand."

"Natalie's father was murdered right here in this town," I said. "On New Year's Eve, 1973."

"How do you know that?"

I pulled out the old newspaper article and handed it to him.

"The Ojibway," he said when he was halfway through. He looked up at both of us and then finished the article. When he was done, he handed it back to me.

"The hat that Alex gave you to give to the Grants," Natalie said. "It wasn't Mr. Grant's at all. It was my father's."

"Are you thinking that maybe Mr. Grant—"

"Yes," she said. "I am."

He looked back down at the article. He slowly ran his fingers over the paper's surface, like he was reading the thing in Braille. "Good Lord," he said.

"Chief," I said, "were you on the force back then?"

"No, not yet. I was a county deputy that year. I remember how it was, though."

"Did you know the chief back then? The one who was arrested?"

"He was gone by the time I got here. The state guys took him out in 1964. It took a while for things to settle down, though, I'll tell you that much."

"How come I never heard about this stuff?"

He looked up at me. "You didn't grow up around here, McKnight. So of course you didn't hear about it."

"Here we go. I'm just a troll."

"What does that mean?" Natalie said.

"A troll, from under the bridge. The lower peninsula, get it?"

"It's not that," he said. "It's more like, if this kind of stuff happened out west, they'd make a big deal about it, you know? The lawless Soo-town, or the little city with the big sins, something stupid like that. They'd turn it into a tourist attraction. But people aren't like that around here. This is Michigan, so nobody makes a big deal about it."

"So do you know anybody who might have been on the force then? Could you maybe find out who the lead detective was?"

He thought about it. "It was probably old Mac Hender-son. I don't know if he's even alive now."

"But you could locate the case file, couldn't you?"

Maven rubbed his forehead. "Oh man, where would those be? Maybe downstairs, maybe in that other storage building. No, wait, we moved everything out of there."

"Chief Maven," Natalie said, "do you think you could have one of your men look for it? We'd really appreciate it."

"I can ask somebody to try, but I can't imagine what you're gonna do with it. The case has been dead for years. Even if you think Mr. Grant was involved somehow . . ."

"Chief, you're a cop, just like me," she said. She was playing her trump card, and I don't know how anyone could have resisted it. "No matter how long it's been, you've got to find out the truth. You know what I mean."

"Just promise me," he said. "Don't go stirring up the Grant family again. With all due respect, ma'am, you don't have a badge in this country. And McKnight, he's not exactly a master of diplomacy."

"I can't promise you I won't talk to them," she said, looking him in the eye. "Not if they know something about what happened."

He didn't say anything. He sat there and watched her as she stood up.

"Besides," she said, "I want that hat back."

Eleven

The sun was going down when we left the station, the snow coming harder, as if the daylight were abandoning us to the grip of winter.

"I'll tell you one thing," I said as we got back in the Jeep. "Any time I gotta talk to him in the future, I'm bringing you with me."

"He seemed all right to me," she said. "A little hardheaded, but you want that in a chief."

"That wasn't hardheaded for him, believe me. That was Maven the pussy cat."

"Men always have to turn things into a pissing contest," she said. "Did you ever try just talking to him? Taking him out for a beer?"

I didn't have an answer for that one. I tried to imagine Roy Maven and me, sitting together at a bar. It made my head hurt even more.

"So where is this place?" she said.

"Which place?"

"Grant's Auto Glass."

I looked at her. "Are you serious?"

"Tell me how to get there."

"It's easy. Take a left out of here, go down a few blocks to Spruce. Another left, then maybe a half mile."

"Let's do it." She pulled out of the lot and onto Court Street, then took the left onto Spruce. We went over the power canal. She kept the wipers on to push the snowflakes off her windshield. A few minutes later, she pulled to the side of the road. Grant's Auto Glass was thirty yards in front of us, the yellow sign glowing through the snow and the darkness.

"What are we doing?" I said. The lights were on in the shop, but I couldn't see any movement through the front windows.

"I just wanted to know where this place was," she said. She leaned forward on the steering wheel. "Not the busiest place in the world."

Just then, one of the two garage doors started to open. The rattle was so loud we could hear it inside the Jeep. When the door was chest high, a man ducked down under it and stepped out into the lot. He was a big man. He wore a down vest over flannel and denim. He had a bright white cast on his right hand.

"That's the younger brother," she said. "What was his name? Marty?"

"That's him."

The man looked up at the snow falling all around him, shook his head, and ducked back into the garage. The door kept opening.

"So let's go," I said. "Let's go talk to him."

"No way, Alex. We're not doing that tonight."

"Why not?"

"Well, first of all, there's no way I can do this if you're around."

"Excuse me?"

"Look at you," she said. "Look at your fists. You're ready to fight him, and you haven't even gotten out of the car yet."

"I'm not going to fight them, Natalie. How dumb do you think I am?"

"Admit it, Alex. You want to bust him up so bad right now. It's all you can think about."

I took a long breath, making myself wait a few seconds before I said anything. "What you said before, about men . . ."

"Yes, exactly."

"If I said the same kind of thing about women . . . You know, women in general do this or that . . ."

"I'd smack you, I know. This is not about that, Alex. If you and I go walking up there, those guys aren't going to talk to either one of us. They'll see you and they'll get their hackles up right away."

"If we just explain to them—"

"That you really didn't make their father walk out into the snow? Sure, that would work."

"Natalie—"

"I'll come back by myself," she said. "I'll try to approach them the right way, maybe flash the badge at them. See if I can get them talking."

"These are not nice people," I said. "I don't like the idea of you coming here alone."

"Tough shit, Alex. Now tell me how to get to the Woolseys' house. I assume it's back this way somewhere?"

She pulled a U-turn and went back the way we came, toward downtown. I stared at her.

"Which way, Alex?"

"Straight for a while. Then take a left on Ashmun."

A few minutes later, we were on the other side of town, parked in front of the Woolseys' house. The last time I had been here, I had plowed the driveway and asked to talk to Chris, and had gotten nothing but a blank look from Mrs. Woolsey. Of course, that was before I had learned she was Simon Grant's daughter.

"Okay, I got it," Natalie said. "I'll come talk to these people, too."

I knew better than to say anything.

"I'm getting hungry," she said. "How about you?"

I kept looking at the house.

"Come on," she said. "You pick the restaurant. Anyplace except you-know-where."

"You don't like the service there?"

"No, I don't like the fact that my father was killed there."

"I'm sorry," I said. I needed another pain pill. "I don't know what I'm saying."

"It's all right, Alex. I'm sorry, too. But you know I'm right about this."

"The Antlers has good hamburgers," I said. "Go back toward downtown."

"Now you're talking."

She swung the Jeep around. When we got to the Antlers, we grabbed a table. The waitress did her best not to stare at my beat-up face. Natalie sat across from me, marveling at all the stuffed animal heads on the walls.

"Charming place," she said.

"Unless you're any wild animal in North America, yeah."

We ordered cheeseburgers and beer. The more I thought about what she had said, the more sense it made to me. With me along, the Grant brothers wouldn't say a damned thing. Of course, I wasn't going to admit she was right.

"What's the matter?" she said.

"I'm fine."

"You're getting tired."

"No, I'm fine."

"You're still not well yet. You should be taking it easy."

"I'm okay, Natalie."

She looked at me again and shook her head.

"I'm sorry," I said. "I think you're right. I am tired."

"Do you have your phone with you?"

"Yeah." I reached into my coat pocket and gave her the phone.

"I should check my machine," she said. She held the phone in front of her, took a deep breath, and then dialed. I watched her as she entered her code and then listened to the messages. The waitress brought us our beers.

After a full two minutes, she turned the phone off and put it down on the table. "Should you be drinking beer, Alex? With the painkillers?"

"Did your mother call?"

She nodded.

"And?"

"She said she can't wait to see me again. And that she quit drinking."

"Did she say anything else?"

"No, just that she wants me to come over as soon as possible."

"Where does she live, anyway?"

"North of the Soo," she said. "Up in Batchawana Bay. I figure I'll have the advantage now. I'm assuming she's pretty drunk right about now, having left that message about quitting."

"Why do you have an advantage if she's drunk?"

"When she drinks, she loses her edge, Alex. Her lies are so ridiculous, you can see right through them. I remember once she actually told me that my father wasn't really my father at all. You want to know who my real father was?"

"Who?"

"Pierre Trudeau."

"The old prime minister?"

"That's the one."

I tried to stop myself from smiling.

"It's okay," she said. "You can laugh. What else can you do?"

"Natalie, I'm sorry you have to deal with this."

"I do want to ask you one favor," she said. "I know I've already put you off once tonight . . ."

"Twice, actually."

"I'm just thinking—"

"You don't want me to go with you when you see your mother?"

"There are reasons why I haven't seen her in five years, Alex. The lies are just one part of it. I had to stay away, for my own health and sanity. She's toxic to me. I don't want to inflict that on you, too. Besides, she was pretty young when she had me."

"So?"

"So if you do the math, she's not that much older than you are. She'd have something colorful to say about that, believe me."

"Natalie, there's nothing your mother can say that's gonna bother me. You've already told me not to believe a word she says anyway."

"It's going to be hard enough seeing her," she said. "I'm just asking you, let me do it alone this time. The next time, you come with me. I promise."

"All right," I said. "I understand."

She picked up her glass and clinked it against mine. I was about to lean over and kiss her, but then the bells went off. They've got these bells behind the bar that are loud enough to give you a heart attack, and they set them off a couple of times every night, with no warning. I had forgotten all about the damned things. The only good news was that I had already drained most of my beer, so Natalie didn't end up wearing too much of it. She laughed. It was the only real laugh I had heard in the short time I had known her. The way things were headed, I had to wonder when I'd ever hear it again.

After dinner, she drove me back to Paradise. We didn't talk much on the way. As we passed Jackie's place, I looked at the warm light in the windows and wished we were headed there for the rest of the evening, to sit by the fire with hot drinks before going to my cabin. Instead, she was going to leave me here alone, then drive all the way back to Canada.

When she pulled onto my access road, I saw that it had been plowed. Good old Vinnie. My truck was outside my cabin, no snow on the windshield. We must have just missed him. He was probably at the Glasgow, wondering how long I'd be away.

"You're gonna be careful," I said. I didn't want to get out of the Jeep.

"I'm always careful," she said.

"Will you call me tonight and let me know how it went?"

"I will."

"No matter how late."

"I promise."

I looked at her. In the dim green light from the dashboard her face was so beautiful yet so full of trouble, it turned me inside out.

"You're the best thing that's happened to me in a long, long time," she said. She kissed me, then gave me a little push, gentle but firm. I opened the door and got out. I watched her drive away. I watched the snow swallow her until I was standing there alone.

I went inside. I took my coat off and looked in the bathroom mirror, freshly shocked by how much damage a man could take and still be standing. The left side of my mouth was still swollen, the bruises making a raccoon's mask around my eyes, the tape still covering the stitches. How a woman like Natalie could even look at this face and say those words. The best thing that's happened to her in a long, long time.

I took my pills. I was more worn out than I cared to admit. I had nothing left. When I went to lie down, it felt like the bed had become a conveyor belt, the Vicodin taking me smoothly away into a land of brightly colored narcotic dreams.

I saw the picture in my mind. It was coming to life. Three men, the dust hanging in the air on a hot afternoon. The older man smiling. The other man, the best friend, watching from the opposite side of the frame. The man in the middle, Natalie's father, in his prime, on a perfect summer day, moving right out of the frame, vamping for the camera, the hat held up with both hands now. Showing off the hat, like he was performing some vaudevillian song and dance.

The whole picture fell apart, then came back together with snow on the ground now. It is New Year's Eve. The men are standing in the snow with no coats. But the hat is perfect, the perfect thing to wear on New Year's Eve. The older man standing behind him is saying something. Somehow I know it is important, but I can't hear what the man is saying.

The other man is gone. It's just the old man and the young man now, father and son, grandfather and father. I need to hear what is being said. But it is drowned out by the sound of a car starting. The car from the picture, a detail I had forgotten about. It is started now. Someone is gunning the engine.

I woke up. I sat up in my bed. Outside, an engine had come to life. It was my truck. Someone was stealing my truck.

No, it was Vinnie. I rubbed my eyes, looked out the window at the snow. Vinnie had come back to plow again. He didn't even know I was home. How could he?

I looked at the clock. That crazy bastard, plowing at

three in the morning. Had I slept that long? It felt like I had just lain down. I heard Vinnie pulling out of my driveway, heard the scrape of the plow against the road.

Then it hit me. Natalie hadn't called.

I got out of bed and picked up the phone. Then I put it down again. She's asleep, I told myself. She didn't call because she got in late and she didn't want to wake you.

The hell with it. I picked it up again and dialed. Outside, the snow kept piling up. It brushed against my windows. The phone rang and rang. Her machine finally answered.

I left a message, told her to call me when she could.

I tried to go back to sleep, but now it was useless. I kept waiting. I listened to the night and the soft snow falling and Vinnie running my truck up and down the road.

I called her again in the morning. I left another message, told her I was wondering how things went with her mother. "Give me a call when you get back in," I said. "I'm worried about you."

I figured I could take my painkillers and lie around and drive myself crazy, or I could get up and get dressed and actually accomplish something. Anyway, there was nothing to worry about. She had stayed over at her mother's house in Batchawana Bay. The snow was getting bad up there. She had done the smart thing and stayed over.

Never mind what she had said about her mother, how unlikely it seemed that she'd spend more time with the woman than she had to. I didn't know how things really were between them. Hell, maybe they had stayed up all night, talking things over. Maybe they had made up.

Maybe.

I took a hot shower, got dressed, drank some coffee. Standing up, moving around, I noticed that I wasn't quite as dizzy now. I felt like I was getting some of my strength back. One look in the mirror, though—okay, so I still looked like hell.

I poked my head outside. The sun was out, but it was a cold and bitter day, below zero, with an Arctic wind whipping down across the lake for good measure. It was the kind of day that showed no mercy, that physically hurt you every single second.

It looked like it had snowed another eight or nine inches during the night before. Vinnie had everything cleaned up beautifully. I should let him plow more often, I thought. He had left the keys on the front seat of the truck, so I got in and fired it up. I drove down to the Glasgow Inn, pulled into the lot, and went inside. A blast of cold air followed me through the door, making everyone look up at me like I was the devil himself.

"Shut the damned door," Jackie said. "You're gonna kill somebody."

"Good morning yourself," I said. "You got any eggs going?"

"Do I have eggs going? Don't you mean, will I stop everything and fix you an omelet right now?"

"Take it easy, Jackie. Are you all right?"

He threw his towel on the bar. "It's minus five degrees," he said. "With a windchill of minus fifty. How could I not be all right?"

"Jackie—"

"You know what I'm gonna do later? I'm gonna get

my beach chair and go sit by the water. It's too nice a day to be inside."

I stood there and watched him for a while. He fussed around the bar and slammed some glasses into a sink full of water. Finally, he asked me what I wanted in my omelet.

"The usual," I said.

"Come back in the kitchen," he said. "I want to ask you something."

I went around the bar and followed him into the kitchen. It was a small galley kitchen, barely enough for two people to stand in, so I stayed in the doorway.

"Are you going to tell me what's going on?" he said. He started chopping up an onion.

"What do you mean?"

"Every once in a while, I gotta make a point of dragging it out of you. I mean, look at your face. You look like the east end of a westbound horse."

"I thought I told you what happened. There was a disagreement at a funeral."

"Alex, come on. We both know what's going on here. Now, I know I've never met this woman. What's her name? Natalie?"

"I'm sorry," I said. "We just haven't had the chance to come by yet." I thought about the night before, driving past the Glasgow, and me wishing we were stopping there to spend the evening by the fire. "She's only been here in town twice, and—"

He put his hand up to stop me. "Never mind that, Alex. I don't care. I'm just saying, you've got this habit of taking on other people's problems. For a friend especially, you'd do anything. I've seen it."

He stopped and put his knife down.

"Hell, Alex, you did it for me."

"I think you're exaggerating."

"I'm not," he said. "I'm not even going to argue about it. I know the way you are. You know it, too."

"So what am I supposed to say, Jackie?"

"Just tell me what's really going on with this woman," he said. "This Natalie, what's her story?"

"You really want to know?"

"Start talking."

I leaned back against the door frame, thinking about it for a second. Then I began. I described my first trip to her house, the awkward beginning of it all, and then the ups and downs over the next few visits. Then the night in the hotel room, the old man, the hat on the floor. All the while he kept working on my omelet, chopping up the mushrooms and the ham, grating the cheddar cheese. He put everything in a shallow skillet and cooked it, somehow making it turn into an omelet instead of a half-burned mess of eggs and whatever else, which was what always happened when I tried to do it myself at home.

I told him about the picture we had found in her basement, the visit to Mrs. DeMarco's house, then finally everything I knew about her mother.

"That sounds familiar," he said. "Are you sure that's not my ex-wife you're talking about?"

"Not unless you're Natalie's real father. Instead of Pierre Trudeau."

"Seriously, Alex. Everything you're saying about Natalie . . . It just gives me a really bad feeling."

Wc went back out to the bar. I sat on one of the stools

and had my omelet while he stood on the other side. He wasn't moving until I heard everything he had to say.

"I've never even seen the woman," he said. "But I can tell, just from what you're saying. She's what, in her late thirties now? Never been married, you say? Hasn't even been in a relationship in a long time?"

"Neither have I, Jackie."

"All this stuff about her mother? How many people do you know who haven't spoken to their mother in five years?"

I shook my head.

"She's got some problems, Alex. Some big problems, going back a long, long way. Sounds like her whole life has been cockeyed. What's that old saying? Never sleep with someone who has more problems than you do?"

"So you're saying what, I shouldn't be with her? Is that what you're saying?"

"No, Alex. Not that you'd listen to me, even if I *was* saying that."

"Then what is it, Jackie? What do you want me to do?"

"I just want you to think about what you're doing," he said. He leaned in closer to me. "Like I was saying, I know what you'll do for a friend. Okay? I know what you'll put yourself through, just to help somebody out. I wouldn't change that about you, Alex. It's one of the things I admire about you."

"Jackie, you're making me blush. You just can't tell with all the bruises."

"Knock it off. I'm being serious here. If you'll go that far to help out a friend . . ." He held his hands out in front of him, about two feet apart, like a man telling a fish story. "Then how much farther will you go for a woman you really care about?"

"Jackie—"

"I'm scared to death for you, Alex. I really am."

He left me sitting there, with those words hanging in the air. After everything I had been through, in all the time he had known me, Jackie Connery had never said something like that to me before.

I finished eating. Then I took out my cell phone and called Natalie. The machine picked up again. Nobody home.

I was starting to get a little scared myself.

Twelve

The cold air hit me again as soon as I stepped outside. I hurried to the truck, slammed the door shut, and got the heater going.

"Okay, now what?" I said out loud. I didn't want to start panicking. It wasn't time to drive over to her house yet. If she wasn't home, that wouldn't do any good anyway. I knew her mother lived in Batchawana Bay . . . But no, how bad would that look? Me showing up on her mother's doorstep, asking to see Natalie, like I was her date for the prom. Apologizing for tracking her down, telling her I was worried about her.

You're driving yourself crazy, I thought. You're imagining the worst, based on nothing.

I didn't want to go back and sit around in my cabin, so I pulled out of the lot and headed toward Sault Ste. Marie. On the way, I called Leon at work. The man who picked up didn't sound too thrilled to be acting as his secretary. When he came on, I asked him who had answered the phone.

"Oh, that's just Harlow."

"Is he your boss?"

"Yeah, sort of."

"He didn't sound real happy, Leon. I don't want to mess up your job."

"Ah, who cares, Alex. It's not what I want to be doing, anyway."

There was an uneasy silence then. We both knew what his dream job would have been.

"How 'bout I buy you lunch again?" I said.

"You on your way in? Sure."

"I'll stop by," I said. With the omelet still in my stomach, I wasn't even slightly hungry, but I needed to see Leon. I needed to be around somebody who believed in good information as the solution to every problem. A half hour later, I picked him up at the motor shop and took him across town. I parked outside the Ojibway Hotel.

"You really want to eat here?"

"It's still the nicest place in town," I said. "Maybe eating here will make me think of something."

"Whatever you say, Alex. Are we gonna have a séance, too?"

"If you weren't doing me so many favors, I'd bust you one," I said. We got out of the truck and suffered the cold air for twenty seconds, then we were inside. My young friend the doorman was nowhere in sight.

There was a new woman at the front desk. And of course there was no old man sitting in the lobby, tipping his hat to me. Everything felt different about the place, like nothing bad had ever happened there. We sat down in the dining room. In the daylight, the view out the big windows was blinding white in all directions. We sat one table from where Natalie and I had been that night. How many days ago had that been?

"You say there was a bar here," I said. "Right here where this dining room is now?"

"A long time ago," Leon said. "Maybe twenty, twenty-five years."

"It's hard to imagine."

"Things were different back then. If you can picture all those men stationed up here at the air bases. Thousands of them. One minute you're in Texas or California—next thing you know, you're in Sault Ste. Marie, Michigan. It's twenty below zero and there's snow up to your ass. If it's December, it's dark eighteen hours a day. I tell ya, Alex. This place . . ."

He looked out the window, like he was conjuring the whole scene in his mind.

"I was just a kid, remember, but even so, I'd hear people talking about it. Places that would be open all night long. Women who'd come up here just to keep the men company. That's what my father called it. Keeping the men company."

"And you're telling me they actually arrested the chief of police back then?"

"The state troopers did. Walked right into his office and put the cuffs on him. Turns out he was being well compensated to ignore certain things."

"Could Simon Grant have been involved in this?"

"Since I last saw you guys, I asked my man at the *Evening News* to run Simon Grant's name. There were a lot of hits, because Grant was involved in the dockworkers' union."

"That's a rough line of work."

"Naturally. There was nothing about him ever being in big trouble, though. Or even getting arrested."

"Anything more on Jean Reynaud?"

"Nothing," Leon said. "But then, the man didn't live here."

"You know, his best friend back then was a man named Albert DeMarco. He was married to Natalie's mother for a while, too."

"Albert DeMarco." He took out his pad of paper and wrote down the name.

"I didn't bring him up when we saw you before," I said. "He's not a good person to talk about when Natalie's around."

"Some bad history?"

"He wasn't her stepfather for very long, but it was . . ." I wasn't sure what to say about it.

"If you're going where I think you're going, you don't have to say it."

"I gotta tell you something, Leon. Every time I think about it, I want to kill this guy. I want to dig him up out of his grave and kill him all over again."

"I hear you, believe me. But listen, my guy knows someone across the river, works at the *Sault Star*. I'll see if he can find anything."

"Thanks, Leon. I appreciate it."

"It's my pleasure," he said. "How's Natalie doing, anyway?"

That was the question of the day, so I had to give him the quick rundown, just as I had done for Jackie. I didn't get the same sermon from him, but I could tell he was just as concerned about me.

"Everything will be okay," I told him. "As soon as she gets back home, I'm sure she'll tell me all about it."

We had our lunch and then I took him back to work. I tried her number again. There was still no answer. I checked my answering machine. Nothing.

There was only one place to go next. I drove up to the City County Building, with a new appreciation for Chief Roy Maven. Say what you want about the man—the state police have never broken down his door to put handcuffs on him.

The receptionist was sitting in the middle of the lobby, with doors on either side of her that kept opening again and again. The poor woman was trapped in a wind tunnel. She had her coat on, and those gloves with no fingers so she could work the phones. I asked her if Chief Maven was around. She told me to have a seat.

"Please tell him that Alex McKnight *and* Natalie Reynaud are here to see him," I said.

She looked on both sides of me, like she was wondering if I had brought an imaginary friend with me.

"Trust me," I said. "Just tell him that."

Nine seconds later, Chief Maven appeared in the lobby.

"Where's Ms. Reynaud?" he said, looking around.

"She had to run out for a minute," I said. "We can start without her."

He gave me a look like he knew he'd been had. "Yeah, let's not wait," he said. "Come on back."

He led me to his office.

"Where's the comfortable chair you brought in for Natalie?" I said. "You should go get it. She could be here any minute."

"Cut the crap, McKnight. Just sit down and tell me what you want."

I sat in the cheap plastic Alex McKnight memorial guest chair. "I'm just wondering," I said, "if you had a chance to find the old police report on the murder."

"Because I've got nothing better to do."

"No, because we asked you, and because it's important."

He rolled his eyes, then opened one of his desk drawers. "I was going to call you today," he said. "I've got it right here."

He pulled out a faded blue file folder and put it on his desk.

"I gotta tell you, though. There's not much to it."

He started showing me all of the materials, beginning with the crime scene photos. The colors were a little washed out after almost thirty-plus years of storage, but there hadn't been much to see in the first place—just a man lying facedown on the ground, a great dark stain on the back of his head and down the back of his overcoat. In one shot I could see a couple of inches of snow under the body, and in another a larger mound of snow running along the side of him. It looked like he had been shot on a shoveled sidewalk. At that moment I was glad Natalie wasn't here with me to see it.

"The autopsy's here," Maven said. "No surprises. Gunshot to the back of the head, time of death around midnight, probably a little after."

"Witnesses?"

He shook his head. "No, it's all here in this report. Henderson interviewed everyone working at the hotel that night, and as many of the partygoers as he could track down. It's midnight on New Year's Eve, so everybody's drinking and making a lot of noise. If you think about it, it's the perfect time to kill somebody."

"So what else is in here?"

"Just some more interviews. He went over to Canada to speak to Mr. Reynaud's family."

"Really? Can I see those?"

"They're a little sketchy," he said, sliding several sheets of paper over to me. "Henderson wasn't exactly Tolstoy when it came to his interview reports. I did find out, though, that he's living in Tampa now. I even have a phone number if you want to talk to him."

"Are you kidding me?" I took the piece of notepad paper from him. It had Mac Henderson's name and a phone number with a 727 area code.

"Tell him hello from me," Maven said. "It's been a long time."

"I don't get this," I said. "Why are you being so cooperative?"

"What do you mean?"

"All this stuff. The old file. The original detective's phone number."

"Why wouldn't I try to help out?" he said. "I'm here to serve the public."

"If it was just me and not Natalie, I wonder . . ."

"I'm offended, McKnight."

"What about Simon Grant? As long as you're being such a mensch, can we find out anything about him?"

Maven ran his hand through his hair. "You've got to remember, McKnight, Simon Grant was an old union man, going back a long way. He was president of the dockworkers' union for seven years, in fact. This was back in the sixties and seventies."

"When Sault Ste. Marie was Sin Central."

"I wouldn't go around saying that," Maven said. "Like I told you before, people around here like to keep that stuff in the past."

"Okay, fine. Just tell me what kind of trouble he got into."

"He really didn't. At least not on the record. He was a material witness to a number of cases back then—menacing, assault, a couple of smuggling cases. The line of work he was in, you almost have to run into that sort of thing."

"Is that all you can tell me?"

Maven put his hands up. "It's a long time ago," he said. "The man is dead. There's not much more you're gonna find out now."

"We'll see about that."

"McKnight, you're keeping your promise to me, right? You're staying away from the Grant brothers?"

"So far, yes."

"McKnight, I swear to God . . ."

"Thank you, Chief," I said as I stood up. I looked him in the eye. "I mean that. Thank you."

"Stay away from them," he said, standing up himself. "Do you hear me?"

"I hear you," I said. "Loud and clear."

I kept hearing him, all the way down the hall, until I walked out the lobby door into the cold air.

When I had the heater going enough to use my hands, I dialed Mac Henderson's number on my cell phone. It rang a few times, then a woman answered. I asked for Mac. She asked me to hold for a moment. A few seconds passed. Then I heard a male voice on the line. It was a deep voice. It didn't sound like that of an old man. I introduced myself, told him that Roy Maven had given me his number.

"Roy Maven!" the man said. "How is that old bird doing? I haven't heard from him in ten years."

"He's just fine," I said. "As mellow as ever."

That got the man laughing. "Roy was a real live wire back in the day," he said. "I don't imagine that's changed much."

"I'm sorry to bother you, sir, but I was wondering if you'd be willing to discuss an old case."

"I've been off the job for almost twenty years now, but go ahead."

"The man's name was Jean Reynaud—"

"Murdered outside the Ojibway Hotel. Shot in the back of the head."

"Okay, I guess you remember."

"I'll tell you why, Mr. McKnight. In twenty-seven years on the police force, I might have seen, I don't know, maybe seven or eight murders? Were you living up there back in the seventies?"

"No," I said, "but I know things were a lot different then."

"Yeah, different is one word for it. But I tell you, even with all that other stuff going on, we never had many murders in town. That's not counting the lake, of course. Old Superior, she'd kill a half-dozen men every year. I'm sure she still does."

"Yes, sir."

"Anyway, what did I say, seven murders? Maybe eight? Every single one of them I solved except one."

"Jean Reynaud."

"Exactly. I got absolutely nowhere with that one. No weapon recovered. No witnesses. The victim has no apparent ties to anyone in the area at all. I mean, absolutely nothing. Really no physical evidence at all, aside from a .45 caliber slug that went right through the back of the poor man's head and out through his face. Aside from that, we didn't have a thing to go on."

"I was a police officer myself for eight years," I said. "Down in Detroit. So I think I know what you mean. There's no such thing as a totally random crime."

"Exactly," he said. "Just what you say. Yet this was as close to random as I ever saw, before or since."

"I saw the old report today. Apparently, you interviewed members of Mr. Reynaud's family?"

"Yes, that's right. Let me see . . . He was a Canadian, right? I had to cross over and go to this little town on the North Channel . . ."

"Blind River."

"Yes, that's right. God, it's all coming back to me now. Isn't it funny how that works? I haven't thought about it for so long . . . I remember, the family had already been notified, of course. This was a couple of days afterward. I went out to this big farmhouse. Mr. Reynaud's parents lived there, and I think he and his wife were living there, too. And their little girl. I remember this little girl running around. She must have been around six or seven years old. An absolute little doll. But it was really kind of heartbreaking, because this girl obviously didn't know what was going on. She kept asking her mother where her daddy was."

"Her name's Natalie," I said. "She's a cop herself now."

"Is that right? I'll be damned."

"So what happened when you talked to the family?"

"I remember talking to the man's father first, I think. He was pretty stoic about the whole thing. He was a real hunk of granite, you know what I mean? One of those old guys who've worked real hard all their lives. They've seen it all, sickness and death. Hard times. He was just trying to keep everyone else from falling apart, it seemed like. He didn't have much to say to me. In fact, I don't think he was real happy to have me there, asking them all these questions. He just wanted everybody to leave them alone."

"I never met the man," I said. "But from what I've heard about him, that sounds like him."

"The mother, she was real upset. Naturally. I mean, this was their only child. The strange thing was she told me that her son had never been to Soo Michigan in his whole life. Which was hard to believe, since they only lived what, a couple of hours away. But no, she said. She never wanted him to go down there, because it was such a terrible place. And I can't argue with them, of course. What am I gonna say? Here I am sitting there in their house, wearing a Soo Michigan uniform, and the only reason I'm there is because their son got murdered as soon as he set foot in the place for the first time in his whole life. It was pretty uncomfortable, to say the least."

"I imagine."

"So next, I talk to the wife. She was pretty young-looking, I remember that. A real attractive woman, too, but I don't know . . ."

"What?"

"I didn't say anything in the report, because, well, I wasn't sure how I'd even say it. She just seemed to be a little . . . off center about things."

"How do you mean?"

"It was hard to put my finger on. I mean, you were a cop. You know how it is when you talk to somebody and everything they're saying adds up, but just the way they're saying it, you sorta get the feeling that everything isn't being said. You know what I'm talking about?"

"I think so," I said. "Are you saying you suspected she was involved in the murder?"

"No, I wouldn't go that far. It's just that . . . God, what was it? All the time I was talking to her, she was telling me that her husband had gone down there to Soo Michigan to go to this bar at the Ojibway Hotel, and had never come back home, and that they had gotten a phone call the next morning . . . And I remember thinking, how come she wasn't mad at him? I mean, on the night itself, when he left her with their kid so he could go all the way down there to celebrate New Year's Eve? She told me everything else about that night, right down to the tiniest detail. I mean, this woman could *talk*. But not once did she tell me how she felt that night. Then even on that day, here I was talking to her about her dead husband, and she's telling me all these other things about how she's gonna have to live with her in-laws, and what's she gonna do with her daughter. Again, not one word about how she was coping with it herself, or how she felt about losing her husband. She would talk about *anything*, but as soon as she got close to her own self, she would stop short. I think that's what gave me a strange feeling about her."

I thought hard about what he was saying. I'd known enough liars in my life. You can't be a cop without meeting plenty of them. For the worst of them, the truly hopeless born liars, maybe this is how it all starts, by keeping a tight lid on your own secrets. By never revealing the truth about yourself. When you've learned to control the truth, then you can start bending it. Just a little at first, then a little more when you see what it can do for you. A lie can open doors for you. Or close them.

A lie can keep you safe.

"Now the best friend, on the other hand," Henderson went on, "he had no problem telling me how he felt about it."

"You talked to Albert DeMarco?"

"Yeah, that was his name. He lived just down the road. As I recall, the two of them were both going to go down to the Ojibway Hotel that night. The way he described it, it almost sounded like a rite of passage for these guys. Everybody in Ontario knew what a wild place Soo Michigan was back then, and especially when your families are telling you never, ever to step foot there. Well, you can imagine what a couple of young men are going to think of that."

"But Jean Reynaud was married."

"Yeah, I know. Either he just needed a guys' night out, away from the family, or maybe stepping out was more of a habit for him. I never really got a line on that one. The one thing that was pretty clear was that Mr. DeMarco blamed himself for his friend's death. He had some reason . . . What was it? He got real sick that day, or something. So Reynaud went by himself. Which struck me as odd, too, now that I remember it. I had all sorts of little alarm bells going off in my head that day."

"Did you press them on it?"

"I tried to. But like I said, I was already in a tough spot, being the ambassador from Sodom and Gomorrah, trying to find out how their man had gotten killed. I needed special permission from the Canucks just to be there in the first place. So no, Mr. McKnight, I never did get anywhere with that case. I still think about it, to this day. Can you tell?"

"I think I'd be the same way."

"You said the little girl became a cop. What happened to the rest of them? The man's parents are gone by now, I'm sure."

"Yes, they are," I said. "So is Mr. DeMarco. I guess he died a couple of years ago. His mother's still kicking around, though. I think she's ninety-six years old now."

"DeMarco's mother? Oh yeah, I remember meeting her. I don't think we talked much, though. She's ninety-six, eh? That's pretty impressive."

"Yes, it is."

"Tell me, Mr. McKnight . . . The fact that you're asking me about this now. Does this mean you might have some new information?"

"I don't know," I said. "Let me throw a name at you. Simon Grant. Does it ring any bells?"

"Simon Grant . . . Simon Grant . . ." There was a long pause while he thought about it. "No, it doesn't. Are you telling me he might have killed Reynaud?"

"I honestly don't know that, sir. But it looks like he may have been involved."

"What does he have to say for himself?"

"I'm afraid he's dead now. He froze to death a few days ago."

"My, it sounds like things are getting interesting up there."

"I promise you, sir, I'll let you know whatever we find out."

"I'd appreciate it," he said. "It's good to close the book on things, even if it's thirty-odd years too late."

"I understand."

"You're gonna say hello to Roy for me, right? The two of you are good friends?"

"I'm not sure you could go that far."

"Well, send my best anyway. What's the weather like, anyway?"

"Cold and snow," I said. "What else is it gonna be?"

"It's eighty degrees here right now," he said. "I was out working on the boat. But I'll tell you, Mr. McKnight, even though it may be paradise down here, I still miss the old Soo-town. There's just something about the place, you know what I mean?"

"I do, sir. Although eighty degrees does sound pretty good right now."

I thanked the man, and promised to keep in touch. I even promised him one more time that I'd give his regards to Chief Maven. But I wasn't about to go do that right then. I called Natalie. The machine picked up. I left another message, told her I had talked to the detective who had handled the case in 1973. I told her I was worried about her and that she should call me as soon as she got home.

You're starting to sound like a nag, I thought. Let the woman be, for God's sake. Maybe she just had a miserable time with her mother, and she wants to be alone for a while.

From there, I went right back to imagining the worst. She had promised me she would call, no matter what. She's not the kind of person who breaks a promise.

What the hell was I supposed to do? I didn't feel like driving back to Paradise. I didn't want to sit around in my cabin. I didn't want to hang out at Jackie's and get another lecture.

I could go visit the Grants, I thought. Or the Woolseys.

No, Alex. You're not the kind of person who breaks a promise, either.

I sat in the car for a while, watching the snow start to fall again. A county car rolled in next to me. The deputy got out of the car and hustled inside to get out of the cold air.

I picked up the phone again and dialed information. "Grace Reynaud," I said, "in Batchawana Bay, Ontario." I had no idea what last name she would be using now. She'd been Grace DeMarco at one time, Grace Reynaud before that. Hell, for all I knew, she was back to her maiden name now, whatever that was. But Reynaud seemed like a good place to start.

The operator found the name, but told me that the number was unpublished. I thanked her and hung up.

I watched the snow some more. I picked up the phone one last time. I dialed Natalie's number and listened to it ring. The answering machine picked up, Natalie's recorded voice asking me to leave a message. I turned the phone off.

Now what, Alex?

I put the truck in gear and pulled out of the lot.

When all else fails, it's time to do something stupid.

Thirteen

Batchawana Bay was a small town, probably the kind of place where everybody knew everybody else. It wasn't that far away. In fact, it was closer than Blind River. After I cleared the bridge, all I had to do was head due north on the King's Highway instead of east. The snow was piled high to either side, but the road itself was clear. I figured I could get there within half an hour, easy.

I passed through Soo Canada, then hit the open road leading north through Heyden and Goulais River. There was nothing to see but white fields and trees bending under great weights of snow, until I finally began to see the frozen expanse of Lake Superior to the west. It was Whitefish Bay, my end of the lake, but seen from the wrong side. I had come all the way around the bay because I was worried about Natalie, because she was heading into a tough situation and most of one day had passed and I still hadn't heard from her. That was all it took.

I would have driven a lot farther. I knew that. I would have done just about anything for her on this cold winter's day, even with the bruises still fresh on my face, with my ribs still hurting and my knee still stiff. Jackie was absolutely right about me. But I couldn't change that. That was the way I was, for better or worse.

As the town of Batchawana Bay got closer, I started to wonder why Natalie's mother was living there. I had been up here before, and it had struck me as one of the loneliest places I had ever seen, the Canadian equivalent of Paradise, Michigan. Of course, maybe that's why she liked it. I'd been down that road myself.

I figured the simplest thing to do would be to stop in at the most likely bar, ask if Grace was around. If it was her regular place, somebody would know her. Hell, *everybody* would know her. If it wasn't, I'd just go on to the next place.

I stopped at a gas station near the public docks. As I stood pumping the gas, I breathed in the cold air and looked out at the bay. The ice stretched as far as I could see. Next to the station was a restaurant, with a long row of windows running along one side. In the summer, it would be a nice place to sit and watch the boats on the water. Today it looked like a nice place to stay warm and get quietly hammered.

I paid the man for the gas and moved the truck to the restaurant lot. When I opened the door, three men looked up from the bar.

"Afternoon, gentlemen," I said. "How's it going?"

"Not too bad," the first man said. He had two empty shot glasses lined up in front of him. A cigarette burned in the ashtray. "Don's in the bathroom, so you'll have to wait a minute."

"Does Don run this place?"

"No, he just cleans the bathrooms as a hobby."

The other two men at the bar laughed. I closed my eyes and counted to three.

"Okay," I said, "so do any of you guys know a woman named Grace?"

"Yeah, we know her," the first man said. "Who's asking?"

"I'm trying to find her," I said. "It's important."

"That didn't answer my question, eh? And what happened to your face?"

The other two men laughed again. This was turning into some real entertainment on a gray afternoon. The first man picked up his cigarette and took a long drag.

"I'm a friend of her daughter's," I said. "Do you know where she lives or not?"

"Her daughter's not alive anymore," the man said.

"What are you talking about?"

"She died a few years ago."

I stepped up to the man. He had the red eyes and nose of a hard drinker and he hadn't shaved in a week. Hell, even with all my bruises, this man still looked worse than I did.

"Let me guess," I said. "Did Grace tell you that?"

"Yes."

"How did she die?"

"Food poisoning. Not that it's any of your business, friend. Who are you, anyway?"

I closed my eyes again, counted to five this time. "Look, I just need to know where she lives. Can you tell me that, please?"

"As far as I know," the man said, "Grace lives right here in this bar. It's the only place I've ever seen her." He nodded his head toward an empty stool at the far end of the bar.

"What's going on?" another man said, stepping out of the bathroom. "Did somebody find Grace?"

"I'm looking for her," I said. "Are you Don?"

"Yeah, who's asking?"

"I'm a friend of Grace's daughter," I said. "Please, don't start with the food poisoning . . ."

"Come over here," he said. He led me away from the men at the bar, toward one of the big windows. "These guys aren't gonna be any help."

"So you know Grace pretty well?"

"As well as anybody," he said. He looked down for a moment, and rubbed the back of his neck. It made me think that maybe he did more for Grace than pour her drinks. "Now, tell me why you're looking for her, because I've been kind of worried myself."

"She hasn't been around today?"

"No, she hasn't."

"I take it that's pretty unusual."

"Yeah, you could say that. This is the first day I can remember that she hasn't been in here."

"Do you know where she lives?"

"Up the road a bit," he said. "Within walking distance. Which is actually . . . well, let's just say it's a good thing on most nights. But anyway, I've called her a couple of times today."

"Did you go over there?"

"Yeah, I did. At lunchtime. Nobody was there."

"Her daughter was coming up to see her," I said. "Last night."

"You mean Natalie?"

"Yes."

"I've never met her," he said. "I guess she wouldn't bring her around here, eh? That would sorta ruin the story about the bad clams."

I was about to smile for the first time that day when I happened to look over the man's shoulder. Outside the window, at the gas station, a man was finishing up at the same pump I had just used myself. He was using his left hand. His right hand was in a cast.

It was Marty Grant.

"What the hell . . ." I said.

The bartender looked out the window. "What is it?"

"Over there, at the gas station."

"You know that guy?"

I didn't have time to answer him. I was already on my way out the door. When I got around to the gas station, Marty Grant had already pulled out. He was heading south. I ran back to my truck and fired it up, skidding my way out of the icy parking lot and onto the road.

You son of a bitch, I thought. What the hell are you doing up here? There's no way it could be a coincidence. No way you're up here doing a windshield job. There were probably a dozen auto glass shops in Soo Canada. Nobody would hire a man from Michigan to drive all the way up here.

I accelerated until I could finally see his truck ahead of me. I'm gonna run you off the road, Marty Grant. I'm gonna run you into the snow and then drag you out of that truck . . .

Wait a minute, Alex. Take a breath. Maybe I should go back, get Don the bartender, go find Grace's house.

No. You heard the man. She's not there.

God damn it, Grant, if you've done something to her. Or to Natalie. I swear to God . . .

I could feel my grip getting tighter on the steering wheel.

Okay, Alex. Take it easy. Just follow the man. Don't do anything stupid. At least not yet. Just settle in and follow him.

But I couldn't stop thinking about it. This is one of the men who beat me half to death. This is the man who swung at me the hardest, so hard that when he missed he'd broken his hand on the bricks.

He's the worst of them. He's the biggest. He's the strongest. God damn it to hell.

I kept following him. It wasn't even an hour on the road, but it felt like an eternity. I stayed a quarter mile behind him, all the way back down the King's Highway to Soo Canada. The sun was going down as he finally reached the bridge with me behind him. I didn't think he had spotted me, even as I pulled in right behind him at the toll booth. He pulled out of the booth and onto the bridge. Another car got between us. When he hit customs, he took one lane and I took another.

I could see that Marty got a quick once-over and was already pulling out onto the road. Meanwhile, I had to wait while the car ahead of me got the full treatment. I was expecting the agent to come out and start ripping the door panels off the guy's car, when finally he was given the all clear.

I pulled up, trying to calm myself down before I spoke to the agent. Looking like a homicidal maniac wouldn't do me much good right now, even though that's about how I felt. The agent asked me the usual questions. I gave him the right answers and was on my way, but by the time I hit I-75, Marty Grant was long gone. No matter, I thought. I knew exactly where to go.

I took the exit and headed downtown, past the Ojibway Hotel, and onto Spruce Street. It was dark now. I pulled into the driveway, right in front of the garage door. I didn't see Marty's truck there, but so what. I parked and got out. After everything that had happened, it was finally time for my own little showdown with the Grant family.

When I opened the door, I saw Michael Grant, the other brother, working on a car. I didn't see Marty anywhere. Michael looked up from his job—it looked like he was doing a full cutout, scraping all the old adhesive out of a windshield bed before putting in the new glass—just in time to see me come through the doorway.

"McKnight?" he said. "What the hell is going on?"

"Where is he?"

"What are you talking about?"

"Tell me where he is."

"Where who is?"

"Your brother Marty," I said. "I saw him in Batchawana Bay."

"What?"

"He was up there. I just followed him back."

"What was he doing up there?"

"That's what I wanna know."

"Look, McKnight . . ." He stepped away from the car and approached me. He still had the scraper in his right hand. "You shouldn't be here."

"Tell me where to find your brother and I'll leave."

He shook his head slowly. "Ain't gonna happen," he

said. "You need to turn around and get out of here right now."

"What happens if I don't?"

He looked at me for a long moment. His eyes were steady until he was about to make his move—the oldest "tell" in the book, the eyes getting wider just before your man pulls the trigger. Apparently, it works for glue scrapers, too. I ducked as he swung it at me and put my elbow into his ribs. That knocked the wind out of him just long enough for me to grab something myself.

There, a crowbar leaning against the garage wall. This will do nicely, Alex.

I picked it up just in time for him to come at me again. He took one look at it and dropped his scraper. "All right," he said. He raised both hands. "All right. Just take it easy."

I didn't feel like taking it easy. Not yet. A new windshield was sitting on a special felt-padded stand, waiting to be fitted onto the car. I swung the crowbar and hit it dead center, sending a spray of glass pebbles all over the floor. What was left collapsed together into a heap, like some sort of folded-up modern sculpture.

He took that in stride. I had to give him credit. "Okay, that's enough," he said. "Put that thing down."

"Where is he?"

"I said put it down."

There was a box leaning against the wall, just the right shape and size. I was pretty sure I knew what was inside. I swung the crowbar and heard the muffled sound of more glass breaking.

"Shit!" he said. "What are you doing?"

"What does one of these babies cost?" I said. "Four hundred dollars? Five hundred?"

I swung at another box and heard more glass breaking.

"I'm calling the police," he said. "You're insane."

"I think you're right. I get that way when people gang up and beat the shit out of me."

I hit another box. It was utterly and completely the most stupid thing I had ever done. I was committing a felony myself and probably screwing up the whole assault case against the three men who had attacked me. I was throwing everything right out the window. Grant made another move, but stopped himself short when I raised the crowbar at him.

"You're a real tough guy with a club in your hand," he said.

"That's good coming from you," I said. "Why don't you call your brother and your brother-in-law over here so we can have an even fight again."

He kept his hands up as he backed away from me. "You're making a big mistake, McKnight."

"I'm sure I am," I said, dropping the crowbar on the floor with a loud clang. "Now it's your turn. Let's see what you've got, Grant."

He took one look at my empty hands and came right at me. I gave him a side step and slipped a punch into his midsection. I followed that with an overhand left that sent him bouncing off the wall. He tried to wrap me up on the rebound, backing me up hard against the car. I got an elbow under his chin and pushed him away, just far enough to hit him again. He started punching back, but I didn't care anymore. I had been carrying this rage around inside me for days, a secret even to myself, subconsciously nursing it and promising it that I'd give it some release. That time had come.

He hit me in the face a few times, hard enough to tear out some of my stitches. I could feel the blood running down the bridge of my nose. But I stayed close to him. I kept driving my fists into his stomach. I could feel him weakening.

He pushed me away and grabbed something off the workbench. A screwdriver. I backed up as he swung it at me. Once, then twice. A man with any sense would have checked out right then, but instead I timed the third swing and locked up his arm. I bent his elbow back, my face just inches from his.

"Drop it," I hissed in his face. "Or I'll break your arm in two."

The screwdriver fell to the ground. When I let go of him, he tried to take one more swing at me. His last. I caught him right under the ribs with everything I had left. That sent him onto his hands and knees. He stayed that way for a long time, trying to breathe.

I stood over him, watching. I wiped the blood off my nose. He kept sucking air, trying to get something into his lungs. He sat down on the cement floor. Finally, he was able to speak.

"Enough," he said. "God damn, enough."

"Just stay right there," I said. "Or I'll kick your head in."

"What the fuck. God damn."

"Where does he live?"

"You can't."

"Where does he live?"

"I'm telling you, McKnight, he'll kill you."

"Sure, whatever," I said. "Just tell me where he lives. He needs to tell me what he was doing up there."

He was still breathing hard. "You still haven't told me what you're talking about."

"Natalie was up there," I said. "That's where her mother lives."

"Natalie who? Who are you talking about?"

"Natalie Reynaud. The woman who was with me at the hotel that night."

"That night . . ." he said. "She was with you?"

"Yes," I said. "I went up there looking for her, because I hadn't heard from her since yesterday. Before I could find her, I saw Marty at the gas station."

"No, it must have been someone else. What would he be doing up there?"

"It was him."

"Just hold on," he said. "There has to be some explanation. What did you say her name was again?"

"Natalie Reynaud."

"Reynaud," he said. "Reynaud."

"You recognize the name?"

"Reynaud," he said. "Yeah, it's familiar."

"Your father apparently left that hat for Natalie," I said. "Do you have any idea why he might have done that?"

He stayed there on his butt. He shook his head slowly and didn't say a word.

"The hell with it," I said. "I'll find his house."

"Where does she live?"

"Excuse me?"

"Natalie Reynaud. You said her mother lives in Batchawana Bay. Where does Natalie live?"

"A little town," I said. "A couple of hours northeast."

"Blind River?"

That stopped me cold.

"Yes," I said. "How did you know?"

"That's where the devil lived."

"Say that again?"

"The devil of Blind River," he said. "That was something my father used to say. That's where I remember the name. Somebody named Reynaud was the devil of Blind River."

"When did he say this?"

He shook his head. "I don't know. It was . . . toward the end there. When I'd go see him. I thought he was just talking nonsense. He was sort of getting that way."

That made me think of Mrs. DeMarco, all alone in her house, living in some phantom version of the far past.

"What else did he say, Grant?"

"I don't remember."

"Tell me."

He thought about it. "He didn't talk to me much. He spent a lot more time with Marty the last few years."

"So maybe Marty has more of the story, you're saying."

He pushed himself up off the floor. "You can't do that, man."

"Says who?"

I was waiting for his last run. When he came up at me, I spun him around and sent him right back into the workbench. He hit the thing hard and started an avalanche of tools.

"You might as well give him a call," I said. "Tell him I'm coming."

I left him there to dig himself out from under the tools

and went back outside. The cold air stung my face like all hell. I was still bleeding. When I got to the truck, I was already starting to feel dizzy. As the adrenaline slipped away, I held on to the door handle, hanging my head, watching the drops of blood collect in the snow.

I got in the truck, grabbed an old fast-food napkin and held it against my eyebrow. I closed my eyes and took a few long breaths. Time to call Leon, I thought. He can find out where Marty Grant lives. The phone rang just as I picked it up. I looked at the incoming number.

It was Natalie's.

"Hello!" I said after I fumbled to hit the TALK button. "Is that you?"

"Alex, what's the matter?"

"Where are you?"

"I'm at home," she said. "Why are you breathing hard?"

"It's a long story," I said. "But you first. Tell me what's going on. Are you all right?"

"Yes," she said. "I'm a little tired, but—"

"Where have you been? You never called."

"Alex, you knew I was seeing my mother last night. I stayed over there."

"Okay," I said. I tried to make myself slow down. "I'm sorry. I don't mean to sound crazy about it. But I saw Marty Grant today. He was in Batchawana Bay."

There was a long silence on the line. "Say that again, Alex. Marty Grant is one of the two brothers . . ."

"The younger one, yes."

"And you saw him in Batchawana Bay?"

"Yes. I don't know what he was doing. I still haven't talked to him yet."

"What were *you* doing up there?"

I hesitated. "I told you," I said. "I was worried about you."

"So you drove all the way up there?"

"It's not that far. It's closer than your house even." Now that I was saying it out loud, it was starting to sound a little ridiculous.

"So what, you saw Marty Grant, but you didn't ask him why he was there?"

"I didn't get a chance. I followed him back here."

"Where are you now, Alex?"

"I'm in front of the Grants' place," I said, looking out at the building.

"You're not going to do something stupid, are you?"

"Too late. Look, Natalie—"

"Alex, I can't believe you."

"Just stop," I said. "This is coming out all wrong. After everything that's been happening, you gotta understand . . . I thought you were in some kind of trouble."

"Alex . . ."

"What's happening with your mother, anyway? How did that go?"

Silence.

"Come on, Natalie. Please tell me."

"It wasn't good," she said. "It really wasn't. I mean, I thought I knew just how bad it could be, but . . . my God."

"What is it? What happened?"

"I wouldn't even know where to begin. I'm too tired to think about it right now."

"You want me to come over?"

There was another long pause.

"She's here, Alex. I brought her with me."

"She's there right now?"

"I couldn't leave her in that house. I had to either try to clean the place up or just bring her here."

"So the two of you were already gone," I said. "If Marty Grant was going up there to find her . . ."

"We weren't there, Alex."

"So I'll come on over. I'll bring some food."

"No," she said. "Please. Give us a little time, okay? I don't think she's ready to see anybody yet. And I need to get some sleep so bad right now. I was up all night. I think I should just call you tomorrow."

"Are you sure?"

"Yeah, I'm sure," she said. "What are you going to do now?"

I was afraid to say.

"Alex, I want you to go home. If you go find Marty Grant right now, you're going to get into big trouble."

"I want to know why he was up there. Don't you?"

"Alex, listen to me. I can't imagine why he'd go up there looking for my mother, but if that's what he was doing, then we'll get to the bottom of it. We'll do it the right way, okay? I'll call him and see what he says. If I don't like what I hear, then I'll contact the police in Michigan."

I let out a long breath. I couldn't think of a good argument.

"You can't be the one doing this, Alex. You know that. You're the one they assaulted. If they're up to something else, I swear, I'll be even more mad than you are. I'll come down on them like the hammer of God. Just promise me you'll go home now and I'll call you tomorrow. Okay?"

"Damn it, Natalie."

"Promise me."

"I'm going."

"Promise."

"I promise," I said. "I'll talk to you tomorrow."

"Good night, Alex."

"Natalie?"

"What?"

"The hammer of God. That's a good one."

"Good night, Alex."

I hit the END button and sat there for a while. I watched the garage, wondering if Grant would come out after me again. He had to see my truck sitting here.

He never did. The sky got darker and the snowflakes started to drift down slowly. The bright light from the garage glowed through the windows. Finally, I put the truck in gear and drove off, back through town, past the Ojibway Hotel again, out onto the open road, toward Paradise.

She had sounded so tired. Beyond that, there was something else in her voice, some great weight of trouble and sadness. I had to wonder if she'd ever let me help her carry it.

I got my answer to that question that very night. I went home and stood in the hot shower, washing away the blood and the windshield adhesive that had somehow gotten all over my arms. Where the stitches had come loose over my eye, I did the best job I could with some butterfly bandages. I sure as hell didn't feel like going to the emergency room to have more stitches put in.

I knew I'd be feeling a little rough the next morning, yet again. It was becoming a way of life for me. I took some painkillers to try to get ahead of it.

I was on my way out the door for a late dinner, already

preparing my excuses for Jackie's inevitable commentary on my new bruises, when the phone rang. It was Natalie.

"I thought you were going to bed," I said.

"Alex."

"What is it? What's wrong?"

"I had to call you," she said. "I couldn't let it wait until tomorrow."

"What is it?"

"I can't do this anymore, Alex. I'm sorry."

"Can't do what? What are you talking about?"

"Us," she said, her voice wavering just a bit. "It's not gonna work."

"I just talked to you a little while ago. What happened?"

"Nothing, Alex. Nothing. I should have told you then."

"We already went through this once before, remember? I know you've got a lot of stuff going on in your life right now . . ."

"Alex, please."

"Is it because I drove up to Batchawana Bay today?" I said. "I mean, I know that was a little crazy, but you've got to admit, the way it turned out—"

"No, Alex. Please. It's not that."

"You're tired," I said. "Come on, just sleep on it and I'll talk to you tomorrow."

"You're not making this any easier, Alex. Please."

"Please what? What do you want me to do?"

"I don't want you to do anything," she said. "I just want you to . . ."

"What, Natalie?"

"We're done," she said, her voice hard again. "That's all I can say right now, okay? We're done for real this time."

"Just like that? I can't even talk to you about this?"

"No," she said. "Do not come over here. Do not call me. Do you understand?"

"You're making it sound like I'm a stalker or something. I don't think I deserve that."

"I'm sorry," she said. "But this is the way it has to be. After a night with my mother, believe me, somebody has to tell the truth to somebody. This was never going to work, Alex. It was never going to work. Will you just believe me, please?"

I held the phone. I looked out the window at the falling snow.

"Natalie," I said, "this can't be it."

"It has to be. I'm sorry."

"I don't believe it. I don't."

"You have to."

"I'll talk to you tomorrow."

"No," she said. "No, you won't. Good night, Alex."

Then she hung up.

Fourteen

The next day was a bad one. The pain woke me up, one pain joined by others in a chorus singing at top volume inside me. I held a bag of ice over my eye, trying to remember when Grant had nailed me there. My ribs hurt where he had tackled me. My knee hurt. My hands felt like the arthritic claws of an invalid, the knuckles swollen and raw.

Worst of all was the feeling that came to me just after I woke up, the biggest sucker punch of all, the sudden realization that the conversation with Natalie wasn't a dream.

I stayed inside all morning. It was the wrong way to deal with it, but so the hell what. I sure didn't feel like going down to the Glasgow. Or seeing anyone. Or talking to anyone. I stayed inside with the ice pressed against my face and a bottle of painkillers sitting right there on my kitchen table. I found myself counting the minutes until I could take another one. A very bad sign, something I'd seen before. But I didn't give one flying rat's ass.

I thought she would call me. I honestly believed that. She would call me. She would tell me it was all a mistake.

It had been her terrible state of mind the night before. She had no idea what she was saying.

Or else she would come over, just as she had before. One knock on the door and she would open it and step inside. Just like the last time.

I had one lousy American beer in the fridge. I killed that, then opened up a bottle of Wild Turkey. I remembered the bottle we had shared at her house. This is Natalie's brand, I thought. I wondered if she was drinking some herself that day, maybe sitting at that big table in the empty dining room with her mother. I wondered if she was feeling bad.

Here's to you, Natalie. Here's to you.

I would have sat there all day, just like that. I would have drunk. I would have filled up my ice bag. I would have counted the minutes until I could take my next pill. That would have been the whole day, right there.

But then it started to snow.

It snowed hard enough that I had to make a choice. I could stay inside all day and let it bury me, or I could go out, no matter how bad I felt, and fight it.

What's it gonna be, Alex? I looked in the mirror. What's it gonna be?

I threw my coat on, went outside, and fired up the truck. I ran the snowplow up and down the road a couple of times, then switched to the shovel. The hard work made me feel sick to my stomach, but I kept going. I punished myself. When I had the last cabin dug out, I leaned over and threw up like Mount Vesuvius all over the snowbank. When I was done, I shoveled it all away and covered it up with more snow.

Then I figured, what the hell. I'm going to Jackie's.

He dropped his towel when I stepped into the place. He stood there looking at me for a long time, then he just shook his head and asked me if I wanted an omelet.

"That would be just what the doctor ordered," I said. "I've got a pretty empty tank right now."

"I see you didn't listen to anything I told you the other day."

"I listened, Jackie. I really did."

"She dragged you right into it, didn't she? Who was it this time? The same three guys?"

"No, just one," I said. "I'm sure he's looking pretty bad, too."

"This isn't a game, Alex. You're gonna get yourself killed."

"You may not have to worry anymore."

"What are you saying?"

"If you don't mind, I'd rather not talk about it right now. Let's just say that Natalie and I are taking a little break again."

I couldn't tell if he was buying that one, but he made me my omelet and brought it over to me by the fireplace. When I was done eating, I put my feet up. I almost started to feel a little better than miserable.

Vinnie came in a little while later. He stood over me, studying my face like an insurance adjuster examining a car wreck.

"Alex," he said, "you're not that good-looking when you're healthy. You can't afford to keep making things worse."

"Thank you," I said. "I knew you'd make me feel better."

"You gonna tell me what happened this time?"

"Eventually. If you sit here long enough."

"Sounds like a plan," he said. He sat down in the other chair and put his feet up next to mine. His face was wind-burned, and now that he had taken the tape off his ear, you could see where the bullet had ripped off a good chunk of it. Between the two of us, we must have looked like the unluckiest pair of losers in the whole world.

Our luck turned even worse when the door opened. Michael Grant stepped in, brushing the snow off his shoulders. He was holding a hat. *The* hat. He looked the place over, stopping when he saw me sitting there by the fire.

"McKnight," he said as he came over to me. There was a big purple bruise on his left cheek, and he had a shiner around his right eye. But aside from that he didn't look half as bad as I did. It didn't make me any happier to see him standing in my bar.

"What are you doing here?" I said.

I didn't bother to stand up. But Vinnie did. Grant gave him a cool, even look and introduced himself. "Alex and I had a little episode yesterday," he said.

"What about at the funeral? Was that an episode, too?"

"No," Grant said. "That was a very bad day for every-one."

"Vinnie, sit down," I said.

He did, with obvious reluctance.

"I asked you what you were doing here," I said to Grant.

"I came to give you this," he said. He held up the hat.

"I don't want it," I said.

"I figured Ms. Reynaud might."

"I wouldn't know. You'll have to ask her."

He looked down at me. "You're making this hard, McKnight."

"How did you even know I'd be here?"

"You're in the book. When I drove by, I recognized your truck out front."

I took the hat from him. "Okay, I've got the hat. You can leave now."

"I need to talk to you. Maybe your friend can excuse himself for a minute."

"Maybe his friend can kick your ass all the way back to the Soo," Vinnie said.

Grant put his hands up. "I came to talk," he said. "That's it. I don't want any more trouble."

"Then you picked the wrong place," Vinnie said.

"All right, take it easy," I said. "If the man has something to say, let him say it."

"Can we talk outside?"

"So we can freeze to death?"

"This'll only take a minute, McKnight. It's about Ms. Reynaud."

I was about to tell him I was officially not interested in that topic anymore, but I figured it was none of his business. "You've got one minute," I said.

"Don't go out there," Vinnie said.

"It's okay," I said. "I don't think he's gonna try anything stupid. Not on my home field."

"Just sit down here," Vinnie said, getting up. "I'll be over at the bar."

Grant didn't look happy about it, but when Vinnie left us alone, he sat down in the empty chair across from me.

"You spend a lot of time here?" he asked.

"You're wasting your minute."

"Look, we don't have to have a Kodak moment here, okay? Let's just say I feel bad about the way things have happened."

"That's big of you."

"You never went over to Marty's house."

"No," I said. "I didn't."

"I called him, told him to expect you."

"Yeah? Sorry if he was disappointed."

"I told him what you told me, about Natalie Reynaud in Blind River. I asked him if he knew anything about her. I also asked him if he was in Batchawana Bay that day."

"What did he say?"

"He said he was up there. You were right."

"Did he say why?"

"No," Grant said. "He said he'd tell me about it later."

"Did he?"

"That was yesterday. I haven't heard from him since."

"Since yesterday?"

"I called his wife. Marty never came home last night. Never called. Nothing. He just disappeared. I've been looking all over."

"So why did you come here?"

"I'm worried, McKnight. I'm running out of ideas. You remember what I was telling you about the devil of Blind River?"

"Yeah."

"I was thinking your friend Natalie might know something," he said. "Have you talked to her about this?"

"Not today."

"I thought the two of you were close."

"Your minute just ended."

"He said one more thing, McKnight. I think it's important."

"What did he say?"

"He said he didn't know the devil's family still lived in Blind River."

I thought about that one. It found its way into my gut and started eating at me.

"Grant," I finally said, "are you telling me—"

"I tried to look her up, McKnight. She's not listed. I had no idea how to contact her."

"I'll call her right now," I said. I told him to stay where he was, then went to the bar and grabbed Jackie's phone. Vinnie and Jackie were both there, watching me. I gave them a little nod of my head and dialed.

The line was busy.

I let him sit over there by the fire for a few minutes while I waited to try again. The line was still busy.

Grant got to his feet just as I was hanging up again. He didn't say a word. He just walked out the door.

I watched him go out, then looked over at Jackie and Vinnie. They were as confused as I was. When I headed for the door myself, Vinnie tried to follow me. I told him to go sit back down. I was just going to see what the hell Grant was doing.

When I opened the door, I saw Grant pacing back and forth next to my truck. It was snowing harder now. There was already a thin white layer on Grant's head.

"What are you doing out here?" I said. I had brought the hat out with me.

"There was no answer when you called her?"

"The line was busy."

"Both times?"

"Yeah, both times."

"I tell you," he said. He started pacing back and forth. "I got a real bad feeling about this. I think we should go out there."

"Are you serious?"

"Come on, you gotta help me. You gotta take me out to her house."

"You *are* serious."

"Yes," he said. "Aren't you worried?"

"I can't believe this . . ." I looked up at the falling snow. Truth was, I was getting just as worried as he was, no matter how things stood between Natalie and me.

"Please, McKnight. I'm begging you."

"Hold on," I said.

I went back inside and called her one more time. The line was still busy. I told Jackie and Vinnie what I had to do. Jackie yelled at me. Vinnie just shook his head. Then I went back outside.

"Let's go," I said. "I'm driving."

"Okay," he said. He got in and we took off toward the Soo.

We weren't even out of Paradise yet when I happened to look over at him. He was holding the hat in his lap and rocking his head back and forth, ever so slightly. It looked like he was wound tighter than piano wire. Then for one quick moment I looked down and spotted something gray and metallic in his coat pocket.

"Hey, look at that," I said, pointing out his side window.

"What?"

I jammed on the brakes and sent him flying into the dashboard. As he was bouncing back, I reached into his coat pocket and pulled out the gun. I had it pointed right at his head before he knew it was gone.

"What the hell's going on?" I said to him. "What were you gonna do with this?"

He caught his breath and looked at me. The gun was two inches from his forehead.

Something was wrong. The gun didn't feel right. It was way too light.

"What the hell?" I said, pulling it away from his head.

"It's not real," he said.

"It's plastic," I said. "It's a cheap plastic toy. What the hell are you doing with a toy gun in your pocket?"

He started to say something. He gave up and shrugged his shoulders.

"Was this gonna be for me? In case I didn't help you?"

He didn't look at me. He picked the hat off the floor of the truck and brushed it off. "I'm sorry," he said.

"I should just beat the living shit out of you right now," I said. "You were gonna pull a toy gun on me?"

"I never would have used a real one. Give me that much."

"Could you be any more of a jackass?" I took my foot off the brake and headed down the road again. "A toy gun. What were you gonna do when we got to customs?"

"I don't know," he said. "Look, I told you I'm worried sick. My brother never disappeared before, okay? I wasn't thinking straight."

I shook my head and kept driving. Grant stayed quiet for a while. The snow started to come down harder. I began to worry about making it all the way out to Blind River. "I don't know why you're doing this now," he finally said. "But I appreciate it."

"Just shut the hell up," I said. "I'm not doing it for you. If your stupid brother is over at her house, or if anything has happened to Natalie, I swear I'm gonna go after all three of you guys, one by one."

He nodded his head slowly. "Fair enough."

I rolled down the window, letting in an icy blast of air. "I'm gonna throw this away, if you don't mind. If the customs guy sees it, he might not be amused."

I threw it into the snowbank, then rolled up my window.

"I hate real guns," he said. "All my life, since I was a little kid. Never went hunting with my father or anything. That was always Marty."

"I'm not too fond of guns, either."

I picked up the cell phone and called Natalie again. The line was still busy. That didn't make sense to me. She wasn't the type of person to sit around talking on the phone all day.

"So tell me," I said, putting the phone down, "if your father said the devil lived in Blind River, I'm thinking that had to be Natalie's father, Jean Reynaud. You ever hear that name?"

"No, I don't think so. I just heard the last name."

"You've got no idea what might have happened between them? Your father and Jean Reynaud?"

"I really don't. Like I said, he might have told Marty something. He was the favorite son, after all."

I picked up on the bitterness in his voice, but I wasn't about to pursue it.

"What about New Year's Eve?" I said. "Did your father ever say anything about that?"

He looked at me. "Which one?"

"There was a party over at the Ojibway, New Year's Eve, 1973. You think your father might have been there?"

"I was a teenager," he said. "I don't remember it, but I wouldn't be surprised if he was there. My father knew everybody."

"Think he might have taken Natalie's father outside and shot him in the back of the head?"

"God, what are you saying?"

"Is it possible?"

Grant just shook his head slowly.

"Let's say he did," I said. "Of course, first he made him take off his hat."

Grant looked down at the hat in his hands.

"You're saying this was the devil's hat?"

"Who knows?" I said. "Maybe we're about to find out."

I kept driving. The snow kept coming down. The wind picked up and drove the snow sideways. Grant didn't say anything for a long time. He sat there and looked at the hat.

We went over the International Bridge. I sure as hell didn't think I'd be coming back this way so soon. This time, the wind and the blowing snow made it downright scary. When I stopped to pay the toll, the man asked me how bad it was, and told me they'd probably be closing the bridge until the wind let up. Then we rolled through Canadian customs and answered the questions, the man taking a hard look at our faces.

"What happened to you guys?" he said. "You both look like something the cat brought in."

"A little disagreement," I said. "We got carried away."

He pressed us a little more, asked us where we were going, how long we'd be in Canada. I told him we were going to the clubs. Eventually, he let us go through.

We followed a snowplow for a few miles through town. When we hit the open road, I passed him and settled in for the long stretch to Blind River. It was still blowing hard.

"By the way," I finally said, "everything your nephew told you, that whole business about me contacting your father, making him come out that night to the hotel, making him go back outside . . . You know he was just covering his ass because he lost track of the poor guy, right?"

"I'm open to that possibility now. I'll say that much."

"Afterward, I was just trying to find out what had happened. That's why I came to the funeral."

"For what it's worth," he said, "when you were getting worked over behind the church, that was me who was telling those guys to cool it."

I thought about it. "I remember somebody saying something like that, but I don't remember anybody actually stopping the other two guys."

"I know," he said. "Like I say, for what it's worth. Which ain't much."

"No."

"We all go to trial in a couple of weeks. I had to put the garage up to make bail."

"That hardly seems fair," I said. "Me, I got a nice four-day vacation in the hospital."

"I'm not saying we're even, McKnight. But you did get your shots in the other day. I'm still feeling it."

I let that one go. I picked up the cell phone and gave Natalie one more try. The line was still busy.

A few miles later, we came to our first accident. One car was right in the middle of the road, pointed sideways, another car pushed into the ditch. I rolled my window down to see if anyone needed some help, but there was nobody around. A hundred yards later, I saw a house, with smoke blowing sideways from the top of the chimney. I figured everybody was inside that house, instant neighbors, waiting for the tow truck to come. I kept driving.

The next accident was just outside Thessalon, another car off the road, this time all the way down a steep embankment. A tow truck was on the scene, the man holding his hand in front of his face to ward off the blowing snow as he hooked a chain to the car's trailer hitch.

"Getting bad out here," Grant said.

"I'm not turning around now."

"The man said the bridge was closing anyway. We couldn't go back even if we wanted to."

We came to Iron Bridge, saw a few more cars abandoned on the side of the road, already covered with six inches of new snow. We passed McKnight Road, but I didn't smile at it this time. We passed the Mississauga Reserve. There was one more stretch of empty road until we finally reached Blind River. As we got closer to the town hall, we could see the trucks parked right on the road itself, next to a telephone pole that had fallen down across the entrance. A half-dozen men were hard at work, all of them wearing orange ski masks. With the lines down and the snow blowing harder than ever, the whole scene looked like the end of the world.

"Looks like the phones are out here," Grant said. "You think that's why her line's been busy?"

"Could be," I said. "Depending on when this pole went down."

"Is her house coming up soon?"

"Couple more miles."

"Okay, good."

He was sitting up in his seat now, nervously turning the hat in his hands again. I was a little uptight myself, with no idea what we'd find at the house. When I got to the driveway, I put the plow down and pushed the snow off, all the way to the barn.

"I don't see Marty's truck here," he said.

"Not at the moment," I said. "Doesn't mean he didn't come out here."

He opened his door and got out of the truck. I did the same, the driving snow stinging my face.

"God, this is painful," he said. "What the hell are we doing? Is anybody even home?"

"Let's go see."

I went up the unshoveled walk to the front door, stepping carefully through the snow. It felt strange to be here now, with officially no relationship with the owner of this house, no good reason to be here beyond a general sense of dread. I wanted to know that Natalie was safe. That was all. After that, I never wanted to see this place again.

I tried the door. It was locked. I rang the bell and heard the faraway chiming in the empty house.

"What do we do now?" he said.

I looked around the place. The windows. If one of them is unlocked . . .

Or wait. The back door. I led him around the house, working hard to get through the deep snow. There at the back, leading into the kitchen, was an old-fashioned

Dutch door. The top section had a large window with nine separate panes. The lower-left pane, the one closest to the doorknob, was broken.

I turned the knob, wishing at that moment like all hell that I had a gun. A real one. I pushed the door open and stepped inside. Grant followed. My stomach was starting to burn. What the hell was going on here?

When we were both inside, I closed the door behind us, shutting out most of the noise of the wind. I could feel a draft cutting in through the broken pane. The room was cold. The power must have been out.

I saw broken glass all over the kitchen floor. The phone hung from its cord.

"Oh man," Grant said as he saw the scene. "What happened?"

I went through the kitchen, crunching through the broken glass. There was more glass in the dining room, with several liquor bottles on the table, one turned over. I did a quick run-through of the rest of the house. In the dim light I didn't see any more signs of violence, but when I was upstairs I noticed that both the bed in the guest room and the bed in Natalie's old room were unmade. It shouldn't have surprised me. Natalie had told me that she had brought her mother back here, but out of nowhere the line from "Goldilocks and the Three Bears" flashed through my mind. Somebody has been sleeping in my bed. What a strange thing to think of at a time like this. The burning in my stomach was getting worse.

"God damn it," I said softly. "God damn it to hell. Where are you, Natalie?"

I went back downstairs to see Grant hanging up the phone.

"It's dead," he said. "Now what do we do?"

"I'm checking the basement," I said. I opened the door and hit the light switch like an idiot. I went back and started opening the kitchen drawers. Somewhere she had to have a flashlight. I opened the silverware drawer, the napkins and candles drawer, the junk drawer. I pushed the pens and pencils around, looking for a flashlight. Come on, I thought. Everyone has a goddamned flashlight.

The next drawer was full of tools. A hammer, screwdrivers, pliers . . .

There. A flashlight.

I picked it up and turned it on. The beam was weak, but it would have to do.

I went back to the basement steps, shone the light down the wooden steps to the concrete floor at the bottom. I could barely see anything. Grant followed me.

I started going down, step by step. The boards creaked.

I'm going to buy her a flashlight, I thought. A good one.

Another step. The air got colder.

As soon as I see her again, I thought, we're going flashlight shopping. And I'm glad I've got this to think about right now because otherwise I'd be scared to death of what I'm going to find down here.

"Natalie," I said out loud, "please don't be down here."

I did a quick scan with the flashlight, through each room filled with the decades of old household items, magazines, newspapers, boxes, and tin cans. Grant followed me from one room to the next, until we finally came to the little closet where Natalie had found all the pictures. But this time there was something strange going on. All the clutter on the shelves had been thrown onto the floor, and the shelves themselves were all slanting away from the wall, like someone had tried to pull them all off at once.

No. That wasn't it. I grabbed one of the shelves and pulled. The whole unit moved in one piece. It was like a door. You couldn't see it before because of all the stuff on the shelves, and the fact that the surface of the door was painted gray, just like the walls.

I pulled it all the way open and looked inside.

"What is that?" Grant said as he came closer. "What's in there?"

I saw something that looked like wax paper. I reached down and touched it. There was something hard underneath. I pulled it out and unwrapped it in the thin beam of the flashlight. The first thing I saw was a long black rifle barrel. I pulled off more of the paper, slick with gun oil.

"What kind of gun is that?" he said.

"It looks like an old Thompson submachine gun."

I shone the light down the barrel. Someone had plugged it with cosmoline to keep the moisture out.

"Somebody knew what they were doing," I said.

"Is that all that's in there? Just guns?"

"Some shells, too," I said, unwrapping an old cardboard box. I lifted another heavy bundle. "This one feels like a shotgun."

"How old are they?"

"Hard to say, but one of the guns is gone." I picked up a wad of loose paper, then dropped it back on the floor.

"Did I tell you how much I hate guns?" he said. "God, this makes no sense at all. What's going on here, McKnight? Where is everybody?"

"That's what I want to know."

I went back upstairs. Something else was wrong here.

Something I couldn't quite place. Besides the broken window and the empty bottles . . .

I went through the ground floor rooms again. Nothing seemed out of place until I got to the living room. The sitting room, Natalie had called it. The couch was one of those awful gold things you saw years ago, covered with plastic. The two Queen Anne chairs made you feel like you had to sit up straight with your pinkies extended. There on the floor next to them was a television set, along with a VCR. Beside those was the empty box they had been packed in.

Her mother was here, I thought. She pulled out the TV so her mother could watch a movie or something. It was probably that or drive each other crazy.

And that smell, I thought. That was the thing that was bothering me. Her mother must have smoked, because the faint, stale smell of cigarettes was still lingering in the air. I saw one of Natalie's salad plates on the floor. It was filled with ashes.

I reached down and picked up an open pack. Virginia Slims, with three cigarettes left.

"Did you find something?" Grant said. He came into the room and looked at the television on the floor.

"Nah, it's nothing," I said. But as I put the cigarettes on the plate, I noticed another pack of cigarettes, this one empty and crumpled up, partially tucked underneath the rim of the plate. I picked it up and tried to smooth it out.

"What is it?"

"It's an empty pack of Camels," I said. "Unfiltered."

The look on his face told me everything I needed to know. I stepped up to him and looked him in the eye. It was all I could do not to grab him by the throat.

"These are Marty's cigarettes, aren't they?" I said.

"They could be anybody's," he said. He took one step backward.

"Anybody's including Marty, right? These are his brand."

"Look, McKnight . . ."

"I've seen enough," I said. "It's time to call the police."

I left him standing there. I knew the kitchen phone was dead, but I could still use my cell phone. I went out into the snowstorm, fighting my way back to the truck. I got in, closed the door behind me, and picked up the cell phone. I waited as the stupid thing tried to find a signal—always a problem when the weather was bad, and especially when the phone lines were down and everyone else with a cell phone was using theirs.

I waited. I looked back at the house. Grant was still in there somewhere. I looked out in front of me.

The barn. The door was wide open. The last time I was here, that door was closed.

I got out of the truck and made my way to the barn. As I got closer, I saw that a great drift of snow had formed in the doorway, extending deep inside.

It was slow going, with the snow nearly up to my waist. I worked my way closer and closer.

I got to the doorway. Today there was no sunlight to come streaming through the gaps in the walls. The barn was dark.

I took a few steps in, waiting for my eyes to adjust.

Somewhere, far away, a voice was calling me. "McKnight! Where are you?"

I was about to answer. Then I stopped.

I saw it for one single second without any idea what it

was, and then everything else caught up. There was a body on the floor of the barn.

Blood.

A body.

A woman.

Blood all over the hair. Blood everywhere.

Something else. Sticking up out of the floor. No, out of the body. A long wooden stick. No, some sort of tool. A farm tool, sticking out of the body.

The damage. The blood. She was butchered with this thing, this old farm thing made of wood and rusted metal.

This body . . . This woman . . .

"McKnight!" The voice again, close behind me now.

I turned and saw him. He stood in the doorway, looking past me at the horror on the ground.

"No," he said. "God, no. Marty, what did you do? My God, Marty . . ."

He turned and started to run away, falling into the snow. He left me there alone with her.

I didn't want to go any closer. But I had to.

I took one step.

Then another.

The hair, spread out around her head. The blade, the long wooden stick, the obscenity of it. I wanted to grab the handle and pull it from her back.

Please, no. Anything but this. Anything.

But wait. I reached down and touched the hair. In the dim light, it looked . . . red. This wasn't Natalie. God, it wasn't her.

I moved around to get a better look at her face. I knew her. I had seen her picture.

It was Natalie's mother. The Irish looks, the red hair. This was her.

This was Grace, the woman I had never gotten the chance to meet, the woman with all of the lies, each one more fabulous than the last. Until now. She would never tell another lie.

I stood there for a long time, looking at her.

Then there was a sound. I looked up to see Michael Grant standing in the doorway again. This time he had the shotgun in his hands, the double-barreled shotgun from the basement.

He hated guns. I had heard him say that more than once today. He hated guns, but not enough to stop him from doing this right now, leveling it right at my head. Twenty feet away. He moved closer to me.

"No," I said. "No."

"I can't let you leave now."

"No."

"I'm sorry, McKnight. I'm sorry."

It came to this, all these years later, since the last time I had looked down the barrel of a gun. Another day, another season, a hot day in Detroit. The feeling was the same.

But this one will be loud. An old shotgun. God in heaven, this will be loud.

"I'm sorry," he said.

He pulled the trigger, and it was all the noise in the world ringing at once, all around me and below me until I reached out to hold it as tight as I could.

Then I let go.

Fifteen

Natalie. I am saying her name. A song with three notes.

Natalie.

She is above me, looking down at me with that smile, that expression both sad and happy at the same time, like it's all a puzzle she hasn't figured out yet.

Natalie.

I can smell her hair. I can feel her fingers touching my face, as light as snowflakes.

I open my eyes.

A wooden roof, high above me in the dim light, a fine powdery snow hanging in the air, melting on my cheeks.

I'm alive.

I sat up quickly, looking around me. My neck hurt. My ears were ringing. God, my ears. I could feel warm blood on my shirt. Was I shot? What the hell happened? He hadn't been more than twenty feet away. There's no way he could have missed.

I touched my neck, where it joined my shoulder. I was bleeding, but . . . What was that? Something hard and jagged, a sudden riot of pain as I felt it. I grabbed on to it, a cry coming out of my mouth before I knew what was happening. It was hot, and slippery with blood, but I held it tight between my fingers and pulled.

God, that hurt. I looked down at the thing as the blood ran warm down my neck. It was a fragment of metal, about a half inch long. What the hell?

Then the rest of it came back to me, all at once. The body on the floor. The long farm tool of wood and metal, like a spear. I looked behind me. I didn't want to move any closer to her. I knew she was dead.

So what had happened? I tried to put it all together in my mind, Grant and me coming up here, the guns in the basement, coming out to the barn, Grant behind me with the gun.

I looked toward the door. There was something on the ground. I tried to get up on my knees, feeling the pain shoot through my neck every time I moved it. I crawled over through the ancient hay and dusty snow. I saw the gun, or what was left of it. It was like something out of a cartoon now, both barrels curled back like banana peels.

It blew up on him. The barrels must have been plugged with the cosmoline, like the other gun I had seen down there. Thank God for fools who don't know any better than to fire a gun that's been wrapped up in a basement for who knows how many years.

Some of the shrapnel had hit me. It was better than getting my head blown off, but it still hurt like hell and it kept bleeding. I tried to get to my feet. I got about halfway, felt like I would pass out, then finally I was standing.

As I looked at the wreckage of the gun again, a sudden thought hit me. Grant was standing right here when it blew up. What happened to him?

The door to the barn was still open, the snow still drifting in. I went to it, moving slowly. I saw blood on the floor, a thin trail of it leading right outside. I followed the trail out into the snow and the wind. It was the last thing I felt like facing, but I knew I had to do something. I couldn't stay in the barn, adding my own blood to the floor, or for God's sake looking at what had been done to this woman.

I started back toward the house, the long fight through the snow. I could see that my truck was gone, and with it my cell phone. I had been in such a rush to get inside, I had left the keys dangling in the ignition. Now Grant was gone. I saw more blood in the snow, leading all the way to where the truck had been. He was hurt, but apparently he could still drive a truck.

I slipped in the snow. The pain ran like a white hot iron spike through my neck. I had to stop for a full minute just to catch my breath.

"Son of a bitch," I said into the wind. "Goddamned son of a bitch."

I started moving again. The snow was collecting on my shoulders. I worked my way to the back door of the house. It was cold inside, but at least I was out of the wind. I went upstairs to the bathroom and looked at myself in the mirror. Very carefully I slid out of my coat, gritting my teeth the whole time. When I was done, I saw that the front of my shirt was soaked with blood. I needed bandages, or at least something to tape myself up with.

I rummaged through more cabinets, found the first aid supplies. Thank God she had a lot of them. I put some gauze squares on my neck, then did my best to tape them in place.

I went downstairs and tried the phone. It was still out. I could wait for the service to come back, keeping warm and trying to limit the bleeding. Or I could try to get out of here. Trouble with that was it was a long way back to the town. Two miles in this weather, in the shape I'm in . . . Not a great idea. Even if I just tried to get down to the road, how long would I have to wait for someone to come by?

I could go the other way, I thought, to Mrs. DeMarco's house. But what good would that do? I'm sure her phone is out, too. For that matter, I hope she's all right over there. She probably has oil heat, but with the power out . . . No, wait, I saw a good wood-burning stove in her kitchen. I'm sure she's staying warm.

Wait a minute. I remembered seeing the medical alert tag, hanging around Mrs. DeMarco's neck. You just press the button and help is on the way.

I went into the guest room. Natalie's mother's open suitcase was on the floor—all these clothes she would never wear again. I couldn't touch them.

I went into Natalie's old room, saw her clothes piled up on the bed. The room was a mess. I grabbed one of her shirts and wrapped it around my neck. All of a sudden I could smell her scent, just as if she were right there in the room with me. I had to stop and close my eyes. I took a deep breath. Then I went back downstairs and headed out the door.

The wind had died down a bit. It wasn't snowing as hard. I had that much going for me. I made my way down the driveway—hell, if I got lucky, I might even see somebody driving a snowplow on the road.

When I got down to the road, I looked in both directions. It was a lonely road to begin with. Now it was like some ancient site where a road once ran, a thousand years ago. I put my head down and kept walking, thankful for the level ground at least, and for the fact that the wind was at my back. I could hear its low moaning along with my own breathing, and nothing else. My feet started to feel cold.

Mrs. DeMarco's house was a half mile down the road, or so I thought. It seemed a lot longer than that as I worked my way through the snow. I was starting to feel like I had made a terrible mistake. But at last I saw a break in the tree line and I knew her driveway was just up ahead.

I trudged on and finally saw her house. The snow seemed to cling to every inch of it. There were no footprints, no signs of shoveling or any human activity. Worst of all, there was no smoke coming out of the chimney.

You're a total idiot, I told myself. She's not here. They came and took her away.

I went up the driveway, just to confirm my fears. I went to the front door and knocked, then without waiting I tried turning the knob. The door was unlocked. I pushed it open and stuck my head in.

"Hello?"

Silence.

I stepped inside. At least I'd get out of the cold for a few minutes before heading back. I'd make apologies later, if it ever came to that.

But damn, it was almost as cold inside as it was out. The heat had obviously been off for hours. I'll make a fire, I thought. Get that stove going, warm myself up.

I went into the kitchen and opened up the stove. I

found a pile of old newspapers and started to crumple them up. I looked around for some wood.

Then I heard the creaking. It was coming from somewhere above me. I stopped and listened.

Nothing.

I opened the pantry door, looking for the wood. Then I heard the creaking again.

It's just the wind, I thought. The house is shifting in the wind.

But then I heard it again. There was someone upstairs.

"I hope that's you, Mrs. DeMarco."

I headed for the stairs and went up slowly, step by step. I made a few stupid jokes to myself about whistling in the dark. After what I had seen in the barn, I'd be whistling for a long time.

When I got to the top of the stairs, I saw four different doors. It was darker here, away from the windows. As my eyes adjusted, I saw an old kerosene lantern on a small table—either an antique for decoration or something the old woman had actually used long ago. There was no time to try to light it now.

I moved slowly to the first door and peeked around the frame. It was a sewing room, with a big black Singer machine, the kind with the treadle underneath. I heard a sound and spun around, ready to hit somebody. But the hallway was empty. I went to the next door and looked inside.

I saw Mrs. DeMarco, standing in her bedroom between a wooden armoire and her big four-poster bed. She was dressed in white undergarments from head to toe. On the bed she had half a dozen outfits laid out, all black.

She turned to look at me. If she was remotely surprised to see me standing in her doorway, she didn't show it.

"I can't decide what to wear," she said.

"Mrs. DeMarco," I said. "Are you all right?"

"I shouldn't have to think about this," she said, staring at the clothes on her bed. "Not today. Someone should just tell me what to wear."

"Mrs. DeMarco, it's so cold in here. Why don't you have a fire going?"

As I moved closer to her, I could see that her skin was blue.

"Should I wear this one?" she said, picking up one of the dresses. It was all black lace, and looked like it should be hanging in a museum.

"You need to get warmed up," I said. As I got even closer, I saw that she was shivering. Her medical alert tag hung from her neck.

"Funerals should be on cold days, don't you think? Somehow it seems fitting."

"I think you're right," I said. "Do you think we could maybe press the button on your tag? For both of us?"

She looked down at it, like she had no idea what it was. "This won't do," she said. She took it off, struggling with it as it got caught in her hair. "I think I need the pearls. What do you think?"

"I agree." I took the tag from her and pressed the red button. I wasn't sure where the signal would go—if there was a station here in Blind River or if they'd have to come from Sault Ste. Marie.

"I've always hated funerals," she said. "Not that anyone likes them, I suppose."

"Come on, we need to get you downstairs. I'll make a fire and get you some hot tea or something."

I was going to pull the blanket off the bed, but then I would have had to move all of the dresses. That probably wouldn't have made her very happy. I saw an old hand-made quilt folded up on top of the armoire, so I took that down and wrapped it around her shoulders.

"I don't have time for tea," she said. "The funeral is in one hour."

"Don't worry," I said. "I won't let you miss it. Let's go downstairs."

"Are you sure?"

"I'm sure."

I led her out of the room and down the stairs, staying in front in case I had to catch her. She took each step with care until we were at the bottom. When I had her sitting at the table, I wrapped the quilt tight around her and started looking for the wood.

"I suppose you're wondering how I'm holding up so well," she said.

"Is there some more firewood around here, ma'am?" The wood holder next to the stove was empty.

"I think I'm probably a little numb," she said. "It's always a shock, no matter how many times you lose someone."

"Yes, ma'am. I'm just looking for the firewood here."

"It's out back," she said. "There's a whole pile out there."

I looked out the back window. If there was a pile of firewood out there, it was covered by an even bigger pile of snow.

"Do you have any dry wood, ma'am? Something that might be stored here in the house?"

"I'm wondering if perhaps I'm not entirely surprised," she said. "That is to say, perhaps this is something that was bound to happen, sooner or later."

I tried to open the back door. The snow had drifted all the way up to the window. Turning, I saw yet another door on the far side of the kitchen. When I opened that, I saw steps leading down into the darkness. This time, someone had the sense to hang a flashlight from a nail in the wall.

"It's such a terrible business," she said. "I think I've always known it would come to a bad end."

I stopped and looked at her for a moment, thinking about what she was saying. I couldn't imagine which funeral she was getting dressed for. Maybe her own son's death had somehow forced its way into her consciousness. She closed her eyes and started to rock back and forth in her chair.

"Okay, I need to get this fire going right now," I said. I grabbed the flashlight and turned it on, saw the firewood stacked neatly, right at the bottom of the stairs. Beyond that was the dead oil burner. I went down to get as much as I could carry, getting another blast of that same old basement smell. When I had a few small logs on top of the paper, I took the book of matches that was sitting on top of the stove and got the fire going. Then I filled the teapot with water and put it on the stove.

"This will take a little while," I said. "Are you okay, ma'am?"

She didn't answer. Her eyes were still closed. I pulled a chair close to her and sat down.

"Mrs. DeMarco, can you hear me?"

She kept rocking back and forth. "What a time," she finally said. "What a time."

"What time are you talking about?"

"What a way to celebrate New Year's."

"The man next door," I said. "Jean Reynaud. Is that who you're talking about?"

She opened her eyes.

"What's happening?" she said. "How did you get here?"

"It's okay, Mrs. DeMarco."

"You were here before."

"Yes," I said. "I've called for help."

I showed her the tag. Then I noticed the receiver unit sitting on the kitchen counter. You press the button, the signal goes to the receiver . . . which was dead. Even if it had a battery, it probably connected right to a phone line. Which was also dead.

Alex, I thought, you are officially the biggest idiot who ever lived.

"Mrs. DeMarco," I said, "someone will come to check on you, right? Your day nurse, maybe?"

"Yes," she said. "Flo will come, eventually. Or the men from the town."

"The fire will be hot soon. We'll get you warmed up."

She looked at me. She looked at my face, the bruises and the tape and the new blood smeared all over my neck.

"You've had some bad luck," she said. "Either that or you don't know how to stay out of trouble."

"Yes, ma'am."

"I'm a little tired now," she said. Her eyes were starting to lose their focus. I put my right arm around her and pulled her close to my body.

"We'll be okay," I said. "Just hold on."

The fire burned. The wind blew. The old woman slept

against my chest. The other woman, Natalie's mother, she was back in the barn, beyond the reach of any warmth at all. Natalie herself . . . I had no idea where she was at that moment. That was a complete mystery.

"Where are you?" I said. "Where the hell are you?"

Sixteen

The truck came, slipping its way up the driveway. As I looked out the window, I saw an insignia on the front grill that read "North Channel EMT." The nurse must have found some way to contact them. Two men got out and knocked on the front door. They were surprised to see me open it.

They took us all the way down to the General Hospital in Sault Ste. Marie. I sat in the front seat while one of the men attended to Mrs. DeMarco in the back. On the way, I told the driver to call the police and to tell them that there was a dead woman in the barn behind the Reynaud house and that Natalie Reynaud herself was missing. On top of all that, I had a stolen truck to report, too.

He looked at me, then back at his partner. Then he made the call.

By the time we got to the hospital, the Ontario Provincial Police were waiting for us. The EMTs took Mrs. De-Marco right into the emergency room, but the OPPs had different plans for me. I had to run through the whole story while the doctor examined me. An officer stayed with me while I got my X-ray. As the doctor sewed up the wound in my neck, he told me the gunmetal fragment had just missed a major artery, and that I should officially consider myself the luckiest human being on the planet.

"Yeah, take a picture of me," I said. "I'm sure they'll use that as the caption."

"This other guy was aiming a shotgun at you," the doctor said. "You're telling me it exploded in his hands?"

"I think so."

He shook his head. "I can't imagine what he looks like right now."

"How did he get away?" I said. "How come I blacked out but he didn't?"

"I couldn't help but notice your other scars," the doctor said. "Not to mention the little souvenir in your anterior mediastinum when I saw the X-ray."

"What about it?"

"When were you shot?"

"In 1984."

"So you've been there before. I've never looked down a gun barrel myself, but if somebody pointed a shotgun at me right now and blasted away, I imagine I'd pass out. Even if I wasn't hit."

"It was a different state of mind for Grant, you're saying."

"The man who fired the weapon? Exactly. He wasn't expecting it. It was a total surprise."

"So how far could he get? I saw the blood on the ground."

"Hard to say for sure," the doctor said. "Only thing I do know is that he'd better be getting himself to a hospital."

It was hard to imagine. I almost felt sorry for him.

When I was all taped up, the doctor told me I could leave if I wanted to. I didn't have a truck, of course, but the police officers were more than happy to escort me from the hospital. In fact, they even had a place for me to stay for a while, instead of going all the way home. In their polite Canadian way they made it quite clear I had no choice in the matter.

Before I went with them, I asked if I could see Mrs. DeMarco. One officer took me up to the sixth floor and let me peek into the room. She was sleeping. She took up such a small space in the bed. I stood watching her for a while. Her mouth was open, her breathing so thin you could barely tell she was alive. I couldn't imagine how her heart kept beating. Almost a century old, this tiny woman in the bed. How much sorrow had she seen in her lifetime? How many hard winter nights like this one?

We left the hospital then. I rode in the back of the OPP car, across town to the main station. There I was shown into an interview room and asked to tell my story again. When I was done they asked me, again very politely, if I wouldn't mind sticking around a little while longer, as there was somebody important on his way down to see me. I had no idea who they were talking about.

They let me lie down on a couch while I waited. I looked at the white tiles on the ceiling for a while, then I closed my eyes. I saw the body on the floor of the barn. The long wooden handle. I saw the two barrels of the shotgun pointed at me.

A noise woke me. I sat up, my heart pounding, ready for the gun blast all over again. An officer had come into the room and switched on the light.

I laid my head down again. My heart rate slowed back

down to normal. I closed my eyes again. This time I saw Michael Grant holding the shotgun. It had already exploded in his hands. He looked down at what was left of the barrels. As he dropped the gun his hands were on fire. He held flames with each hand and the smoke rose to the ceiling of the old barn. He reached out to touch me with his burning hands.

I woke up then. There was a hand on my shoulder. The face looking down at me was familiar—the white hair, the rugged features.

"Mr. McKnight," he said.

It came to me. It was Staff Sergeant Moreland, Natalie's superior officer from the Hearst Detachment. I sat up and rubbed my eyes.

"What time is it?" I said. I looked out the window.

"It's around eight in the morning."

"Oh man," I said, touching my neck. "I need some more drugs."

"Perhaps we can talk first?"

He sat down at the table. He was moving slowly, and looked almost as worn out as I felt. I got up and joined him.

"Did you drive all the way down from Hearst?" I said.

"Yes, as a matter of fact. I take it you remember me."

"You're Natalie's commanding officer."

"Do you remember what I told you the last time I saw you?"

"You told me to go back to Michigan and to never set foot in Ontario again."

"I think it was more like a suggestion," he said. "But yes, that was the general idea."

"And obviously I didn't."

He rubbed his forehead. "Mr. McKnight, you understand why I said that, don't you? You were involved in the worst homicide case I've seen in thirty-eight years on the Provincial Police force."

"With all due respect, sir. I'm not sure 'involved' is the right word."

"You were there, eh? You were right in the middle of it. Obviously, the whole thing took a toll on Constable Reynaud. When she went on administrative leave, I was hoping she'd be able to put it all behind her. Imagine my surprise when I find out now that she's missing and that her mother has been murdered with an old ice hook."

"An ice hook?"

"Yes. For moving blocks of ice around, when they used to cut them out of the channel. Someone stuck it right through her, McKnight, all the way to the floor. Once again, you're right in the middle of everything."

"Sergeant Moreland, I don't know what happened to Natalie, but—"

He put his hands up to stop me. "If you're involved in some relationship with Officer Reynaud, that's none of my business," he said. "Never mind what I'd say to my own daughter about it, who happens to be around the same age."

I shook my head and looked away.

"But enough of that," he said. "When she's back home safe, then you and I might talk a little more, eh? Right now, I'm sure you'll agree, our first priority has to be finding her."

"Of course."

"Naturally, we're also trying to find the man who tried to kill you. His brother, too. I'm told that's the person you were both looking for when you came up here?"

"Yes, that's right."

"I'd like you to tell me everything that happened," he said. "I know you've already been through this."

"You want to hear it yourself," I said. "I understand."

"Take your time."

I went through it one more time for him, starting with Simon Grant in the hotel and ending with the scene in the barn. He listened carefully to every word. Even though he had a pad of paper and a pen, he never wrote anything down.

"Go back to Marty Grant," he said when I was done. "You say you saw him in Batchawana Bay?"

"Yes, when I went up looking for Natalie and her mother."

"You have no idea why he might have been up there?"

"No, I don't."

"And you have no idea why he might have gone to Natalie's house, assuming he did?"

"No, other than what his brother said about the devil of Blind River."

"The devil of Blind River," he said. He slowly tapped on the pad with his pen.

"I'm thinking that had to be Natalie's father."

"But you never talked to Grace Reynaud about this?"

"I never talked to her about anything," I said. "I never got to meet her."

"At least not alive."

"No," I said. "Not alive."

"We've been in contact with the police in Soo Michigan," he said. "Apparently you know the chief down there, Roy Maven?"

"We go way back, yes."

He came as close to a smile as he was going to. "So I hear. In any case, they're looking for both of the Grant brothers down there. They've spoken to the rest of the family, but they're not getting much cooperation."

"I'm not surprised. They seem like a pretty tight family."

"Apparently, they told Chief Maven that they weren't going to say a word to him. That's exactly how they put it."

"As opposed to telling him that they had no idea where either of the brothers were?"

"Right. It sounds like they know *something,* but they're not talking."

"Have you checked the hospitals? I was talking to the doctor about that gun, the way it exploded. Michael Grant is probably hurting pretty bad right now."

"Naturally," he said. "But we haven't heard anything on that yet. We haven't found your truck yet, either."

"So what's next?"

"I'm going to give you my card," he said, reaching into his pocket. "I'm going to put my home number on the back. If you think of anything else that might be helpful, call me immediately."

"That's it?"

"An officer will take you back to Michigan," he said. "You'll need to call someone to meet you at the bridge."

"You came a long way just to hear my story."

"I needed to see you in person," he said. "You said you were an old cop, right? I'm sure you can understand."

"I suppose I can."

"Natalie Reynaud is one of my own. You know that."

"Yes, Sergeant."

"If anything happens to her . . ."

He didn't say anything else. He didn't have to.

He called an officer to come pick me up. While I was waiting, I gave Vinnie a ring on his cell phone again. He didn't answer. So I called Jackie at the Glasgow.

"Jackie," I said when he picked up. "Is Vinnie there?"

"Alex, you damned fool, what the hell is going on there?"

"I'm coming home, Jackie. I'll explain everything."

"I told you, God damn it. Did I not tell you this would happen?"

"Yes, you did. Let me talk to Vinnie now."

"You don't have the sense God gave a turnip, you know that? I'll be waiting right here, Alex. I'm gonna kick your stupid ass all over this bar."

Good old Jackie, I thought. He knows me too well.

"Jackie, is Vinnie there or not?"

"No, he's not. I haven't seen him since yesterday. Do I need to come get you?"

Wait a minute, I thought. Wait one goddamned minute.

"Alex, are you there?"

"Yeah, sorry. I'm here."

Jackie knows what I'd do to help him out. Him or someone else I cared about. That's why I got the big lecture in his kitchen.

"I'll come pick you up," Jackie said. "Just tell me where."

"No need," I said. "I've got a ride. I'll see you soon."

"The cops are bringing you all the way over to Paradise?"

"Yeah, no problem. I gotta go, Jackie. See ya soon."

I hung up.

"God damn," I said. I went to the window and looked

out. It wasn't snowing. "God damn, it's the same thing all over again."

It all came back, the last time someone had done this to me. Jackie had been in real trouble, and he was about to do something incredibly stupid. He was going to try to take matters into his own hands.

He didn't want me to be a part of it. He pushed me away. He told me he didn't need my help, that I'd just screw everything up, as always. That I should just stay out of his business.

It hurt me when he said that. It was supposed to hurt. He was driving me away, for my own good. Because he knew if I got involved, I'd go all the way down the line with him, maybe even farther. I'd be in just as much danger as he was.

"Did you do the same damned thing, Natalie? Is that why you pushed me away?"

I went back to the pay phone and dialed a different number. A man answered with the name of the motor shop and asked how he could help me.

"I need to speak to Leon Prudell," I said. "Is he there?"

A few seconds later, he was on the phone.

"Leon, it's Alex. I know I've been asking you for a lot of favors lately . . ."

"Name it."

"I'm in Soo Canada right now. I was hoping you could pick me up at the bridge."

"What happened, did your truck break down?"

"It's a long story," I said. "I'll tell you when I see you."

"I'm on my way," he said. "You want me to come right now?"

"You think you could run home first?"

"I guess so. Why?"

This is why I was calling him. Besides the fact he could get up here a lot faster, besides the fact he was my ex-partner—Leon Prudell always had the right tool for the job.

"I'll wait for you on the American side of the bridge," I said. "Bring a gun."

I stood outside the little duty-free shop, a hundred feet from the tollbooth. My head still hurt. My neck still hurt. It was too cold to be standing outside, but what the hell. I wanted to be cold. I wanted the wind to hit me in the face, maybe knock some sense into me.

Natalie needed my help. She pushed me away and I let her. Now she was gone.

I looked out over the edge of the bridge. The St. Marys River was frozen and covered with snow. Beyond that was the lake, where the ice ended and the water began, water so cold it would kill you in a minute. It would pull you down all the way to the bottom, to the hard granite, a thousand feet deep. Nobody would ever see you again.

It's too easy to disappear around here, that's the thing. If it's not the lake, it's the land around it, nearly three thousand miles of jagged shoreline, the trees, the empty places, the great wild north all around you, with an international border running through the middle. In the winter you can walk right across the ice, start the day in one country and end it in another.

I remembered all the people who had vanished up here, intentionally or not. All the people I had known myself, even Jackie for a few horrible hours, until we rode out onto the lake to find him.

Now it was Natalie. The Grant brothers, too. There was a connection. There had to be. Find them and you find Natalie. That's the one thing I kept holding on to.

Find them.

Leon showed up, driving his little red car. He pulled over and I got in.

"My God," he said. "Look at you. I didn't think you could look any worse."

I knew Chief Maven would want to see me first thing. For about half a second, I thought about having Leon take me there. "Go to the Grants' garage," I said. "It's on Spruce."

He didn't move. He kept looking at me.

"Come on, Leon. Let's go."

"You gonna tell me what's going on?"

"Did you bring it?"

"Tell me why you need the gun, Alex. Or I'm not giving it to you."

"Just go," I said. "I'll tell you on the way."

He headed downtown while I went over the whole story again. He stopped me when I got to the part about going over to Natalie's house with Michael Grant.

"You and Grant together?" Leon said. "I thought he was one of the guys who attacked you."

"Call it an uneasy truce," I said. "But it gets worse. Natalie's mother was there, in the barn. Someone had killed her."

"Alex, my God. Do you think Marty Grant did it?"

"I don't know. I can't imagine *anyone* doing this to her. I mean, if you had seen her . . ."

"But somebody did. Go on."

"Michael Grant followed me out to the barn. He had taken an old shotgun from the basement. It had been put away, with Cosmoline in the barrels. This guy knew enough to put shells in it, but that's all he did. So the barrels exploded."

"So if he hadn't been a complete idiot about cleaning the gun—"

"I wouldn't be here right now."

"Where is he now?"

"He drove off in my truck," I said. "Nobody's seen him, or his brother for that matter. The police say the family is refusing to talk about it."

"They're protecting them. It's only natural."

"I think they're probably getting them in even more trouble than they're already in, but they didn't ask me my opinion."

"What about Natalie?"

I shook my head. "No idea. They're looking for her, too. Maybe there's something we can do that the cops can't."

"I'm not sure what you mean," he said. But he didn't press it. He kept driving. When we got to the Grants' garage, the place was deserted. As we slowed down, though, we couldn't help but notice another car parked a hundred yards down the street.

"They're watching," I said.

"Of course."

"Let's try the Woolseys' house. It's over on Twenty-fourth."

"Let me ask you something," he said as he turned around. "What are you planning on doing with the gun?"

I didn't say anything.

"Are you thinking about putting a gun to Mr. Woolsey's head and making him tell you where the Grants are?"

"We have to find her," I said.

"Very bad idea, Alex."

"Leon, he's the only lead we have."

"I'm not giving you the gun."

"Leon . . ."

"You're not thinking right," he said. "You've got to stop and get your head on straight. You're not going to be any help to her if you start acting like an idiot."

I didn't argue. I knew he was right. As usual.

"Let's just go see what's going on over there," he said. "If they're not talking to the police, I'm sure they've got another car watching them."

We got to the south side of town and headed west down Twenty-fourth Avenue. When we got to the Woolseys' house, we saw four cars in the driveway, the same driveway I had plowed myself a million years ago, back when life was a hell of a lot better and the only mystery to solve was why some old man would leave a hat in a hotel hallway. Another obvious surveillance car was parked out on the empty road.

"There he is," Leon said. "It's hard to hide around here."

At that very moment the front door opened and Mr. Woolsey stepped out onto the porch. Looking at him, even from this distance, the whole scene at the funeral came back to me. Woolsey was the man who had thanked me for plowing his driveway, and then led me behind the church. He had offered me a cigarette and walked with me while his two brothers-in-law sneaked around the other side.

He stood there on his porch without a coat on. His arms were folded and he was staring right at us. The door opened again and a woman poked her head out. Woolsey turned and said something to her. She closed the door.

"It looks like they've got the whole family over here in one house," I said. "They're sticking together."

"Yeah, probably the whole family, Alex. The kids, everybody."

"I hear you," I said. "What if we got Woolsey to come out to the street?"

"Our friend over there in the unmarked vehicle will be watching."

"Let him watch."

"No, Alex. It's not the right play."

"Leon, I have to do something."

"Okay," he said. "Just think. How else could we approach this? You say the whole family is probably in there. Who are we talking about?"

"Everybody," I said. "Michael's wife, Marty's wife, the kids. Woolsey and his wife. And Chris, I assume."

"You assume. He's a college kid, isn't he?"

"Yes," I said. "I suppose he could be over in his apartment."

"All by himself. Without a bunch of other people around."

"He's got a roommate. I met him when I was trying to find Chris to ask him some questions, back before I even knew he was Simon Grant's grandson."

"You remember where his apartment is?"

I looked at him. He was way ahead of me, as usual. "Go to Easterday," I said.

As he pulled out onto the road, we passed the unmarked vehicle that had been staked out there. The driver did a professional job of not looking at us as we passed.

When we got across town, I directed Leon to the apartment building. We were on campus now, so there were many vehicles parked all up and down the street. It was hard to tell if one of them had a police officer sitting in it.

We got out of the car. Leon followed me as I went to the same door I had knocked on once before. Street level, facing the road. The roommate answered, just like the last time. He still looked about fourteen. He was still working on the goatee and not getting anywhere. He still had his long hair tied up on top of his head with a rubber band.

"Is Chris here?" I said.

"Nope."

"Think he'll be back soon?"

"No, don't think so."

"Do you remember me?" I said. "I was here once before."

"I remember," he said. "You left a card."

"This is my partner, Leon."

The kid nodded to him.

"I've got something important to ask you," I said. "Do you have any idea where Chris is right now?"

I watched his eyes. Basic cop training.

"No, I don't," he said. He blinked and looked over my shoulder toward the street.

"He's not at his parents' house?"

"I don't know, man. Really."

He sneaked a glance at the door, like he'd very much like to close it.

"I never caught your name," I said.

"It's Russ."

"Can we come in and talk to you?"

"I told you. I've got no idea where Chris went."

"Just for a minute," I said. "Please? It's important."

He didn't look too happy about it, but he stepped back and let us in. The place wasn't too surprising as a college apartment. The furniture had been handed down a few too many times, and the brown carpet was probably a couple of years overdue for replacing. There were posters on the wall with rock groups I had never heard of.

"You like the Wallflowers?" Leon said to him.

"That's Chris's poster," he said.

"I saw his dad play once," Leon said. I had no idea what he was talking about, but I figured he was trying to strike up some kind of rapport with the kid.

"Was that before or after the Civil War?"

Leon smiled at that. So much for the rapport. "I think Bob Dylan was post–Civil War."

"Look, I'm sorry, I just don't know what you guys want from me."

"Please sit down," I said. "I'll tell you why we're here."

He sat down on one of the chairs. Leon and I took the couch. It gave a little bit more than I expected. I grabbed Leon's shoulder to keep myself from sinking.

"I know you live with Chris," I said. "Are you his friend, too?"

"We get along okay. He's a pain in the ass sometimes."

"But you're his friend."

"Sure."

"If you knew he was in trouble, would you help him if you could?"

"Of course."

"Well, he's in trouble right now. We just have to find him before he gets in any deeper."

"I told you guys—"

"We're not the police," I said. "We're not going to arrest him. If we find him, all we'll do is bring him back safe."

"Chris took the car and left, okay? He didn't tell me where he was going. I swear to God, he didn't say."

The kid was looking me right in the eye. It sounded like he was telling the truth—and maybe pushing that particular truth a little too strongly.

"Chris didn't say where he was going," I said. "But you know."

He looked away.

"Come on, guys," he said.

"Russ, we don't want Chris to go to jail," Leon said. "We don't want you to go to jail, either."

"What are you talking about?"

Leon stood up. "I'm talking about aiding and abetting, Russ. I'm talking about complicit knowledge of Chris's whereabouts when every police officer on both sides of the border is looking for him and his two uncles."

Leon went over to the kid and looked down at him.

"Do you know Michael Grant or Marty Grant?"

"No, man." He was starting to get a little rattled.

"You've never met either one of them?"

"I think you should leave now," he said.

"I'm not going anywhere," Leon said. "If you don't know either of these men, why are you willing to go to jail for them?"

"You're crazy."

"Chris I can understand," Leon said. He got even closer to the kid. "Chris is their nephew. He *has* to do something stupid to try to protect them."

"But you don't," I said. I figured it was about my turn. I stayed on the couch and kept my voice even. I smiled at the kid. "Why would you mess up your whole life for two guys you've never even met?"

"I'm not," he said. "I've got nothing to do with this. I told you."

"You know where he is," Leon said. "I can tell you're lying. If I can tell, imagine what's gonna happen when the police take you in?"

The kid looked at Leon for one second, then back at me. Perfect. I'm your man, Russ. Talk to me.

"Why would the police take me in?" he said.

"I'm surprised they haven't already," Leon said. "You're the roommate, for God's sake. They always bring the roommate in."

Easy, I thought. Don't overdo it.

"He's right," I said. "The police will know in a second. I'm telling you, Russ . . ."

Say his name. Make eye contact.

"You gotta let us help," I said. "Come on, Russ. Be smart. Tell us where Chris is so we can help both of you."

"Oh man," he said. He closed his eyes and rubbed his forehead.

Leon took a step back. A little positive reinforcement.

"He told me his uncles were in trouble," Russ said. "Marty disappeared and Michael went looking for him. Then I guess Michael freaked out and shot somebody.

That happened yesterday. Now Marty and Michael are both missing."

"Yes," I said. "Go on."

"Chris was all upset. He was thinking maybe they were hiding out, you know, like they were afraid to come home."

"Yes?"

"He said he wanted to find them, so he could help them. Whatever that meant."

"Yes?"

"He even took my car, in case somebody was watching him."

"Where did he go, Russ?"

The question hung in the air for a long moment. Russ closed his eyes again.

"He didn't say where he was going."

Leon took a step forward again. "But you know where."

"Mackinac Island," he said. "Okay? I think he went to Mackinac Island. His family has a place there."

"You've got to be kidding me," I said. "Mackinac Island? In February?"

"It's a good hiding place," Leon said. "Who'd think of looking there in the dead of winter?"

"You know where this house is on the island?" I said.

"I was there once," Russ said. "Last summer. I don't know the address or anything."

"Just give us the general idea."

He described going up the long hill toward the Grand Hotel, passing the hotel and then going farther up, beyond the string of million-dollar homes overlooking the water. There in the woods were a few older, smaller houses. As best as he could remember, the Grants' place was just past the fork in the road, the third or fourth house on the right.

"We appreciate it," I said. "I promise you, if Chris is there, we'll bring him back."

Russ thanked me, looking a little like a wrung-out dishrag. Then we left.

"The old good cop, bad cop routine," I said as he got back in his car. "Guess it still works."

"It works on smart-ass college kids who don't know any better," Leon said. "You hear that crack about the Civil War?"

I shook my head. "Mackinac Island, huh? What do you think?"

He put the car in gear and pulled away.

"Only one way to find out."

Seventeen

Mackinac Island. That's where we were headed. If it wasn't February, we'd be taking one of the ferries leaving from St. Ignace, and we'd be two people out of the thousands that make the crossing every day. We'd be going there because it's a great place to be on a warm summer day, this island with no cars whatsoever, just bicycles and horse-drawn carriages, with the Victorian houses and Grand Hotel, with the main section of Huron Street where you can buy the world famous fudge in every other store. This was the place my father took me to when I was eight years old, the place I could have dreamed of taking Natalie to for a long weekend, back when I thought we'd still be together past Memorial Day. But in February, Mackinac Island was the last place I'd think of, for the simple reason that the place doesn't really exist at that time of year at all.

"Is anybody gonna be there?" I asked him. "Isn't it deserted now?"

"I think there's a couple hundred people who live there year-round," he said. "They keep a few of the horses around, just watch over things until the season starts again."

"I know they've got some sort of Christmas festival over there, but after that . . ."

"It's pretty dead, yeah. By now, the ferries can't even run anymore."

It was fifty miles to St. Ignace, straight down I-75, an easy trip for a change, with no snow falling. The sun was even trying to come out. When we got down there, we drove over to the little airport and saw a plane leaving just as we pulled in.

"Son of a bitch," I said. "Was that our plane?"

"Might have been. We'll have to ask."

There was only one small building, so it wasn't hard to find the ticket counter. The woman told us they were sending out two more planes today, the first in about an hour.

"With all the snow we've been having," she said, "we've had to cancel a lot of flights this week. We only had one flight yesterday. And there's more snow coming tonight. So we thought we'd better move some people while we can."

We bought our tickets for twenty-five bucks apiece and sat down in the little waiting area. There was a big window where we could watch the runway, and a kiosk full of pamphlets for all the local attractions. I picked up one and looked at it. Something about the Antique Wooden Boat Show. I put it back. Just for the hell of it, I went over to the pay phone and tried Natalie's number again. The phone rang and rang until I hung up.

"I wish I knew where she was," I said to Leon. "She's a cop, for God's sake. It's not like she doesn't know how to get help if she needs it."

"We're doing what we can," he said. "If we find either of the Grants out there, maybe he'll have some answers."

"God, I hope so. I swear, Leon, I can't help imagining the worst."

"Don't think that way," he said. "You'll use up your energy. Just stay in the moment."

Stay in the moment, another Leon-ism. But as usual he was right. The hour passed like slow death, but finally the other plane was ready to leave. A few other people had arrived by then, and we all piled into the little twelve-seater Cessna. The last time I had been in a small plane like that, it had been up in Canada when everything was getting turned inside out. I tried not to think about it. Meeting Natalie had been the only good thing that had come of that whole nightmare.

The little plane took off and banked hard into a stiff wind off the lake. "Another storm coming!" the pilot yelled to us. "Just what we need, right?"

The other passengers looked at each other with good-natured Michigan smiles. I stared out the window and saw a line of trees leading right out onto the lake. I nudged Leon and asked him what they were.

"Those are old Christmas trees," he said. "They use them for trail markers."

"What trail?"

"It's a trail for snowmobiles to get out to the island. I hear guys at the shop talking about it. It's about a five-mile run. Some riders get really nervous being out on the ice that long."

Everyone else in the plane was looking out the windows on the other side now, as a ray of sunlight had broken through the clouds. Below us, the great Mackinac

Bridge was glowing in shades of green and gold. On another day, it would have been a breathtaking sight and I actually would have enjoyed it.

Within a matter of minutes, we were descending. The pilot put the plane down on a runway that looked no longer than a quarter mile, pulling up next to a building even smaller than the one at St. Ignace. A sign read WELCOME TO MACKINAC ISLAND INTERNATIONAL AIRPORT.

I took a peek inside the building. There were more people trying to get off the island today than trying to get on. It looked like some of them would have to wait until the next plane. I scanned every face in the room. With my luck, Marty would be flying off the island on the same damned plane.

"It's been a long time since I've been here," I said to Leon. "And I don't think I've ever been up here on the airstrip. How far away are we from Huron Street?"

"We'll take a taxi," he said. In this case, a taxi was one of the handful of horse-drawn carriages that kept working through the winter. There were two of them waiting by the airport building, and they were both going down to Huron Street. So we hopped aboard one of them with some other passengers and rode into town.

"Where are you gentlemen staying?" the driver asked us. He didn't have to do much. The horses seemed to know exactly where they were going.

"We're just poking around, sir," Leon said.

He looked at us like we weren't quite sane. "The last flight's going back in a couple of hours," he said. "You flew all the way out here, but you're not spending the night?"

"If we end up staying, are there some rooms available anywhere?"

He looked back and forth between us again. "Yeah, I'm sure there are. A few places stay open during the winter. None of them are very big, but things are pretty quiet right now. Just a few snowmobilers around."

"Oh good," I said. "I love snowmobiles."

"But you don't have sleds on the island, do you?"

"Never mind. Just drop us off by the Grand Hotel."

"It's closed, sir."

"I know that. We're just looking for a house up that way."

"Those houses are all closed, too."

"I know," I said. I wanted to take the crop out of his hand and hit him in the head with it. "Just drop us off by the Grand. We'll be fine."

He shook his head and turned around. The two horses kept going, moving slowly down the long hill. The trees on either side of the road were thick with snow, like we were riding down through a long white tunnel. The air was cold and wet, with a fine mist of snow sifting down from the branches. The trip ended up taking longer than the plane ride. When we were finally down on Huron Street, the carriage stopped to let out the other passengers at one of the hotels that stayed open in the winter.

"We'll get off here, too," I said.

"I thought you wanted the Grand Hotel," the driver said.

"We want to look around a little bit first," I said. "Here is fine."

I paid the man. He drove off, still shaking his head.

The street was quiet. It was like some kind of polar

ghost town, with virtually every storefront closed up and sealed over with plastic. Some of them still had Christmas decorations out. It looked like the entire town had been abandoned on December 26. We saw another horse-drawn carriage down the street, this one with a single horse and one rider. Then the whole quiet scene was torn apart by the sudden roar of a motor. Two snowmobiles came around the corner and raced down the empty street.

"What's with that?" I said. "They can bring those right down the street? I thought this was the island with no motorized vehicles."

"All bets are off in wintertime," Leon said.

"Great."

"You're thinking they might be down here somewhere? Instead of up at the house?"

"It was just a thought. They've gotta come down here to eat once in a while, right?"

We took a look in the one grocery store on the eastern end of the street, then walked down past all the closed fudge shops and ice cream parlors, past another small hotel that was open, another that was closed. Finally, at the end of the street we saw a restaurant with the lights on. It looked warm and inviting. It even had a fireplace like Jackie's. I took a good look inside.

"Are you ready to go find the house?" Leon said.

"I'm ready."

We left the restaurant and started up the hill. As long as there weren't any snowmobiles buzzing around, there was an eerie calm as we walked between the great trees and the unlit streetlamps. The Grand Hotel itself, the granddaddy of all hotels, was a huge white and green monolith at the top of the hill. The walk was tougher than it looked.

I had to stop at the top to catch my breath, leaning over with my hands on my knees. Up close the hotel was even more imposing. The world's largest front porch, which held hundreds of rocking chairs during the summer, was now completely empty except for a thin layer of snow.

We walked its length in silence. From our vantage point we could see all the way out onto the frozen surface of Lake Huron and the Mackinac Bridge in the far distance. A cold wind kicked up and spurred us on. Beyond the hotel there was a string of big Victorian houses, sharing the same magnificent view. But each one of them looked closed up for the season and utterly deserted. The snowmobile tracks on the road were the only sign that anyone had been here since the seasons changed.

We followed the upper road, passing one million-dollar house after another until the road went into the trees. From one house to the next, the view of the lake became obstructed, the property value going down by about three quarters. These were the older, smaller houses that hadn't been bought up by the people with money to spend on remodeling. The road forked.

"We go right?" I said. "Is that what he told us?"

"Third or fourth house."

The houses were close to the road, but set back behind trees so thick with snow it felt like we were walking into an ice cave. We couldn't hear the wind anymore. We walked by the first house, then the second, then the third. All three were locked up tight with plastic sheets on the windows. More important, we couldn't see any footprints leading up to them in the snow.

"We're protected from the wind here," I said. "You'd think we'd see some tracks."

"You're right," Leon said. "Look."

As we came to the fourth house, we could see the line of churned-up snow leading to the front door.

"You think that's Chris in there?" Leon said.

"Let's go find out."

"You gonna just walk up and knock on the front door?"

"No, first I'll look in the window. Then I'll knock. Any chance of you giving me that gun now?"

"Here," he said. He took out his Ruger from his coat pocket. It was the same gun he had loaned me once before, after I had thrown my service revolver into the lake. "When this is all done, we're gonna replace your old one. You shouldn't have to use a loaner every time."

"I keep hoping I'll never need one again."

"I'll go around back," he said. He pulled out his gun, too.

"Your wife is really going to kill me," I said. "I promised her I wouldn't get you in trouble again."

"This isn't trouble. This is just a little social call."

I slapped him on the back, then walked through the trees to the house, stepping through the deep snow. When I got to the door, I looked through the little window. I saw furniture covered in white sheets. I tried the doorknob. It was locked.

What the hell, I thought. I knocked on the door. Nothing. I knocked again. I waited. I was beginning to wonder if we'd have to break into the place. Then I remembered Leon's lockpicking skills. Knowing him, he'd have his tools with him. I was about to go around to the back when I heard something from inside. It sounded like the pounding of feet on a wooden floor.

Before I could look in the window again, the front door flew open. Chris Woolsey came running out, just in time for me to stick my foot out. He fell face-first into the snow.

"Help!" he screamed into the cold air. "Somebody help me!"

"Go ahead and yell," I said, grabbing him by the collar. "They might hear you on the bridge."

"Let go of me! Somebody help!"

I put the gun away and gave him a good smack across the face. That seemed to settle him down a little bit. Leon came out the door, sliding in the snow.

"Anyone else in there?" I asked him.

"No," Leon said. "Not as far as I can tell."

"What's the deal?" I asked Chris. "Are you alone?"

"Go fuck yourself."

I smacked him again. "I'm starting to enjoy this, Chris. You better talk to me."

"I'm alone," he said. "There's nobody else here."

"Okay," I said. "Let's go inside and talk."

I pushed him back through the door and onto one of the covered chairs. "First question," I said, leaning over him. "Do you know where Natalie is?"

"Natalie who?"

I had to try hard not to hit him again. "Natalie Reynaud. The woman who was at the hotel with me."

"I haven't seen her since that night. I swear."

"Okay, next question. Your Uncle Marty—"

"He's not here."

"I can see that," I said. "Is that why you came out here? Were you looking for him?"

He didn't say anything. He looked out the door like he wanted to make a break for it again.

"We know this is your family's house," I said. "That's why you came here, right?"

"How do you know this is our house?"

"Your roommate told us."

"Oh, man. That piece of shit."

"He was trying to help you out," I said. "Both of your uncles are in serious trouble. You thought if either of them were gonna hide out somewhere, this would be the place. Am I right?"

"Yeah," he said. He wiped his nose on his sleeve. "Uncle Marty disappeared two nights ago, and Uncle Michael disappeared yesterday, after he . . ."

Chris looked at the bandage on my neck.

"Fuck," he said. "After he tried to kill you, I guess."

"But you haven't seen either one of them here?"

"No. Not really. I mean, I think Marty *was* here."

"How can you tell?"

"*Somebody* was here. There was some food on the table, and one of the beds was slept in."

Leon came into the room, holding an ashtray. "Are these yours?" he said to Chris.

"No, I don't smoke."

"Let me guess," I said. "Camel unfiltereds."

"You got it," Leon said.

"That's my Uncle Marty's brand," Chris said. "He must have come here, but he wasn't around when I got here yesterday. I've been waiting, hoping he'll come back."

"The rest of your family is all camping out at your parents' house," I said. "Do they know you're here?"

"Hell, I don't know. I left a message on the machine,

told them I was going out looking. They could probably figure it out if they wanted to."

"You seem to have a real communication problem in your family," I said. "Like when you told them I was the guy who made your grandfather come to the hotel that night."

He looked down at the floor.

"Now would be a good time to tell me everything you know," I said.

He shook his head.

"I don't give a shit about your uncles right now," I said, "but Natalie is missing, too. I'm trying to find her. I swear to God, Chris, I will beat you right here and right now until your eyes bleed."

"Okay," he said. He wiped his nose on his sleeve again. He kept looking at the floor. "Okay, man. It all goes back to my grandfather, and some stuff he told me just before he . . . I mean, when he was still around. I'd go over there a lot, just to see how he was doing, sit with him for a while. Especially lately, since I'd been working at the hotel, which was right around the corner from him. That one night I went to see him, that was the first night where we were starting to get all that snow. I was talking to him about it, and I just happened to mention that I had carried some bags for a woman at the hotel, who had just driven all the way down from this town in Canada called Blind River. I asked her that in the elevator. I said, I hope you didn't have to drive much in this weather, and she said, excuse me, I know how to drive in the snow and I came all the way down from Blind River."

"That was the night before I got there," I said.

"Yeah, I guess so. Anyway, I tell this to my grandfather because we were talking about the snow, and he says, Blind River, that's where the devil lived. And I'm like, what are you talking about, Grandpa? I thought he was joking, but he got real serious and he said, I'm not making a joke, Chris. As far as I'm concerned, Blind River's where the devil lived. Then he asked me what this woman's name was. I said, I've got no idea. And he said, well if you get a chance, find out. I'd be interested to know."

"Let me guess," I said. "You looked her name up on the room registration."

"No, it wasn't like that. I didn't go snooping around. I just asked Gail at the front desk. I said, hey, who's that lady from Canada? I think I might know her. And Gail told me her name."

"Okay, go on."

"So I stopped in to see my grandfather on the way to work that morning, because my mother had made him something to eat. I told him, that woman's name is Natalie Reynaud. My grandfather says, Chris, please tell me if you're making a joke now. Is that woman's name really Natalie Reynaud? I said, yeah, do you know the name? He said, I know the last name all right. That's the devil's name."

"Did he say anything more about the devil? Like what this person did to earn that title?"

"No, I asked him about that, but he wouldn't tell me. He said he wasn't going to pass it down to me, whatever that meant."

"Did he happen to say anything about killing the devil?"

"No, what do you mean?"

"Never mind," I said. "Just go on."

"He did say that the devil was dead now. Then he went into the bottom of the closet and dug out this old hat. He said, see this? This is the devil's hat right here."

"He didn't say how he got it?"

"No, he didn't."

"Okay," I said. "Keep going."

"So later, when I'm at work, he shows up all dressed up in his suit. I'm totally freaking out, because there's no way he should be out walking around on his own like that, especially in bad weather. There's a guy, even, who's supposed to be keeping on eye on him over in the apartments. I asked him where Tony was and how come he was out. He said don't worry, he just wanted to see the old hotel because all he does anymore is sit around in his apartment. So here he is sitting in the lobby, saying hello to everyone. He was happier than I'd ever seen him, you know? I figured, why not? This was good for him. I'd let him stick around and then I'd take him back home later. I had no idea he was gonna go out wandering in the snow. I swear to God."

"Why didn't you stop him? Didn't you see him leave?"

"No, I didn't."

"You were the doorman. How can you not see him leave?"

"I wasn't down by the door."

"Was it a maid or a waitress in the restaurant?"

He mumbled something.

"What did you say?"

"I said it was a waitress."

"Okay, so what happens next? You know your whole family is gonna kill you, so you look for somebody else to pin it on."

He started to say something, but stopped.

"At least you're not denying it," I said. "I'll give you that. Is there anything you want to tell us? About your grandfather or your uncles? Or anything?"

"No," he said. "That's all I know."

"Come on, then. We're going."

"I can't," he said. "I've got to wait here, in case Marty comes back."

"Does he have a snowmobile?"

"No."

"Well, the last flight is coming in soon. We'll go see if he's on it. If he's not, then he's not coming back here today at all."

Chris didn't look too happy about that, but he didn't say a word. He followed us out the door and down the road, past the Grand Hotel and down the hill toward town. The clouds were coming in thick and filling every corner of the sky, casting everything in a strange, muted light. We caught another horse-drawn carriage on Huron Street. This time there were no other passengers. We went back up to the airport, passing through the long white tunnel of trees, the air feeling colder by the minute. Chris was hunched over in his seat like a kid on his way to the principal's office. We got there just in time to see the plane landing. I watched each passenger getting off—a young couple who stepped off looking up at the sky like maybe this whole trip had been a mistake. An older man behind them. Another man, young and big, about Marty's size—my heart raced for one second until I saw it wasn't him. There were no Grants getting off this plane.

We got on with a few other people, all of us getting off the island on the last flight before the snow came. We touched down in St. Ignace, got into Leon's car with Chris folded up in the tiny backseat. He wrapped his coat tight around his body.

"Are you taking me home?" he finally said.

"I thought you might want to tell your story to the police," I said.

"That actually sounds better than telling it to my parents right now."

"Okay, then. Just sit tight for a while."

"I lost him once before," he said.

"Excuse me?"

"I lost my grandfather on the island, a couple of summers ago. I was supposed to be watching him and he wandered down the hill. They found him on one of the ferries."

"Yeah, so?"

"So my father just about killed me. I mean, he really beat the hell out of me."

"You're in college, Chris. Learn how to take care of yourself. Or go to the police."

"I know, I'm just saying . . . I shouldn't have lied about it this time."

"You're right," I said. It was another lie to think about as we drove the fifty miles back to Sault Ste. Marie. The snow hadn't started yet. It felt like it was waiting to gather its full strength before hitting us again. All the while I kept looking out the window at the endless line of snowbanks as they whizzed by us. A long trail of white leading nowhere, with no answers at the end. The sun went down, and with it most of my hopes. It would be the second night with no way to find her.

We rolled into the Soo and headed straight across town

to the City County Building. Leon parked in the back lot. Chris pried himself out of the backseat and stood rubbing his legs. I put a hand on his back and pointed him toward the door. He walked in with us and stood there with his arms folded while I told the receptionist we needed to see Chief Maven right away. That's when it all went to hell fast. Maven came out of his office and down the hall, moving like a lineman rushing a quarterback. Behind him was one of his officers.

"McKnight!" he said. "Where the hell have you been?"

"I'm sure you remember Chris Woolsey," I said. "He has a few things to tell you."

"Of course I remember," he said as he turned to Chris, his voice losing about half of its venom. "Please go with Officer Donovan. He'll talk to you."

Chris gave us one last look and went with the officer. Maven watched him leave. When he was gone, Maven turned and stepped in about six inches from my face.

"There was a state trooper over at the Woolseys' house," he said. "He says you two clowns showed up there today. What the hell were you doing?"

"You know what I was doing."

Maven stepped away from me. He took his chief's hat off, ran his fingers through what was left of his hair, looked at Leon for a moment, then at me. "I'm not going to say anything else, McKnight. I give up. You and your chauffeur need to go see Sergeant Moreland right away."

"Why?" I said. I felt a sick chill in my stomach. Please, don't let it be Natalie. "What happened, Chief?"

"They found your truck," he said, "with Michael Grant inside."

The way he said it, I didn't even have to ask. But Maven answered anyway.

"He buried the truck in a snowbank," he said. "Then he bled to death."

Eighteen

We crossed the bridge and found the police station. Staff Sergeant Moreland was standing at the door with his head outside, looking up at the snow. When he saw us coming, he held the door open without saying a word. He pointed down the hallway.

"In here," he said, directing us to an interview room. The bright fluorescent lights hurt my eyes. "I was just watching the snow come down. It's hard to believe there's any left up there."

I wasn't sure if he was just trying to put us at ease with the small talk. He let Leon sit down next to me. Right away that told me something. If he wanted to put us through the ringer, he'd do us each separately.

"You would be Mr. Leon Prudell," Moreland said, extending his hand. "Chief Maven tells me you were Alex's old partner, back when he was a private eye."

"Very briefly, sir."

"I saw Alex just this morning," he said. "I didn't imagine I'd have the pleasure again so soon."

"We'll do whatever we can to help," Leon said.

"That's good to hear. As you know by now, we found Michael Grant. He ran off the road into a ditch. It didn't take long for the snow to cover him. When the plow came by, it buried him completely. Somebody else ran off the road in the same spot this evening, bumped right into him. If that hadn't happened, God knows when we would have found him."

"Where was he found?" I said. I couldn't help thinking about the whole family gathered at the Woolseys' house.

"Just west of Iron Bridge."

"He didn't make it very far then."

"I'm surprised he could drive at all," Moreland said. "He basically had no left hand anymore. He had tried to wrap it up with an old rag."

I could picture that rag in my mind. It was tucked into a pocket on the driver's side door. Last time I used it was to check my oil.

"There were deep lacerations in his face and shoulders, too," Moreland said. "He must have been losing a lot of blood, even with the low temperature."

"Sounds like he never had a chance," Leon said. "That shotgun ripped him apart."

"We recovered your cell phone as well," Moreland said. "It looks like he tried to call for help. There's no record of the call ever going through."

I wasn't sure what to think at that point. It was a horrible way to die, bleeding to death, trapped in the snow. But if the gun hadn't exploded, I would have been dead myself.

"That leaves Marty Grant," Moreland said. "And Natalie, of course." He closed his eyes for a moment. "In any case, Chief Maven tells me you two were busy today. You traced the nephew out to Mackinac Island?"

"Yes," I said. "It looks like Marty was there. But not anymore."

"I'm sure the Michigan guys will keep looking."

"What about you guys? Have you found any leads here?"

He looked up at me. It seemed like he was more weary than annoyed. "We can't find any trace of her," he said. "All we can find are trucks and dead bodies."

"I know this isn't the most important thing in the world right now," I said, "but when do I get the truck back?"

"We've already been through it. I don't see why you can't take it with you now."

"Are you serious? In Michigan I probably wouldn't see it for a month."

"It's around back," he said. "I'll take you to it."

"I appreciate that."

There wasn't much more to say, so he showed us out. Leon waited for me in the parking lot while I went around to the back lot with Moreland. He unlocked the gate and led me to my truck. It was parked beneath a flood lamp mounted high on a wooden pole, the snow flying heavy now in the cone of orange light. My truck looked amazingly unharmed by its ordeal, aside from a dent in the snowplow.

"We cleaned it up a little inside," Moreland said, "after we took some samples. But you might want to take it someplace for a better job."

Only in Canada, I thought. They actually cleaned it up for me.

He gave me the keys. I opened the driver's side door.

My cell phone was sitting on the dashboard. The seat was still damp, and the heavy metallic scent of blood hung in the air.

"Did you guys happen to find a hat in here?" I said.

"That old hat you told me about? I think Grant had it on his head when they found him. I'm sure it's in the lab right now."

"That's fine. It's not important."

"You still have my card?" he said. "You'll call me if you get any more ideas? Maybe *before* you go chasing them this time?"

"I'll try," I said. "But I don't think I can promise you."

I wasn't sure if he accepted that, but he let me go. I started it up and pulled around to the front, next to Leon's car, and rolled down my window. As Leon leaned out, I could see his breath in the cold night air.

"Thank you," I told him. "Again. I really owe you."

"It's nothing, Alex."

"Go home to your wife," I said. "Tell her I'm sorry."

"We'll be fine," he said. "Call me tomorrow."

I watched him pull out of the lot and head for home. I didn't move. I sat there as the snow collected on my windshield. It was getting late, I was tired, and if I had had any sense at all, I would have gone right home and gone to bed.

I couldn't. I had to do something.

I could go out to Natalie's house, I thought. Drive all the way out there in the snow to look through her empty house again. Looking for what? I had no idea. The house and the barn would be closed up now, anyway, both places taped up as official crime scenes.

There's nothing you can do, Alex. There's nowhere else you can go.

I finally pulled out of the lot and started driving. I found a gas station and pulled in to fill up the tank. The snow kept falling. I watched the liters click by, five quarts apiece. I went in and paid the man. He looked at my bruised and taped-up face, asked me if the hospital knew I had escaped. I told him he was wasting his comedic talent working at a gas station.

The hospital, I thought as I got back in the truck. I could go see how Mrs. DeMarco is doing. That would be one small thing, at least, instead of driving straight home. The General Hospital wasn't far away, so I figured what the hell. Even though it was late, I could at least ask about her.

I drove over and parked in the emergency room lot, went inside, found an elevator, rode it up to the sixth floor. I walked up to the nurse's station.

"Sir, can I help you? If you're a visitor, you really need to come back tomorrow."

"I'm just wondering about Mrs. DeMarco," I said. "Is she still on this floor?"

"I recognize you now," she said. "You're the one who brought her in."

"Yes, ma'am. How is she doing?"

"Not too bad, considering. Celia will be sorry she missed you. That's Mrs. DeMarco's day nurse. She was here a little earlier, dropping off some things."

"Well, I was just driving by, anyway. I don't want to disturb her."

"Why don't you go peek in her room? She was awake a little while ago."

"Maybe I'll do that," I said. "Although it's a little hard to have a conversation with her. I think she's pretty much just living in the past now."

"That's actually a very common symptom of dementia," she said. "As the memory breaks down, you get stuck in one particular time of your life. Sometimes it's a good time. Sometimes not so good."

I thought about that for a second. I imagined myself as an old man, living one traumatic day of my life over and over.

"She was talking about a funeral," I said. "In fact, she was getting dressed for it."

The nurse shook her head. "The one thing you really can't do is try to talk her out of it, if you know what I mean. You can't try to convince her she's being delusional. The best you can do is just reassure her that everything's going to be okay."

"I understand," I said. "Thank you."

I went down the hall to her room and knocked softly on the door. I didn't hear anything, so I pushed the door open and looked inside. Mrs. DeMarco was in her bed, the back tilted up so she could see out the window.

"Mrs. DeMarco?"

Her eyes were open. She didn't say anything. For a moment I thought she was dead.

"Mrs. DeMarco?"

She turned her head slightly. "It's you again."

"Yes," I said. "How are you feeling?"

"Where am I?"

"You're in the hospital, ma'am."

"Did I faint?"

"No, not really. You just had a bad day. The power went out."

She nodded her head and looked back out the window. "It's been a bad winter."

I thought about what the nurse had said. "Mrs. De-Marco," I said, "what year is it?"

"It just turned 1930, dear."

"I'm sorry," I said. "That was a silly question."

"No, I get the same way," she said. "The years go by so fast."

I wasn't sure what else to say. I stood up and went to the window. I watched the snow falling. I thought about Natalie, wondered again for the thousandth time where she was at that moment.

Wait a minute. She said 1930.

"Mrs. DeMarco," I said, turning back to her, "when you were talking about New Year's Eve before . . ."

Her eyes were closed.

I stood there for a while. Just as I was about to leave she moved again.

"Where's Albert?" she said. She picked her head up, like she was about to try to get out of the bed.

"Your son?"

"Where is he?"

She thinks he's a little kid, I thought. This man who had already lived his entire life, this man who had done horrible things to Natalie and God knows who else. He was dead now, and the world was undoubtedly a better place without him. But what could I say to her?

"He's just fine," I said. "Don't worry about Albert."

"Are you sure?"

"Yes, I'm sure."

She seemed to accept that. She laid her head back down.

"Mrs. DeMarco," I said, "do you feel like talking about what happened on New Year's Eve?"

"I told them not to go," she said. "I told them."

"Who did you tell?"

"Warren and Luc. I had a bad feeling about it. You should be with your family on New Year's Eve."

It was the same thing she had told us before, the first time I had met her. We'd thought she was talking about the night Natalie's father was murdered. But that would happen a good forty years later.

"Who are Warren and Luc?" I said.

"My husband, Warren," she said. "And Luc Reynaud."

Luc Reynaud. That would have to be Natalie's grand-father.

"Mrs. DeMarco, do you know anyone named Grant?" It was a shot in the dark, but why not?

"Yes. They were there, too."

"Where is this, ma'am?"

"Out on the ice," she said. "The ice run."

"The ice run?"

"I told Warren and Luc not to go. They didn't listen to me."

For the first time, I was seeing some connection between the Grants and the Reynauds, but it didn't go back to a murder in Sault Ste. Marie three decades ago. It went back a lot further.

"They never listened to me," she said, as she started to shake. I took her hand. It felt like the most fragile thing I had ever held.

"It's okay," I said. "It's okay."

She took a long ragged breath and then laid her head back on her pillow. I tucked her blanket around her neck.

"I'll let you rest," I said. "I'll come back and see you again soon."

She didn't say anything else. She closed her eyes and was still.

When I went back out, I confessed to the nurse that I might have put some stress on Mrs. DeMarco with my questions.

"I'm sure she'll be fine," the nurse said. "She's an amazing woman. If you think about it, she's seen most of the twentieth century. You should see some of these pictures."

"Which pictures?"

"In here," she said, pointing to a cardboard box behind her. "Celia brought this over. She wasn't sure what was going to happen now, if Mrs. DeMarco would even be going home or if she'd ever work for her again. She didn't want all this to get lost, you know, if somebody comes in to clean out the house."

"Would you mind if I took a quick look?"

"I don't see why you couldn't," she said. "Here." She picked up the box and put it on top of the desk.

The contents weren't organized in any way. The photographs were jumbled together among the old newspaper clippings, sports ribbons, report cards, Mrs. DeMarco's marriage license from 1923—the whole mess a tattered paper trail from a long, long life. Just looking through it made me feel sad. This was all she had left. She didn't even have most of her memories anymore. They were cut off at 1930. A lot of this stuff in the box she wouldn't even recognize now.

I found some of the color photographs. They were the same kind of washed-out old Polaroids, like the one Natalie had of the three men. A young girl was blowing out birthday candles. I looked at it for a few seconds before I realized the young girl was Natalie, maybe twelve years old. It hit me in the gut like a sucker punch. I recognized her mother in the picture, and her stepfather, Albert DeMarco. A younger Mrs. DeMarco stood behind them, next to a woman who must have been Natalie's grandmother.

"Are you okay?" the nurse said.

"Yes," I said. "I'm sorry. It's just . . ." I shook my head. At that moment I would have given everything I owned just to see Natalie one more time, and to know that she was safe.

"I should get out of your way," I said. I flipped through a couple more pictures, the colors getting brighter and clearer as the subjects got older. The last one I looked at was a picture of Mrs. DeMarco standing next to a man. It took me a moment to realize it was her son, Albert. That sick feeling hit me in the stomach again, the same thing I'd felt every time I had seen this man's face. Someone had made them pose together in front of a fireplace, Albert wearing a grim, impatient smile.

I put the picture back in the box. Then I picked it up again. I looked at the two faces again. Mrs. DeMarco looked old, but there was a fullness and a color in her face. I was guessing this picture was taken maybe ten years ago. So Albert DeMarco had to be about sixty years old here. A rich and successful man, looking bloated with food and success and an easy life. And that "hurry up and get this over with" smile.

I stood there and looked at the picture for a long time.

Something about it bothered me. I couldn't figure out what it was.

"I hope you'll come back and visit her," the nurse said. "I don't imagine she'll be getting too many visitors."

"I'll do that," I said. I kept staring at it. God damn it, I thought, there's something about that face . . .

"It's such a shame," she said. "She should live in Nevada. God knows he could afford to move her there."

I looked up at her. "Excuse me?"

"I'm just saying, it's a shame."

"You said he could afford to move her there. Who are you talking about?"

"Her son," she said. "Mr. Moneybags."

"Albert DeMarco?"

"That's the one."

"I thought he was dead."

"That would be news to Celia. He's the man sending her the checks every month from Nevada."

I looked at the picture again. In one sickening moment it all came together.

I knew this face looked familiar. I had seen it somewhere, not long ago.

When I was standing there at the airport, looking carefully at each person to see if one of the Grants was getting off that plane . . . The young couple first, looking up at the sky. Then the older man behind them, with that same look of impatience, the exact same face as in the picture I was holding in my hands.

I thanked the nurse and ran. She must have thought I was crazy, but I didn't care. I ran down the hospital corridor, pressed the elevator button, waited for all of two seconds and then hit the stairs. I went down the six floors and then out into the night. I got into my truck and picked up my cell phone.

The snow was coming down hard now. There was already a thick coat of it on my windshield. I waited to see if the phone would pick up a signal. When it did, I dialed a number. Then I stopped. I hit the button before the call could connect.

No, I thought. I can't call Leon again. He just got home. He's explaining everything to his wife. Now I'm gonna call and ask him to come out again in the middle of the night? I can't do that.

There's only one other person I can call. Maybe a better choice anyway. Leon's a good friend, a good ex-partner, but there's one other person in this world who's gone down the line with me even farther.

I dialed the number. He answered on the second ring.

"Vinnie," I said. "I need help."

"Tell me what you want me to do."

"I need a snowmobile."

"You hate snowmobiles."

"Not tonight. Does your cousin Buck still have one?"

"He's got two."

"He's got a trailer?"

"Yes. Where am I going?"

"St. Ignace, by the point," I said.

"Where the trail leads out onto the lake?"

"Yes, that's the place. Vinnie, I know it's a tough night to come out, but it's important."

"I'll be there," he said. Then he hung up.

I cleared off the windshield, pulled out of the lot, and drove into the falling snow.

He's alive, I thought. God damn it, he's alive.

It didn't make any sense to me. Natalie wouldn't have lied about that. She wouldn't have lied about anything. But her mother . . .

That's it. Of course. Somehow her mother made her believe he was dead. Another lie, like Natalie's dead dog, like the story she told those men in the bar about Natalie dying from food poisoning. This lie was the worst of all. But why?

I gunned the accelerator, pushing the truck as fast as it could go on the icy road.

The hell with it, I thought. I can figure it out later. Right now I have to get out there. Not only is Albert DeMarco very much alive, he's out on Mackinac Island right now.

And if I had to guess, I'd say that probably means one thing . . .

Natalie's out there, too.

Nineteen

It was pushing midnight when I finally hit St. Ignace. I wasn't sure where the hell I was going, but I knew there had to be a parking lot somewhere on the shoreline. I worked my way south, staying close to Lake Huron until I finally found the parking lot they used for the ferries in the summer. Now there were about a dozen vehicles in the lot, all covered with snow. There was no sign of Vinnie, or anyone else for that matter. It was the loneliest place on earth, because who'd be stupid enough to go out on the lake on a night like this?

I stopped the truck and kept the engine running. I put my head against the steering wheel and felt everything start to spin around me.

Just close your eyes for a little while, I thought. Save your strength.

A sudden knock on my window woke me up. Vinnie looked in at me. I checked my watch. It was twelve-thirty.

When I opened the door, I saw that he was wearing a snowmobile suit. Behind his idling truck was a double trailer. I got out and watched him back both machines down the ramp.

"Vinnie," I said when he was done, "you brought two sleds."

"That's right," he said. "You think I'm gonna let you go alone?"

"I appreciate it, but listen—"

"We're losing time, Alex. Don't fight me. Just get your suit on."

"I don't need a suit."

"See, you need me already. If you don't put this suit on, you'll be a Popsicle by the time we get across."

I took the suit from him and slipped it on. It was big enough for two of me. "Whose is this?" I said.

"It's Buck's. It's big on him, too. Here's your helmet."

He handed me a snowmobile helmet with a visor. When I put it on, I was sure I looked exactly like an astronaut.

"Alex, are you gonna tell me why we're doing this?"

"At least one of the Grant brothers was out there to-day," I said. I pointed to the east. Somewhere out there the island lay embedded in ice and covered by the dark-ness. "Now Natalie's stepfather is there. The man who was supposed to be dead. I think Natalie's probably out there, too."

"Good enough for me. Let's go."

"One second," I said. I went back into the truck, un-locked the glove compartment, and pulled out Leon's Ruger. He had left it with me when we went up to see Sergeant Moreland. I had lied about it both times I crossed the border. Now I was glad I had held on to it.

"I don't have a gun," he said.

"I hope you won't need one."

"You know exactly where we're going?"

"I just follow the trees to get out there, right?"

"Yes. I mean once we get to the island . . ."

"The Grants' house," I said. "That's the only place I know."

"Okay, then," he said. "Lead the way."

"Whatever happens, I owe you big."

He gave me one nod of his head, then flipped down his visor and got on his machine. I did the same. It was already idling with a low growl, making me feel like I was sitting on some kind of wild animal.

Lights, I thought. Where the hell are the lights? I fumbled around with the buttons for a few seconds until Vinnie reached over and hit the switch on the left handle. The lights were shining on the back of his trailer until I finally gave it some gas and pulled away, heading toward the end of the lot. The headlights reached out into the night now, finding only snow on the ground, then snow in the air, and beyond that nothing but darkness.

I drove off the end of the lot, quickly losing any sense of perspective. It was just a vast slope of snow, leading down and down until it was flat. I had no idea if I was on land or water. I wasn't seeing any markers, either. I kept pushing the damned thing forward, trying to spot something in front of me. Anything. I kept bogging down in the deep snow, until I finally figured out that speed was my friend. I twisted the throttle back and stayed up on top of the snow, even though I had no idea where I was going.

I saw an arc of light to my left. Vinnie was breaking off and heading on a different course, so I swung over that way and finally picked up the line of trees. I fell in behind him, content to let him lead the way for a while. One tree flashed by, then another, then another. Vinnie was kicking up a great white cloud behind him. It was starting to stick to my visor. I tried to wipe it off with my left hand, which sent a bolt of pain through my neck.

The next thing I saw was a tangle of bare branches and then everything was turned upside down.

When I opened the visor, I was looking straight up at the falling snow. My neck hurt like all hell, but aside from that I seemed to be fine. The snow had acted like a big pillow. I heard Vinnie circling around. He pulled up next to me and helped me to my feet. I looked over and saw the tree lying sideways. It was just as Leon had told me, an old Christmas tree that somebody had stuck in the snow. In the glare of Vinnie's headlights I could still see some tinsel hanging on the branches.

"You okay?" he said.

"I never hit a tree in the middle of a lake before," I said. I rubbed my neck as I got back on the snowmobile. Then we were off again.

The snow seemed to get even deeper as we worked our way toward the island. I could feel the treads fighting hard to move through it. The wind rushed by. Five miles, I thought. It's only five miles.

The ride seemed to last forever. The snow kept falling, as though it would never stop. If the trees hadn't been there to guide us, I would have sworn that we were lost, riding around in great looping figure eights all over the frozen surface of Lake Huron.

Finally, a great mass started to take shape ahead of us, darker than the night itself. It grew larger and larger, until we could make out buildings and the faint glow of streetlights.

We rounded a corner by the big wall of boulders that formed a breakwater during the summer months. We rode right up past the docks where the big ferries let off the passengers, on the east end of Huron Street. At least we were right in town this time and didn't have to ride all the way down from the airport.

We hit a big bump as we rode up onto the street level. There was probably some official snowmobile ramp somewhere else, but that was the least of our problems. I headed down the middle of Huron Street, Vinnie right behind me. The street was empty. It looked even lonelier than the last time I had been there.

One hotel in the center of town seemed to be open for business. Every other building was dark, until we got to the restaurant at the end of the street. I pulled over and came to a stop in front of it. Vinnie pulled up beside me. There were a dozen other snowmobiles parked along the street here. It was obviously the only place to be on a February night on Mackinac Island.

I got off the sled and stretched for a moment. I was stiff and cold, even with the space suit on.

"Is this where we're going?" Vinnie said. He took off his helmet and shook out his long hair. The snow clung to his suit, making him look like a walking snowman.

"No, it's up the hill," I said, pointing to the road that led up to the Grand Hotel. The huge building looked even more foreboding at night. "I just wanted to stop for a second, so we can figure this out."

"What's the plan?"

"I'm not sure if we should take the machines all the way up," I said. "The noise will give us away."

"There's a few other snowmobiles here. We won't be the only people buzzing around."

"You may be right," I said. "Although the house is way up there, just past the Grand Hotel. Everything's locked up tight."

"If it's on the main road, I'm sure the riders go up there. Even at night. You know how it is."

"You're right," I said, remembering all the times I had lain awake at night, swearing at the snowmobiles tearing down the trail behind my cabin. "It would be a long hard walk in this snow, too."

"You need something before we go up?" he said, nodding toward the front window of the restaurant. "Some water? Some food in your stomach?"

"No, I'm good," I said, which was far from the truth, but I didn't feel like waiting another minute. I took one glance inside the place, seeing the warm light, the men sitting around the fireplace, other men drinking at the bar. It made me feel even colder.

"Okay," he said, putting his helmet back on. "Let's rip it up."

I brushed the snow off my helmet and lifted it over my head. Then I stopped dead.

"Alex," Vinnie said from behind me. "Are you all right?"

Inside the restaurant, sitting against the back wall . . .

It was Natalie.

I didn't believe it at first. I thought maybe after everything that had happened that day, I was having some kind of hallucination. But then she moved. She looked up and took a quick scan of the room before going back to her drink. It was her.

"Alex, what is it?"

"She's here."

"What?"

"She's here," I said. "Come on."

He looked confused as all hell, but he put his helmet on his sled and followed me into the bar. From one second to the next, the air felt seventy degrees warmer. It smelled of cigarette smoke.

"Gentlemen!" the bartender called to us. "Wipe off the snow, please!"

I ignored the man. I walked through the room in my ridiculously large snowmobile suit, leaving a trail of snow with every step. The faces were all turning to look at me, but she hadn't seen me yet. She didn't know I was twenty feet away from her and closing in.

She didn't notice me until I was standing right next to her. When she finally looked up at me, it all hit me at once. This was the woman I had spent every waking hour worrying about, the woman I had almost killed myself trying to find. Now here she was, sitting at this table. The light picked up the red in her hair. She stared at me with those green eyes until finally she cleared her throat and spoke.

"You're here."

There were seven or eight things I wanted to say. I picked one. "So are you."

"Hello, Vinnie," she said, looking past me. "Did Alex drag you all the way out here?"

"He didn't drag me," Vinnie said.

"Natalie," I said, "everyone's been looking for you."

"Who's everyone?"

"All the police in Michigan and Ontario. Your old commander. Me."

"I haven't been gone that long."

"Natalie, he's alive."

"That suit's a little big on you," she said.

"You already know that, don't you . . ."

"Yes."

"And your mother . . ."

"Don't, Alex. Please don't talk about that, okay? I'm trying to hold everything together here."

"I was there," I said.

She looked at me. "You saw her?"

"Yes."

"I shouldn't have left her alone," she said. She looked at the bottom of her glass. "By the time I got back, it was too late."

"For God's sake, what's going on?"

She didn't look up.

"Natalie, please," I said. "Tell me why you're here."

"I've got a better idea," she said, standing up and grabbing her coat. "I'll let our old friend Simon Grant tell you."

Twenty

She led us both through the bar, out onto the cold street. The snow was falling even harder now. There was nothing but the faint light coming from the front window, a light at the small hotel in the middle of the block, another far down at the end of the street. Everything else was dark. Empty buildings. Mountains of snow.

We stopped to breathe in the cold air, all three of us. Outside the bar it was quiet. A faint wind made the snow swirl around our heads.

"Natalie, what are we doing?"

"You'll see," she said. "You have to trust me."

"What do you mean, Simon Grant's going to tell us? He's dead. I mean, not like your stepfather. I went to Simon Grant's funeral."

"Please, Alex. Just come with me before you say anything else."

I turned to Vinnie. "Just go," he said to me. "She asked you to trust her."

"Vinnie, you come with us," she said. "I'd like you to hear this, too."

She set off down the street, back toward the center of town, moving quickly down the path we had just cut with our sleds. I zipped up my ridiculous suit and tried to keep up with her. I was tired, more tired than I wanted to admit to myself.

"Where are we going?" I said. "The Grants' place is up the other way."

"We're not going to the Grants' place," she said.

She stopped in front of the hotel in the middle of the block, the Chippewa. She pulled the door open and held it for us. A woman came to the counter in the tiny lobby, rubbing her eyes and looking past us, out the front door.

"Still snowing out there?" she said. She was a big woman, in her sixties. I would have bet anything she was an Ojibwa.

"You could say that, Mrs. Larusso," Natalie said. "We're going up to my room for a while."

"Are you sure, hon? We have other rooms, you know."

"No, we'll be fine."

"We always have empty rooms in February."

"We'll let you know if we need one, Mrs. Larusso. Thank you."

"Natalie," I said, "why are we going up to your room?"

"Just shut up for once," she said. "Please. Just stop talking."

"Natalie . . ."

"I swear," she said, taking my hand in hers, "if you say one more word, I'm gonna hit you right in the mouth."

She hit the elevator button, waited exactly one second, and then opened the door to the stairwell.

"I always hated elevators," she said, and pulled me into the stairwell. Vinnie followed. As we went up the stairs behind her, I couldn't help but think of the last time we had been in a hotel together, and everything that had happened since then. Her room was on the third floor. It was small, dominated by a queen-sized bed with an elaborate iron frame. She took her coat off.

"Natalie," I said. "Will you please tell us what's going on?"

"Take that stupid snowmobile suit off," she said. "You, too, Vinnie."

"All right," I said. "If that means you're finally gonna talk to us." I unzipped the suit.

"Sit down," she said, "and watch this."

There was a television on top of the dresser. She turned it on. A commercial was just ending, then the Red Wings game came back on. Before I could say anything, she picked up an overnight bag from the floor and pulled out a videocassette.

"Will you both sit down, please?"

When we were both sitting on the edge of the bed, she put the videocassette into the VCR port that was built into the bottom of the television. The hockey game was replaced by a hospital room. A man was sitting up in a bed, his hands folded in his lap. He was looking at the camera.

"What is this?" I said. Then I recognized the man. He was a slightly younger Simon Grant.

Another man appeared. It was Marty Grant. His face loomed huge in the frame as he adjusted the camera angle.

She hit the fast-forward button. The two men stayed in place, Simon Grant in the bed, Marty in the chair next to him. Their heads and hands moved in a blur as Natalie scanned through the tape.

"Martin, I know why you're doing this," Simon Grant

said as soon as the tape speed went back to normal. "You think I'll be dead by the end of the week."

She hit the fast-forward again. "Simon Grant had a heart attack about ten years ago. Marty wanted to get a tape of him talking about his life, in case he wasn't around much longer."

"How did you get this?" I said.

She looked at me. "Marty gave it to me."

Before I could ask her anything else, she put the tape back to normal speed again. "Okay, this is about where we want it," she said. "Listen."

Marty was laughing hard at something his father had just told him. "You gotta be kidding me, Pops. She actually fell for that?"

"Only for fifty-five years. God bless her."

"Okay, if that's the best thing you ever did in your life," Marty said, "then tell me the worst thing you ever did."

Natalie moved away from the television. She went to the window and looked out at the darkness as the tape kept playing.

"That's a tough question," the older man said.

"It's just between you and me," Marty said, sneaking a wink at the camera.

"I lived a long life, son."

"Come on, Pops. How bad could it be? It's not like you ever killed somebody."

There was a long silence.

"Yes, son, I did."

Marty stopped smiling.

"Pops . . ."

"I'll tell you about it, Martin. I think it's about time."

"You're serious?"

"Let me tell you something about hate, son. I've learned a lot about hate in my life. Hell, I lived on it for years. It's what kept me going, every day, when I was a young man. I hated how poor I was when I was growing up, how I didn't have a father. How I had to go out and work from when I was ten years old. This was during the Great Depression, you understand. You don't know what it was like back then. I'm glad you don't. I'm glad you never had to see times like that. A man would do anything just to earn a little money, so he could feed his family. I hated having to live like that, and seeing what it was doing to my mother, how it was making her an old woman when she was forty. Later on, when I was working on the docks, I hated the men I was working for. I hated the way they took advantage of us whenever they could, like we were nothing more than animals."

Marty Grant was leaning forward in his chair, his elbows on his legs. He didn't move an inch. He sat there and listened to his father.

"I suppose, looking back on it, all that hatred in my heart, it was sort of like a fuel, if you know what I mean. It kept me going. I don't know if I would have been able to survive, or work so hard, or later, when I was in the union . . . We had to fight so hard, son. Maybe I *needed* that hatred. But damn, what it did to me. What a price to pay. All those years . . ."

Natalie kept looking out the window. She was as still as Marty's image on the tape.

"There was one man in particular, son. This goes back to 1929, when they still had Prohibition. People used to bring liquor across the border all the time. I bet you didn't know that a lot of the rum-running happened right here on the border between Michigan and Ontario. Most of it was down by Detroit, of course. That's where the gangs were. Capone's men and Bugs Moran and the Purple Gang . . . God, you can't even imagine, son. It was a different country back then. Anyway, my father and his brother, they got involved in this. They knew these other men in Canada who would bring good whiskey across. My father and uncle would meet them and pay them for the whiskey, and then they'd sell it. In the summer, they'd come over in these wooden boats. Then, when the river froze, they'd bring it over on a sled."

Mrs. DeMarco's words came back to me. The ice run.

"There was one night . . ."

Simon Grant stopped. He cleared his throat.

"It was New Year's Eve, the last night of 1929. The Ojibway Hotel was still brand-new. They were having this big party. I guess the manager there had been asking my father if he could get some whiskey for him, but the weather had been so bad . . . The men from Canada couldn't get through, not until the weather broke on New Year's Eve itself. I don't know how much my father felt like doing it that night, but the money must have been good. He and my uncle went over to get it . . ."

Grant stopped again. He coughed a few times and then kept going.

"I was just a little kid, you understand. I didn't hear the real story until later. Apparently, what happened was, some of the gangsters down in Detroit finally got wind of what was going on up here. They hadn't been bothering with it way up here in the U.P. But now with the new hotel and the big parties and everything . . . Somehow they heard of this big load of whiskey coming across. They knew exactly where the meeting would be, out on the St. Marys River. They took the whiskey and the money and they killed everybody. My father and my uncle, they never came home. That was December of 1929, remember. The stock market had just crashed a couple of months before that. The next few years . . . The next few years were tough, son."

Grant shook his head slowly.

"My little sister . . ."

Marty finally looked up at him.

"Her name was Victoria. She would have been your aunt. You never got to meet her. She died of pneumonia when she was eight years old. I was ten. She was . . ."

He had to stop for a while.

"God, how long ago was that?" he said. "You should have seen this little shack we were living in. It wasn't fit to be a henhouse. My little sister, she was just . . ."

His voice broke.

"This angel. I remember her like . . ."

He put his hand in front of his face, then let it fall back to his lap.

"So when, 1972 . . . That's forty-three years later. You were in high school back then. I get this call from a man named Albert DeMarco."

I looked over at Natalie. She didn't turn around.

"This man tells me, all these years later, that his father was out on that ice, too. He knew all about it. He told me something else that I had never heard before. He told me that the gangsters let one of the men live. That man must have made a deal with them. My father and uncle get killed . . . the man's partner, Mr. DeMarco, he gets killed . . . and Luc Reynaud, he's the one man who made it back home—he works directly with the gangsters from that point on. I asked this man why he was telling me this now. He says it was something he thought I should know. Of course, I knew there was more to it. Eventually, this Mr. DeMarco, he gets around to telling me that the Reynaud family was fabulously wealthy, that they had all this money from way back, during the last few years of rum-running, supplying the gangsters in Michigan, buying gold during the Depression . . . this whole story the man's telling me. A big house and horses, a whole estate up there in Blind River, Ontario. All this built up on that one night Reynaud sold out my father and my uncle, and DeMarco's father, too. He tells me all this and then he finally gets to the point. Luc Reynaud's spoiled brat son, Jean Reynaud, was coming down for a big party at the Ojibway on New Year's Eve. He told me if he was in my shoes, he'd want to know about it."

"Pops," Marty said, finally speaking up. "Are you telling me this was the man . . ."

"DeMarco wanted me to kill him. That was pretty obvious. I told him I didn't run errands for cowards, told him if he wanted Reynaud dead he should kill the man himself. That's what I told him. But at the same time . . . let's just say I was curious about meeting the son of the man who killed my father. So I went to the hotel that night. There he was, all dressed up. He was real smooth. He had this old hat on. A gray homburg. I went up to him at the bar and I introduced myself. I asked him if he knew who I was. He said no, he didn't. I told him I liked his hat. He told me it had belonged to his father. I asked him if he knew how his father had made all his money. He sort of looked at me funny, and then he told me that his father had made all his money by milking cows. I asked him if he was sure about that. He put his two fists up, started moving them up and down, like he was milking a cow. He said, that's where the milk comes from, sir. Just like that. He started laughing. Then he bought me a drink. He slapped me on the back and said, Happy New Year to you, sir. Then he walked away. I just sat there for a while, thinking about what he had said, drinking the beer he bought me. Milking cows, he said."

Simon Grant stopped for a while to let that sink in. Marty Grant stared at the hospital floor.

"When it was just about midnight, he came over and slapped me on the back again. He asked me if he could buy me another drink. I said, no thanks, but you should come outside and see the fireworks over the river. We went out in back. He asked me where the fireworks were. I said they're right here and I shot him in the head."

"You had a gun," Marty said.

"Yes."

"You brought it with you, I mean."

"I always carried a gun. I told you, it was a rough place back then."

"Pops, I can't believe any of this. I can't."

"That next summer, I went out to Blind River. First thing I wanted to do was see this big Reynaud estate that DeMarco had told me about. It was just a little farm-house. Jean Reynaud was telling the truth. His father *did* make his money milking cows. That fancy suit he had on that night, that hat . . . those were probably the only nice clothes he owned. I knocked on the door, but nobody was home. I'm not sure what I would have done if Luc Reynaud had been there. I mean, this whole story about him getting rich off the gangsters, it obviously didn't happen that way. But still, he was the one man who came home alive that night. My father was murdered out on the ice. And DeMarco's father. They died on the ice and they stayed there all winter until it melted. I don't know exactly how it happened, but I would have sat old Luc Reynaud down and made him tell me. Then when he was done, I would have told him I had taken away his son, just like he had taken away my father."

"What if he had nothing to do with it?" Marty said. "What if the gangsters just decided to let him go?"

"I don't think that could have happened, son. You've got to remember who we're talking about."

"Pops . . ." Marty shook his head.

"I ended up going to the next house down the road, and it turns out that was the DeMarcos' house. I met Albert's mother, this tiny little woman living all by herself. She was friendly, so I got to talking to her. I asked her some questions about her family. She told me about her husband, and about Luc Reynaud coming back alone that night. For some reason, she didn't think that was suspicious. Or maybe she did. Hell, maybe she knew exactly what had happened and she just wasn't gonna say it. Not to me. Anyway, I asked about her son, Albert. Turned out he had just gotten married to Jean Reynaud's widow. I even got to see their wedding picture. Grace, her name was. What a beauty. All of a sudden it made sense to me. This man had used me. He wanted Jean Reynaud out of the way, and he knew I was the only other man in the world who could hate that family as much as he did. So now I hated all of them. The Reynauds. The DeMarcos. I hated myself, too. It never ends."

Simon Grant coughed a few times and then he reached over to his son. Marty Grant didn't move.

"Now that I've told you this, Martin . . . I know I'm getting close to the end of my life. I hope you'll see what a life of hating can do to a man. I hope you'll let me take it right to the grave with me, son. Please bury it with me. You gotta promise me one thing, too."

Marty looked up.

"You can't tell your brother Michael about this. You know how he is."

Both men sat there for a long time, not saying a word. Finally, Marty got to his feet and came toward the camera. The last shot was Simon Grant alone in his hospital bed. Then the tape ended.

The hockey game came back on. I paid no attention to it. Vinnie sat next to me in silence. Natalie stood at the window. In my mind I saw the photograph again. The three men. Luc Reynaud in his gray suit, Jean Reynaud in light linen, holding the hat over his head like a trophy.

Because he had just taken it from his father—his father's gray hat that went perfectly with his gray suit. It had been on his father's head, and now it was on his, his young wife taking the photograph to record the moment forever.

"The devil of Blind River . . ." I said.

"It wasn't my father," Natalie said, finally turning around to look at me. "It was my grandfather."

"The devil's hat, filled with ice and snow . . ."

"He wouldn't do that, Alex. Not my grandfather."

"It was so long ago," I said. "There's no way to know what really happened out on that ice."

"He wouldn't sell out his partner like that. Or set up those other men."

"It doesn't matter. Just tell me, what does all this have to do with you being here on this island? And Albert . . ."

"He's here," she said. "Somewhere."

"Why? What does he want?"

"That's an easy one," she said. "He came here to kill me."

Twenty-one

A lone snowmobile roared by on the street below. The sound got farther and farther away until it was gone.

"This is why Marty Grant came looking for us," Natalie said. "He wanted my mother to have a copy of this tape, so she'd know the truth. Albert killed her first husband."

"Natalie . . ."

"He killed my father, Alex."

"He didn't kill anybody," I said. "Simon Grant did."

"Try telling that to Marty. Albert set the whole thing up. He's the one who made it all happen."

"No, Natalie. He just pointed Simon in the right direction."

"It doesn't matter, Alex. Whatever happened, Marty wanted my mother to know. Obviously, he didn't want to tell anyone while his father was still alive."

"He came looking for your mother? Is that why he was up in Batchawana Bay?"

"Yes," she said. "That was the day you saw him up there. I didn't know anything about it at the time. I had already come to get her out of that house."

"So I followed him back to Michigan," I said, "and got into it with his brother at the garage. Michael said he told Marty about that, and about you. He even told him that you lived in Blind River. That's the last time he heard from him."

"Yes, that makes sense, because he showed up that night. God, what a horror show that was."

"Natalie, what did he do?"

"It wasn't him so much. I mean, all he did was tell me he wanted to see my mother, said he had something important to show her. I didn't like him being there, but he said it would mean a lot to her. She came to the door and started talking to him. The next thing I know we've got the VCR pulled out and he's showing us this videotape. You can't imagine, Alex . . . what I was thinking of while I was watching that. When it was done, I said to him, okay, I'm glad I know this now, but I wish I had seen this tape while Albert was still alive so I could have beat his head in with my hockey stick."

"God, Natalie. And you had no idea he's still alive . . ."

"No, that was my little surprise for the evening. Marty told me that he had looked up Albert DeMarco. He's living in the States now, out in Las Vegas. He's got all these real estate deals going on, building houses. He owns part of a casino, too. He's gotta be what, over seventy now, but he started over with a young wife, two kids in high school—you know, buying himself a new life. Marty said he was going to send him a copy of the tape, just to let him know that his past wasn't a total secret."

"What did you say, Natalie? What did your mother say?"

"You have to remember, Alex, this was the biggest lie

she ever told me. But as good as she is at lying, she's just as good at explaining herself after it all falls apart. She did it for me, she said. To make me feel better. To help me forgive her, all these years later. And you know what? I wanted to believe he was dead. I really did. So one drunken night, two years ago, she calls me up and she tells me the monster is gone. She wants to see me. She wants to be with me again. She wants to be my mother again . . ."

Natalie stopped to wipe her face with her hands.

"Two years, Alex. Two years I thought he was dead. I was up in Hearst, remember. Way the hell up there. What was I supposed to do, start calling people to make sure he was really dead?"

"Okay, so then what?"

"I just had to get away from her. I went outside for a while, just walked around, freezing my ass off. I almost went down the street to Mrs. DeMarco's house, like I did when I was twelve years old. But I couldn't, you know? That was Albert's house, too. It was like I couldn't escape him, no matter what I did. He'd always be there haunting me. So eventually, I just went back inside. Marty was gone already. I got in a big fight with my mother, told her I wished she was dead . . ."

She stopped again.

"And then I called you," she said. "I called you and I told you it was over between us. I'm sorry, Alex. I just didn't want you to be a part of it anymore."

"You should have told me what was going on," I said. "I would have helped you."

"I know that."

"So why didn't you?"

"It was my problem, Alex. You've already been through enough for me. My God, just look at you."

She reached out and touched the bandages on my neck. "What's this, anyway?"

"I'll tell you in a minute," I said. "Just finish your story."

"The next day, my mother was up early. She was actually cleaning the house if you can believe it. She acted like there was nothing going on, but I knew better. I finally got it out of her. When she was alone with Marty the night before, they hatched up this plan. They were gonna blackmail Albert."

"With what? That videotape?"

"That's what I said. It's an old man talking about something that might have happened thirty years ago. Albert would just laugh at her. You know what she told me?"

"I'm afraid to ask."

"She told me that nothing on that videotape was a surprise to her. Albert had told her the whole story a long time ago. A full confession. You know what else? Apparently, Albert paid Simon Grant ten thousand dollars in cash after he killed my father. He was a full accessory, before and after the fact. My mother would be willing to testify to all of this in court."

"But Simon didn't say anything about money on that tape. And why would Albert—"

"Alex, did you hear what I just said? This was *my mother's* story."

"I'm sorry," I said. "Of course. But you're telling me she'd actually say all of this under oath?"

"She'd tell it to a lie detector, Alex. She really would, and I'm sure she'd pass."

"Okay, so what happened next?"

"I told her it would never work. Albert would know it was all a lie. But then it occurred to me that Albert would also know how good a liar she was. That's when I started getting a headache. Anyway, the plan was that Marty Grant would come out here to his house on the island and call Albert, and tell him he had twenty-four hours to get out here with a hundred thousand dollars. He didn't want my mother to be here, but he wanted her to stay by the phone so he could call her when Albert got there—you know, in case he needed to hear it from her directly. If he didn't show up, they'd go to the police in Las Vegas, the Gaming Commission . . . they'd even send copies of the tape to his wife and kids. It was all a big bluff, of course. The whole thing. I told her they were both crazy. And now . . ."

She looked out the window.

"They didn't know who they were messing around with, Alex. They had no idea."

"So what did you do?" I said. "How did you end up out here?"

"My mother didn't have Marty's phone number. She just knew he was going to call her. So I took the tape and I told her to stay put. I came out here to give it back to him, and to tell him to forget the whole thing, to leave my mother alone or else I'd find a way to have him arrested. When I got out here, it wasn't hard to find his place. It's such a small island, and Mrs. Larusso downstairs knows everybody. When I got to the house, it was empty. But I knew somebody had been there. I started to get a bad feeling about it. I called back home, but nobody answered. That didn't make any sense, because I knew my mother . . ."

She swallowed hard.

"I knew she was waiting by the telephone. But I just figured . . . I don't know, maybe that she was drinking again, that she was passed out somewhere. So I left. I caught the next plane out and drove back to Blind River. When I saw what had happened to her . . ."

"We got there later," I said. "Michael and I came out to the house."

"Michael Grant?"

"Yes. When we found your mother, Michael panicked. I remember him saying . . . what did he say? Something about Marty, no, why did you do this . . ."

"He thought Marty killed my mother?"

"I don't know what he was thinking," I said. "He tried to kill me. He grabbed an old shotgun from your basement, from that stash of guns in the closet."

"What happened?"

"The barrels exploded. He bled to death."

She closed her eyes. "God," she said. "When does it end?"

"Natalie, what did you do after you found your mother? Why did you come back here?"

"I called him, Alex. I knew Marty was able to contact him, so I called information out in Las Vegas. He wasn't listed, but they had a number for his company. The De-Marco Group. I called and I got this woman on the line and I told her Albert needed to call me right away. I gave her my name, told her he'd know who I was. It didn't take more than five minutes, Alex. He called me back. All of a sudden it was that voice on the phone, that voice I hadn't heard in thirty years. He pretended he had no idea why I was calling. I asked him what kind of man would do that to a woman he once loved so much? He said he had no idea what I was talking about. He had been there in his office all day, he said. I told him he hadn't changed one bit. He was still getting other people to do his killing for him. He asked me if I was about done because he's a busy man, and I said, no, I'm not done. I'm going to call your wife and tell her what you did to me when I was a kid, and what you did to my father . . . and my mother. I'm going to tell her everything I know about you so she won't feel so bad when I come out there and kill you."

"What did he say to that?"

"Not a word, Alex. Not a word. I told him I was heading back down to Mackinac Island. I told him I'd have the last copy of the videotape with me, and if he wanted it, he had to come get it."

"Why here?"

"I couldn't stay in that house," she said. "Not with my mother there. I figured this was as good a place as any. Nice and isolated. Just me and Albert."

"There's no way he'd come alone," I said. "You know he's got somebody else here."

"Maybe," she said. "I honestly don't know. For me, maybe he'd come by himself. He still thinks of me as that twelve-year-old girl."

"No," Vinnie said. It was the first thing he had said since we had come up to this room. "He wouldn't come alone. Not if he's a born coward."

"Wait a minute," I said. "When I saw him getting off that plane . . ."

I tried to bring it all back in my mind. Standing there in the airport, looking at every face.

"There was another man with him," I said. "He was big."

"That's at least one other man he has," Vinnie said. "Who knows how well armed they are? We'd be fools to go out trying to find them."

"You're right," she said. "We have to stay here. At least for now."

"You've got to be kidding," I said. "We're sitting ducks."

"No, not here," she said. "They're probably up at the Grants' house, waiting. If we go up there now, we'll be playing right into their hands."

"That's true," Vinnie said.

"I'm so tired," she said. "I haven't slept in two days."

"If we do this in the morning," I said, "you have to promise me something."

"What's that?"

"You have to promise me that we're going to do this together. We're going to be smart about it, and if it looks bad, we're going to bail out."

She didn't say anything.

"Promise me," I said. "We're together, no matter what."

"Okay," she said. "I promise."

"What do you think, Vinnie? Are you up for this?"

"I'm with you," he said, looking at Natalie. "You know that, Alex."

"We should try to get some sleep," Natalie said.

"Good idea," Vinnie said. "I'll go see the woman downstairs about another room."

He stood up, went to the door, then looked back at me. "Alex, you gonna stay here?"

"Yes, he is," Natalie said. "If that's okay. I'd rather not be alone."

"I'll see you in the morning," he said. Then he left.

"I'm sorry," she said. "I didn't even ask you if you wanted to stay."

"It's okay. If you don't want to be alone . . ."

"It's more than that."

"Natalie, I don't know where we stand right now."

"Show me what happened."

"What?"

"I can see the bandages. Show me where you got shot."

"I didn't get shot," I said. "It was a piece of metal, from when the shotgun exploded."

"Show me." She pulled me to my feet.

"Natalie . . ."

She shushed me. She unbuttoned my shirt and touched my neck. "My God," she said. "Look what happened to you."

"It's not that bad."

She shook her head. "After everything you've done for me, this is what you get."

I took hold of her hand. "We're going to make everything right," I said. "We'll do that tomorrow."

She kissed me.

"Why did you come here?" she said.

"I had to."

"I pushed you away so hard. What kind of a man would do that?"

I didn't say anything.

"I'm glad you're here," she said, her voice barely above a whisper now. "That much I know. This is better."

She pulled my shirt off my shoulders. I reached my arms around her and held her tight. I put my nose in her hair and breathed in her perfect sweet scent.

"Everything's going to be okay now," I said. "I promise."

She spun me around and pulled me down onto the bed. I kissed her, again and again. We pulled the rest of our clothes off. We made love on top of the covers and then under them when it got too cold. It kept snowing outside, more and more white flakes coming down like it would bury us forever.

Afterward I held on to her tight. She was breathing deeply. She was falling asleep in my arms. I tried to say something. This is how it should be. I am in bed. I should stay awake for a while, think about what we're going to do tomorrow. No, I should sleep. Sleep.

The wind blew. The sound turned into the faraway droning of an engine. A snowmobile. Then the sound became the wind again.

"Natalie," I said, finally finding my voice. I reached for her. There was nothing there. My left arm was being pulled upward now. It made my neck hurt.

"Natalie."

A clicking noise. I know that sound. I've heard it before, a long time ago.

What's wrong with my arm? I reached with my other hand and heard the noise again. A light came on, blinding me. I felt the pain in my neck again. Pain and what was that? Something cold on my wrists. A metallic rattling. Almost like . . .

Handcuffs. I squinted at the bright light and looked up at my hands. I was cuffed to one of the iron railings at the head of the bed.

"What's happening?" I said. "Natalie, where are you?"

There was movement beside the bed. I shook my head and blinked.

"Natalie!"

"I'm right here," she said.

Everything came into focus. She was standing in the center of the room, putting her clothes on.

"What the hell's going on?" I said. "Why did you handcuff me to the bed?"

"I'm sorry."

I pulled at the cuffs. The iron rail was as strong as a prison gate.

"I broke my promise," she said. "I told you I'd never lie to you."

"Natalie, listen to me. Just let me go, okay? We can talk about this."

"You know, it's funny," she said. "I think I understand my mother a little better now."

"Please, Natalie. Let me go."

"A lie really does have a lot of power, doesn't it? It makes everything easy."

"No. Come on."

"I had to wait until she was dead to see that."

"For God's sake, Natalie . . ."

She pulled her sweater on over her head.

"He sent someone to kill her, Alex. He'll kill you, too, in a second. You know that. We can't run away. He'll find us and kill both of us."

I yanked hard on the cuffs. The metal bit into my skin.

"Natalie . . ."

"I'm sorry, Alex. I'm glad we were together. One last time. I wasn't lying about that."

She took her service automatic from her bag, checked it, then put it in her coat.

"Do not do this," I said. "Please, for the love of God . . ."

"You'd do the same thing, Alex."

"No. No, I wouldn't."

"If you were me," she said, reaching into the bag again, "yes, you would. We're the same, Alex. You understand me perfectly."

"No. Natalie. Please."

She brought out another gun. It was a revolver.

"Do you know what this is?"

"Natalie . . ."

"It's my grandfather's favorite gun. It's an old Webley Bulldog, from World War I."

"Please, you can't do this."

"My grandfather's gun. It was locked away in the basement. But don't worry. I know how to clean an old gun."

She took one step closer to me. I tried to grab her.

"I have to go now," she said.

She stood there for a moment, just out of reach. She looked at me one last time.

"I love you, Alex McKnight."

Then she was gone.

Twenty-two

I pulled at the cuffs until my wrists were bleeding. No matter how hard I tried, I couldn't bend the metal bed frame. There was only one thing left to do.

I started yelling.

"Help! Help! Vinnie! Can you hear me? Vinnie!"

I stopped to catch my breath, then started again.

"Anybody! Help! Get me out of here! Help!"

I yelled as loud as I could until my throat was raw. I kicked at the wall again and again, making as much noise as I could. There was no way anybody could sleep through it, and yet when I stopped, everything was silent again.

"Vinnie! Where the hell are you? Vinnie!"

I collapsed in the bed, breathing hard.

God damn it, I thought. I am such an idiot. She's going to go out there and get herself killed because I'm the biggest idiot who ever lived.

Just as I was about to start the noise again, I heard a knock on the door.

"Hello in there!" someone said.

"Who's there?"

"It's Mrs. Larusso, from the front desk. Are you okay in there?"

"Mrs. Larusso, thank God. You've got to get me out of here!"

There was a pause.

"Are you locked in, sir?"

"I'm handcuffed to the bed! You have to help me!"

Another pause.

"You're handcuffed to the bed, sir?"

"Please! Just come in!"

I heard her fumble through her keys for a moment. The door finally opened. She poked her head into the room. Then she screamed.

"You're naked, sir!"

"Please, ma'am. Where's Vinnie?"

She stayed just behind the door. "The gentleman who was with you?"

"Yes! Please go get him."

"I put him in the room next to you, sir."

"Where is he?" There was no way he wouldn't have heard me, not if he was right next door.

"I don't know, sir. Can you tell me why you're hand-cuffed to the bed?"

"I don't have time. Please. Do you have a hacksaw?"

"I'm sorry. I don't know what to do here, sir. That woman you were staying with, Miss Reynaud, she's with the police, isn't she?"

"Ma'am, please!"

"I thought I saw a badge in her purse, when she paid me for the room."

Oh God. Think, man. Think.

"Okay," I said. "Look, I'm a little embarrassed. That badge wasn't real. We were playing a game here, and it got a little carried away. Can you please help me now?"

"Where is Ms. Reynaud?"

"She must be down at the bar, having a drink. Please, ma'am."

"The bar is closed."

"She's with Vinnie," I said. "They went out for a walk. It's all part of the joke, see? But I really, really have to use the bathroom right now, ma'am. I don't want to ruin your nice bed. Please, please, go get a hacksaw."

"It's three o'clock in the morning," she said. "I don't like any of this, I have to tell you."

"I'm sorry, ma'am. Please, I can't wait any longer."

"I'll go get the saw and let you out. But if you've done anything to that bed frame . . ."

"Hurry!"

I shifted around my legs to cover myself with the blanket as well as I could while I waited for Mrs. Larusso to find her hacksaw. Minutes passed. Hours. Days. At long last, I heard her coming down the hallway again.

"Are you covered up now, sir?"

"Yes! Please come in and cut this off."

She peered around the door. "You know, I was sleeping," she said. "I really don't appreciate this."

"Okay, I'm sorry, ma'am. Please hurry."

"I'm not sure how to do this. Where do I cut?"

"Here," I said. "Right on this chain, between the cuffs." I pushed one hand through as far as I could, and pulled with the other.

"My husband is better at this kind of thing," she said. "He's on the mainland tonight. He missed the last plane."

"I'm sure you'll do fine," I said. "Just cut right there." I had to try very hard not to yell at her. That wouldn't help her move any faster.

"Okay, let me try," she said. She took one slow drag of the hacksaw across the chain, making a microscopic notch in the metal.

"Give it a little speed," I said. "It's all in the motion."

She tried to saw faster.

"That's it," I said. "Back and forth, back and forth."

She got into the rhythm. Then she stopped.

"Look at this mess," she said. "We're getting metal dust all over the sheet."

"I'll clean it up, I swear. Please hurry."

"I don't know what kind of game you were playing," she said as she started again. "Handcuffing somebody to a bed. That doesn't sound right to me."

"Never again," I said. "I promise. That's it. Keep going, just like that."

"I think we're almost there."

"Ma'am, let me ask you again. This is very important. Did you see either of my friends leaving?"

"No," she said. "I told you, I was in bed. I have a room right behind the front desk."

"Okay, I understand."

With one last stroke of the saw, the chain broke open. The handcuffs were still on my wrists, of course, but now my arms were free to move again. She screamed when I jumped out of the bed, scrambling for my clothes.

"Let me leave first, for Heaven's sake!"

"Thanks for your help, ma'am." I threw on my pants and my shirt, laced my boots on over my bare feet. I was just about to step into the big snowmobile suit, said the hell with that thing. Grabbing the gun out of the pocket, I ran out into the hallway and down the stairs.

When I got outside, the cold air filled my lungs. The snow had let up, lonely flakes drifting slowly from the sky. There was no wind. Everything was quiet. I ran down the street to the restaurant. It was dark. I had left my snowmobile in front. But now it was gone. Vinnie's was gone, too.

Son of a bitch, I thought. They couldn't have gone together. Maybe Natalie took one of the sleds, then Vinnie followed her? Why the hell didn't he come get me? Was he afraid he'd lose her? At that moment, it didn't matter. What mattered was that I was down here at the bottom of the hill, and Natalie was up at the house.

I started running. I still had the gun in my hand, so I tucked it into my pants. The handcuffs were rubbing my wrists raw. Within a quarter mile, I was gasping for air. My boots started to slip. Another quarter mile and I was in real pain. I slid on a patch of ice and fell face-first into the snow.

Get up, I said to myself. You goddamned broken-down worthless piece of shit. Get up and help her. I pushed myself up, the snow hanging from my eyebrows. I wasn't cold. I couldn't even feel it.

I got back on my feet and ran. I was almost up the hill, the Grand Hotel looming above me. I knew that was the halfway point. The ground would be level once I got there. Everything would be easier. I pushed myself harder and harder. I couldn't breathe anymore, but I kept running.

I got closer and closer to the hotel. Keep going, Alex. Keep going. Every second counts. I had two hundred yards to go now. Then a hundred. Then fifty.

When I got to the top of the hill, I had to stop for a moment. My lungs were on fire. I stood there with my hands on my knees, trying to breathe.

Almost there, I thought. Almost there.

I set off again, along the front of the hotel. It rose above me like a huge black cliff. All the happy summer people long gone. The men and women all dressed up, playing croquet on the big lawn. The children in the pool. The horses. There was nobody here on this dark road except me.

I tried to pick up the pace again. I ran up the street, past the million-dollar Victorians until I could finally see the woods ahead of me. I couldn't see the Grants' house yet.

Natalie's there, I thought. She has to be. And Vinnie?

Damn, he doesn't even know where the house is. He's never been here before. Unless he followed her. I hope to God he followed her.

I made myself slow down as I came to the edge of the woods. I had to catch my breath. You can't sneak up on somebody when you're wheezing like a goddamned asthmatic.

I left the road before it went into the trees. I'll take a shortcut, I thought. I'll come at it from the back, in case somebody's watching.

The snow was deep. It was hard work, making my way through it. By the time I got to the first house, my pants were soaked. I leaned against the house, catching my breath again. There's this house, I thought, then two more. The Grants' house is the fourth.

Another thought hit me with a sudden jolt. What if nobody's there? What if everything's going down somewhere else on the island? Somewhere I don't even know about?

God damn it, no. It has to be here. This is the only place.

I left the first house, cutting my way through the snow, going from tree to tree. I still couldn't see the Grants' house yet.

Please be there, I thought. Please be there.

I stopped again at the second house. For a moment, I thought I heard something ahead. It was hard to tell with my own heart pounding in my ears.

I kept going. One tree to the next tree to the next. Finally, I saw a light.

It was coming from the house. Someone was there.

I stopped and listened.

Nothing.

I took the gun out of my pants. I moved slowly now, stopping behind each tree. I could see the house clearly now. There was at least one light on, in a room on the ground floor. But none of the outside lights were on.

I thought back to when I had been there before. We talked to Chris there, in the main room, on this side of the house. Did we leave a light on? I didn't think so, but I couldn't be sure.

One way to find out, I thought. I've got to get to the house so I can look inside.

I stayed down as low as I could. The snow helped hide me. It muffled any noise, too. For once in my life, I was thankful for two and a half feet of snow on the ground.

As I passed the second house, I thought I could make out a break in the snow. It looked like a long line, leading from the Grants' house, right toward me. A trail maybe. Someone had come this way, not that long ago.

I stopped and listened. Then I moved around a great,

fat tree and saw the path in the snow right there in front of me.

What the hell? It just stopped. Somebody had come through here, then what? Turned around?

Wait a minute, what was this? I thought I saw something in the snow. Something dark. As I moved toward it, I felt myself tripping. As I reached down to catch my balance, I put my hand on it.

Fabric. It was a coat.

Dear God, I thought. I felt the body. I moved up to the head and pushed the snow away. I couldn't see who it was.

Please, no. Don't let it be.

I touched the face. It was as cold and hard as stone. A man's face. The head was tilted at an impossible angle, the neck cut wide open.

He's been dead for a while, I thought. He's frozen solid. I bent down to look closely at the man's face.

It was Marty Grant.

You poor bastard, I thought. This is what happened to you. You called DeMarco and this is what happened.

I was about to get up when somebody spoke.

"Don't move."

I turned to see who it was.

"I said don't move. If you move again, I'll put a bullet right through your left eye."

A man was standing there. He had a gun pointed right at my face. He was dressed in white winter camouflage.

"Okay," he said. "That's better. Now we're going to go inside. I think there's someone in there who'd like to meet you."

Twenty-three

The first thing I thought of was my gun. Then I noticed he was holding it. I must have dropped it when I went down on my hands and knees to look at the body.

"Right this way," he said. "Please don't try anything stupid." He spoke with a French-Canadian accent. He was definitely not the man I saw getting off the plane with DeMarco.

He waved me in front of him. I started walking.

"What's with the outfit?" I said. "You think you're a commando or something?"

"Shut up and keep moving."

"You specialize in Arctic warfare, right? What's your unit called again? The JTF2?"

"I told you to shut up."

"I think I've got it now," I said. "You're not a real soldier at all. You're one of those losers who likes to dress up and pretend."

He didn't say anything. If I'd knocked him even slightly off balance, that was one small thing in my favor.

"You must have been the first man here," I said. "De-Marco sent you to kill Marty Grant. He was a big man, wasn't he? It's a good thing you had a gun."

As long as I had him out here alone, I had a chance. If he got me into that house, I was probably a goner.

"You should really shut up now," he said. "Or I'll show you exactly how I killed him."

"I'm not nearly as big," I said. "Put the guns down and we'll see how tough you are."

Come on, I thought. Try something right here. Take a swing at me.

He didn't. He kept walking behind me. He led me to the front door of the house and told me to open it. I did. He stepped in behind me. The bright lights hit my eyes.

"Who do we have here?" a man said.

As my eyes focused, I saw Natalie sitting at a table. She still had her coat on. Across from her was the man who had spoken. It was Albert DeMarco. Now that I could see him up close, it was hard to believe he was in his seventies. A well-preserved sixty-year-old, maybe. Another man stood directly behind Natalie. This was the big man I had seen getting off the airplane.

There were two guns on the table in front of De-Marco, Natalie's automatic and her grandfather's Webley Bulldog.

"Have a seat," he said. "What an unexpected pleasure."

I looked at Natalie. When our eyes met, I could see her lips trembling. She was trying very hard to keep her composure. She opened her mouth to say something. She couldn't do it. She shook her head.

As I sat down next to her, I gave the man behind her a better look. Six foot five, maybe 240 pounds. He looked strong. His high cheekbones and close-cropped hair made him look like a German boxer.

I turned and looked back at the man in the white camouflage. He was barely five foot six in his army boots. Not even 150 pounds. He had long black hair tied in a ponytail. Now that I could see his face, he looked at least half crazy.

"I was sure Natalie would bring along some help," DeMarco said. "I did, too, of course. I'd like you to meet my troubleshooters."

"Please tell me you really don't call these guys your troubleshooters."

He smiled at me. The skin around his eyes didn't move. It was all plastic surgery, I thought. The hair is probably fake, too.

"I think you should know," I said. "Speaking of men, I've got seven others with me. The whole place is surrounded."

He laughed. "Natalie, is this the best man you could find? I hope you're not paying him too much."

The man in white wasn't laughing at my little bluff. He looked back at the door. Then he went out.

One man out of the room, I thought. One less gun.

And somewhere out there, I hope to God, Vinnie is watching.

"I didn't hire Alex," Natalie said.

He smiled again and looked at me. "Now I understand," he said. "You always did have a thing for older men."

I wanted to hit him so badly. Just one shot. But no, that was the wrong thing to think about. I had to stay cool, no matter what.

"Let Alex go," she said. "He has nothing to do with this."

"Did he bring the videotape with him?"

"No," she said.

"Where is it?"

"In a safe place. I'll tell you if you let Alex go."

"Stop it," I said. "I'm not going anywhere."

Come on, Vinnie. Where are you?

"Let me ask you something," he said. He picked one of her guns off the table. "You see, this gun I understand. This is your regular police-issue Sig Sauer P229."

He looked at it carefully, like a man at a gun shop. Then he put it down. It was twelve inches away from him. A good four feet away from me.

No, don't let him see you looking at those guns, I thought. If he notices that, he might take them off the table.

"But this other gun . . ."

He picked up the old Bulldog and weighed it in his hand.

"This gun is interesting. Note the distinctive shape of the barrel. And only five rounds. Very unusual."

He looked down the sight line. The gun was pointed at my chest.

"It does have a good feel to it," he said. "I'll say that much. But why two guns? It doesn't make any sense to me. Do you have any theories, sir?"

"A little extra firepower," I said. "She didn't know how many men you'd have on your payroll."

I sneaked a peek at the man standing behind Natalie. He looked down at me with cold eyes. No emotion at all. His huge hands were hanging at his sides, eighteen inches from Natalie's neck.

"My guess," DeMarco said, "is that this gun right here has some special significance."

Natalie was watching him handle the gun.

Look at me, I thought. Please, Natalie.

"It's an old gun," DeMarco said.

Look at me, Natalie.

"A Webley Bulldog. It's a classic."

Finally, she did. I gave her a quick smile. I raised one eyebrow. He's out there, I said in my mind. Read my thoughts, Natalie. He's out there. We have to be ready.

"I'm thinking this gun has to be at least seventy years old," DeMarco said. "Maybe more. Hell, this gun is probably older than I am."

I tried to put myself in Vinnie's place. I'm outside, I see one man coming out. He's the perimeter. Take him out if I can? Look in the window? Which would I do first? What do I do if I see Alex and Natalie in the room with these two men?

"In fact," DeMarco said, "I'll bet you that this gun belonged to Luc Reynaud. Am I right?"

A better question, what would Vinnie do if he looked in the window and saw the two guns lying on the table? Would he figure those were our only chance?

"If I had to guess," DeMarco said, "I'd say that this was Luc Reynaud's favorite gun, the gun he took with him everywhere. You had to watch out for yourself back then. Life on the border could get pretty dangerous."

I have to get light on my feet, I thought. I have to be ready to react in a split second.

"You know what else? I think there's a very good chance that this gun right here is the very same gun Luc

Reynaud used to kill my father. Wouldn't that be something?"

He put the gun on the table and spun it.

"I wonder if my father even saw it coming," he said. "I wonder if Luc Reynaud looked him in the eye before he killed him and took all the money. Or if he just shot him in the back."

The gun kept spinning.

"My grandfather didn't do that," Natalie said.

"Your grandfather was the only man who came back alive," DeMarco said. "Except for the gangsters, of course."

"They must have killed him," Natalie said. "They killed him because he tried to do something stupid. Or because he was an ugly, evil snake, just like you."

DeMarco smiled again. The gun spun slower and slower.

"Whatever I am," he said, "your grandfather made me."

"That's a lie," she said.

"Oh yes, Natalie. You know it's true. It all goes back to Luc Reynaud."

Okay, I thought. This is good. Everybody is looking at the spinning gun. The other gun, Natalie's automatic, that's closer to me. That's the gun I have to go for.

The Bulldog came to a slow stop. The barrel was pointing right at DeMarco's stomach.

"Let's try that again," he said. "This time for real. Did you ever play Spin the Bottle when you were a kid? Now we're going to play Spin the Gun That Killed My Father in Cold Blood. Unless you'd care to tell me where that videotape is . . ."

Come on, Vinnie. Now would be a perfect time.

"Natalie? Mr. McKnight? Do you have anything to say?"

Right now, Vinnie. You have to be out there. You have to help us.

"All right, then," DeMarco said. "Let's see who gets it first."

He spun the Bulldog.

This is it, Vinnie. With or without you, I've got to make my move.

Spinning.

DeMarco is focused on it. When I make my move, he'll reach for that gun first. He has to.

Spinning.

No external safety on the Sig Sauer. Double-action trigger. Just grab it and fire.

Spinning.

I can do this. I am fast. I am lightning.

Spinning. It's starting to slow down.

You're an old man, DeMarco. No matter how many times you've had your face lifted, you still have old-man reflexes.

Spinning slower. Slower.

Everyone watching it spin.

Then a sound. Outside. A muffled shout.

DeMarco looking to his right, toward the door.

I explode. Over the table. DeMarco's face, showing surprise. His right hand reaching out, first for the Bulldog, then the automatic, his fingers touching it.

But it's mine. I take it from him in that hundredth of a second. I roll onto my back. I fire the gun. Once. Twice. Right over Natalie's head. I hit the big man in the chest. He has no idea what has just happened to him. He's looking down at his chest like somebody has just played a cruel joke on him.

DeMarco's hands on my face now, digging at my eyes. I bring my arms back, two fists, two handcuffs still on the wrists, one gun. I hit him in the nose and feel it give. As I sit up, he's already going down. The blood is already coming out.

"Natalie, you okay?"

"Yes," she said. "Go!"

"Here," I said. I slid the Bulldog to her. The man behind her had a hand on her shoulder. He was bending over like he had just dropped something. As he pulled his hand off her body, he folded up and collapsed.

I rolled off the table and ran to the door. As I put my shoulder into it and pushed it open, I ran right into Vinnie. He had a gun in his hand.

"Alex," he said. "Are you all right? Where's Natalie?"

"Inside," I said. "Where's the other man?"

I saw him before Vinnie could answer. He was on his hands and knees in the snow, almost blending in with his white camouflage.

"How'd you get his gun?" I said.

"It wasn't easy," Vinnie said. "This guy got Natalie before I could do anything. I didn't have a weapon, Alex. Then you came later, from the other side. I was starting to think we had no hope."

"How'd you know to follow her in the first place?"

"Come on," he said. "She's the worst liar I've ever seen."

I was about to say something else. Then I saw the man in white going for his pant leg. I saw the ankle holster. I saw a flash of silver.

"Drop it!" I said.

But he was already swinging it. I shot him four times. I stayed there in my pose for a long time, the gun still pointed at the spot where he had been. Vinnie went over to him, leading with his gun. He took one look down at the man and relaxed.

"He's done," he said. "I wish he didn't tie his hair back like that. It makes him look like an Indian."

I let out a long breath. I had just killed two men. Six gunshots rang in my ears.

Then, from somewhere inside the house, we heard the seventh.

I rushed back inside, with Vinnie right behind me. Natalie stood with the Bulldog in her hands. DeMarco's chair was tipped over. His body was still in it, as if he had sat back down before he died.

"Natalie."

She didn't look up.

"Natalie," I said. "He went for your gun, right? You had to shoot him."

She kept looking down at him. She didn't move.

"Natalie, am I right?"

Nothing from her. Nothing.

I stepped up to her.

"Tell me," I said. "He went for your gun. You had to shoot him."

She finally moved. She looked at me.

"Yes," she said. "He went for my gun. I had to shoot him."

She looked back down at him. Natalie had shot her stepfather right between the eyes.

Twenty-four

The sun came out on Valentine's Day. I woke up early. The bright light on the snow didn't make my head feel any better. It had been a long night at the Glasgow. I had sat with Jackie and Vinnie by the fire until it was time to close the place. Jackie had a few drinks. So did I. Vinnie had his usual 7-Up.

When I had said good night to him in the parking lot, Vinnie had told me he was already thinking about working on the cabin with me again, the one that had burned down. I told him I'd be ready as soon as the weather broke. I thanked him again for everything. I didn't have to make a list for him. He knew what I was talking about.

A few hours of sleep later, here I was heading out again. I drove to the Soo and met Leon for breakfast. It felt good to see him without having to ask him to look up something for me. No mysterious hats to photograph in the parking lot. No newspaper articles about murders that happened thirty years ago.

I gave him his gun back. I told him I hoped I'd never have to borrow it again.

After breakfast, I drove across the bridge to Canada. The sun was still shining. When I pulled into the General Hospital parking lot, Natalie was there waiting for me. She was wearing a sweater and a leather jacket. Blue jeans. She looked better than ever. She gave me a quick kiss, then we went upstairs to the sixth floor.

When we got to the station, there was no nurse there. We walked down to Mrs. DeMarco's room and looked in. The bed was empty.

"Mr. McKnight?" I turned and saw the nurse, the same nurse who had been there the night I had paid my visit.

"I'm sorry," she said. "She went early this morning."

I thanked her. There was nothing else to say.

"Do you know who I could give this box to?" she said. It was the box she had shown me before, with all the photographs and documents.

"I was her stepgranddaughter for a while," Natalie said. "I think I'm as close to family as anyone."

I was surprised to see her take the box. I carried it down to her Jeep for her. We sat together in the front seat while she looked through it. I couldn't help thinking about everything she had been through, the whole history of three families and how it all went back to one night on a frozen river. She passed quickly through the pictures of Albert, the newspaper articles, the report cards. She stopped when she got to the picture of herself as a twelve-year-old, blowing out the candles at her birthday party. "Everyone's gone now," she said. "I'm all alone."

"What are you gonna do with all this stuff?"

"I don't know," she said. "This is the last thing I need, another box of old stuff to take with me."

To take with me. That was the one thing we weren't

talking about. None of us had faced criminal charges. Not me. Not Natalie. Not Vinnie. But Natalie was an OPP officer, on administrative leave. In another two days, she would appear before a review board. They would decide whether she was to be reinstated. If she was, they'd almost certainly reassign her. Her old commander, Staff Sergeant Moreland, had told her he wished he could transfer her to the Mounties and send her to the Yukon. He was probably only half joking.

I didn't know what she'd say to the board, what she'd tell them about what had happened in that house on the island. That was the other thing we weren't talking about.

"What do you want to do now?" I said.

"It's Valentine's Day," she said.

"So we should do something special."

"Damned right we should. Let's go."

"Where are we going?"

"You'll see."

We left my truck in the parking lot. She drove me across town to one of the big ice arenas.

"I played here once," she said as we pulled in. "A big tournament. I think I had eight minutes in penalties."

"Why are we here now?"

"Why do you think, genius? Come on."

She took me inside. The rink was reserved for open skating all day, with a Valentine's Day special discount for couples.

"It's been a while," I said.

"Me, too."

They tried to give her white figure skates. She pushed them right back to the man. "Real skates," she said.

A few minutes later, we were on the ice. We went slow at first. I was still getting my strength back, after everything I had been through. The bruises were finally going away. I was no longer scaring children in the streets.

We went a little faster as we got warmed up. We held hands and skated in big circles. When the ice finally cleared ahead of us, she let go of me and skated ahead. As I watched her, I thought about what I was feeling, for the hundredth time that day. Part of me wanted her to go back to the police force, to find her way back into the real world, no matter where that took her. Part of me didn't.

In a way, I knew exactly what she was facing. I had been in a similar situation once myself. I ended up leaving the Detroit police and moving to Paradise, Michigan. I rented out cabins and went down to the Glasgow Inn every single night. That's how it turned out for old Alex. But then, I didn't have someone around to love me.

She picked up speed. Three strides and she was already a blur. She went into the corner and turned hard. There was no net on the ice, but she circled around where it would have been and came out the other side like she was fired out of a slingshot. She skated like a hockey player, head down, shoulders square to the ice—but so graceful it took my breath away. Her hair was sailing behind her. She was smiling.

She went all the way around the ice, dodging anyone in her way. When she came back to me she dug her skates into the ice and sprayed me.

"How's that?" she said.

"You were flying."

"Damn right I was."

I took her hand again. I kissed her right there in the middle of the ice. Then we kept skating. We skated together, around and around, until it was time to go home.